MATTHEW RIEF

LEGEND IN THE KEYS
A LOGAN DODGE ADVENTURE

FLORIDA KEYS ADVENTURE SERIES
VOLUME 8

D1524028

Exotic Latitudes
Press

Logan Dodge Adventures

Gold in the Keys
(Florida Keys Adventure Series Book 1)

Hunted in the Keys
(Florida Keys Adventure Series Book 2)

Revenge in the Keys
(Florida Keys Adventure Series Book 3)

Betrayed in the Keys
(Florida Keys Adventure Series Book 4)

Redemption in the Keys
(Florida Keys Adventure Series Book 5)

Corruption in the Keys
(Florida Keys Adventure Series Book 6)

Predator in the Keys
(Florida Keys Adventure Series Book 7)

Legend in the Keys
(Florida Keys Adventure Series Book 8)

Join the Adventure!
Sign up for my newsletter to receive updates on
upcoming books on my website:

matthewrief.com

PROLOGUE

Key West
January 1905

Henry Flagler stood at the end of the old wooden dock, glancing at his pocket watch as a ship steamed into port. He was in his mid-seventies and had a thick white mustache and short white hair. He wore an expensive black suit and matching top hat.

As the steamer was being tied off, the captain, a tall Norwegian man dressed in his blue uniform, strode across the gangplank and headed straight for Flagler. Reaching into his front pocket, he grabbed a small package and handed it to the businessman without a word. The two men exchanged quick glances while Flagler felt the weight of the package, then slid it into his own pocket.

If either of them had directed their gazes toward

the main deck of the steamer, they would've seen three Cuban deckhands observing their quick transaction. One of whom, a wanted criminal named Julio Lopez, had an old silver revolver secured out of sight under his waistband.

Satisfied, Flagler nodded to the captain, then turned and climbed into the passenger seat of his custom White Steamer automobile. The driver took him down the dock onto the dirt-and-sand downtown streets. There were few cars on the island. Most walked or used the trolley, which Flagler's driver had to avoid during the drive over to his house.

Key West had a population of just over twenty thousand residents, making it the largest city in Florida. In the 1850s, US Senator Stephen S. Mallory had dubbed it "America's Gibraltar" due to its strategic location right at the mouth of the Gulf of Mexico. The island had a bustling economy fueled by fishing, sponge diving, cigar-making, shipbuilding, salvaging, and its status as a naval port.

Flagler's temporary residence was a white Victorian-style mansion just a few blocks from the waterfront. When the wheels stopped and the driver opened his door, Flagler headed inside, then up to the highest part of the house. Three stories up, he stepped out and turned his gaze to the east. From up in the crow's nest, he could see all the way to Marathon on a clear day.

In the quiet of the moment, the genius businessman let his mind wander. The following day, Flagler and his Florida East Coast Railroad executives would announce to a group of the town's leading citizens that he was going to bring his railroad to Key West.

"What kind of man tries to build a railroad across

the ocean?" he asked himself for what felt like the thousandth time.

Flagler was seventy-five years old. He'd accumulated over sixty million dollars over the course of his illustrious life. He made a small fortune every month from his Standard Oil holdings alone. It was expected that a man his age would slow down and step away from the realm of ambition. People thought he should spend his days back at his Palm Beach estate, sitting in a chair and admiring the view until the end of his days. But that wasn't Henry Flagler. He had a strong passion for progress, a clear vision of how things could be, and a work ethic that few could comprehend, let alone match.

Looking out over the city and the surrounding ocean beyond, he thought back to his humble business beginnings in northern Ohio. The naysayers had been prevalent when he'd turned his sights to oil—when he'd embarked on an ambitious endeavor that would transform him and his friend John D. Rockefeller from wide-eyed ambitious young men in their twenties into two of the richest men in the world.

When Flagler had turned his attention away from oil years later, there had also been writers, politicians, and fellow businessmen who'd urged him not to try and turn a muddy settlement in Biscayne Bay into a city. In less than ten years, he'd transformed Fort Dallas, a middle-of-nowhere town with just a few hundred hardy settlers, into a sprawling city he called Miami.

He looked off to the east at the islands of the Lower Keys.

I've made a living out of doing the seemingly impossible. And I'll do it again.

He was resolved. Firm in his convictions and dedicated beyond comprehension to making his visions reality.

He smiled, then reached into his pocket and pulled out the small package the captain of the steamer had handed to him back at the dock. Untying the strings and unfolding the packaging, he grabbed a beautiful massive yellow diamond and held it up to the afternoon sunlight.

A gift for his third wife. A little token of his affection.

He smiled and shook his head.

As if the millions I've spent on her over the past four years haven't been enough.

After a quick examination of the incredible stone, Flagler wrapped it back up in the packaging. Stepping back down into the house, he called in two of his assistants.

"I trust you with this, Cedric," Flagler said, handing the package to one of his assistants.

The diamond was to be taken to a local jeweler who was to work day and night for a week to turn the stone into a necklace.

Both of his assistants were in their early thirties, well dressed and with athletic builds. Once they had their orders, they took the diamond back outside and hopped into the car.

"To McLusky's," Cedric said to the driver.

The driver started up the car and accelerated them toward the center of the island. A few blocks from Flagler's house, a man suddenly ran over and jumped onto the vehicle. It was Julio Lopez, and he had his revolver pressed hard into the driver's chest.

"Drive into that alley," Julio said in his best English.

When Cedric protested, the young raggedly dressed Cuban cocked back the hammer.

"Do it now," he said.

The driver's hands began to shake. He accelerated and smashed a trash can as he turned sharply into the narrow alley. Motoring between two shops, he hit the brakes and idled right in front of a row of barrels filled with rainwater.

Just as they stopped, Cedric nodded to his companion, who reached for a weapon of his own. But before he could draw it, a second Cuban appeared from the corner of the alley and smashed a baseball bat against the side of his head. He grunted and jerked sideways from the unexpected blow. The assistant let go of his weapon, and it fell to the dirty ground.

As Cedric jumped to his feet, preparing to retaliate, a third Cuban appeared right behind him. He grabbed the well-dressed man from behind, choking him out and forcing him to the ground.

"We were working on the ship," Julio said. He still had his gun pressed against the driver. "We saw the jewel." With a swift slam of his weapon, he knocked out the driver, then stepped out of the car and held a hand out to Cedric. "Give it here."

Outnumbered, the man had no choice. He reached into his pocket, grabbed the small package, and handed it to the Cuban. After lowering his weapon, Julio unwrapped the package and eyed the glistening diamond. He smiled, then dropped it into his pocket.

Without another word, the angry Cuban with the baseball bat stepped over and bashed Cedric's head in with the barrel. He fell to the ground, blood oozing from his mouth.

As the three Cuban deckhands headed for the

road, Cedric forced his body to work despite its protestations. He reached for his ankle, grabbed a Browning pocket pistol, and took aim through blurry eyes.

Crack!

Gunpowder exploded, sending a .25 ACP round into the back of one of the Cubans. Cedric rapidly fired off another shot. Suddenly, two men were down, leaving only Julio on his feet. The Cuban dove for cover around the corner of the alley. He just managed to slam on to the sidewalk and roll awkwardly as a third bullet flew right past him.

The city looked like a kicked ant hill. People on both sides of the street scattered from the danger as Julio rolled to his feet.

"Stop right there!" a booming voice called out from behind him.

It was followed by a deafening high-pitched whistle. It was a local police officer. A tall, middle-aged man with a mustache and a heavyset frame.

Julio didn't have to turn around to know who it was. The moment he regained his balance, he took off in the fastest sprint of his life. He weaved in and out of a few running people, grabbed hold of a utility pole to redirect his momentum, and turned down a cross street.

The officer drew his weapon and took off after the fast young Cuban. Julio pumped his arms as fast as he could, his lungs burning and his heart pounding as he tried to put as much distance as possible between himself and the officer.

He knew that he couldn't escape. No matter how fast he ran, other officers would join in, and he'd be tackled to the dust, convicted, and receive a hefty sentence. No, the only way to get out of it would be to hide. To take cover and let the city cool off before stepping out and making his escape.

Rounding another turn, he spotted a second officer a few blocks down.

Now or never.

He took a sharp right, ducked down below a wooden fence, then made quick work of a fire ladder that led up to the roof of a hotel. Three stories up, Julio caught his breath and looked around, making sure no one had seen his desperate climb.

Once in the clear, he searched the roof for a hiding place. But it was completely empty aside from a rainwater collection system and a line full of drying clothes.

Soon someone will come to collect these clothes.

Looking across at an adjacent building, he spotted nothing but piles of scrap metal and tarps on its roof.

That's more like it. I can hide there until dark and slither away.

Julio made sure that no one was watching, then climbed up onto the edge and jumped as far as he could. It was only a six-foot gap, but he slipped and hit his head against the adjacent building's wall. Spinning around, he couldn't grab hold of the ledge and free-fell thirty-five feet to the ground below.

He landed hard, with a loud grunt and an even louder crack. He curled up and cried out as his hands wrapped around his lower leg, which was bent at a grotesque ninety-degree angle. His tibia and fibula were both severely broken, and he couldn't stand, let alone run.

Through a break in his cries, he heard footsteps approaching. He whipped his body around, trying to ignore the pain as he scanned for his lost weapon. He froze when he realized that it wasn't the police.

Instead of walking over to detain Julio, a blurry figure bent down, grabbed something off the ground, then put it in his pocket and walked off. Julio was confused for a moment, then he reached a shaking hand for his pocket and felt nothing. The diamond was gone.

He cried out in pain and despair as the figure disappeared around the corner. Then, his consciousness faded.

~ ~ ~

Two years later, Alfred Hastings lay on his deathbed at his small home in Key West. The seventy-one-year-old was suffering from tuberculosis and knew that his time was coming soon. With no living relatives, he chose to reveal his greatest secret to the only one who would listen. He reached a weak hand into a leather-bound notebook beside him and pulled out a folded piece of paper.

"This is the first clue to the whereabouts of the Florentine Diamond," he told his nurse. "It's a rare and valuable diamond. I have kept it hidden all this time, and now, I leave it to you."

The nurse thought Alfred was growing delirious. She'd heard the legend of the lost Florentine Diamond but had never given it any merit. She was about to prepare an extra dose of medication when he stopped her.

"No," Alfred said. "I see it in your eyes that you do not believe me. But it is true. Follow the clue. It will lead you to a buried gold compass. Solve the riddle on the back, and it will lead you to the next clue. Eventually, you will find the diamond. You will have enough money for the rest of your life." He coughed a few times. "I leave it to you because you have been kind to me."

The young nurse saw the look of passion in the dying man's eyes. She accepted the clue and pressed a hand to the dying man's cheek.

"Okay, I believe you," she said.

Alfred nodded. He closed his eyes, then opened them again. His eyelids were getting heavy, his breathing more and more difficult with every passing second. But he was glad to see his clue in the hands of the young nurse.

Maybe she'll find it. Maybe someone will find it and it will change their lives.

Alfred died moments later. The young nurse followed the clue a week after but reached a dead end when she ran into massive construction crews on Key Largo. The location where the next clue, a gold compass, was buried had recently been dredged. The miles of embankments created fill for the raised sections of the railroad, and the compass was gone.

Instead of being found by the nurse, the compass had been picked up by a laborer from New Jersey. Excited by the find and not knowing its secret value, he'd stashed it away, taken it up north as soon as he could, and pawned it off.

ONE

Miami
Labor Day 1935

Douglas McCabe was walking along the bustling downtown streets when he saw it. He craned his neck, his legs froze in place, and his jaw dropped open. Stepping through a thick crowd of holiday weekend tourists, he stopped in front of a blanket that was laid flat on a patch of grass. The blanket was covered in antique trinkets, and in the middle, he spotted a gold compass.

McCabe was a tall, slender Irishman in his early forties. He wore white pants, a white dress shirt, and a thin gray sport coat. A first-generation American, he'd emigrated twenty years earlier with his wife and had made a living bartering and selling with his childhood friend, Caleb O'Reilly. The two men eventually opened their own shop, but the Depression had hit them hard, and they were on the brink of bankruptcy and starvation.

This changes everything, he thought as he eyed a set of initials carved into the side of the compass.

After decades of rummaging through the bowels of antique stores, flea markets, and pawn shops up and down the East Coast, his heart stopped as he gazed upon the object that could drastically change his life if he played his cards right.

Shielding his eyes from the tropical afternoon sun, he knelt down and reached for the compass.

"Payment fos," an old Jamaican man said from the other side of the blanket.

He sat cross-legged and tapped McCabe with a long piece of bamboo to keep him from touching his prized merchandise.

McCabe's eyes shot up. He hadn't even noticed the man. He'd been too transfixed by the find. When his eyes met the old man's, he saw a look he knew very well.

McCabe had spent years buying and selling antiques for a profit. He knew the art of the poker face and almost always used it to his advantage when haggling. But the moment he laid eyes on the compass, he'd fallen off the radar. He'd displayed his desire, and it put him at the mercy of the seller.

"How much?"

"Ten dollars," the man replied.

Ten dollars? That's three times what it's worth.

It didn't matter. McCabe needed it, and he'd get it even if he had to sell his soul.

He took one more long look at the compass, his eyes focusing on the initials carved into its side.

A.J.H.

McCabe reached into his pocket, pulled out the money, and handed it to the seller. The old man's eyes lit up, and he gave McCabe the compass.

As McCabe walked off, he read the inscription on the back, and his hands began to shake.

This is it. My break has finally come.

The inscription on the back was a riddle. Though he couldn't figure out its meaning right away, one part of it was clear: he needed to get to Key West.

He glanced at his watch. It was four in the afternoon. The train station was just a few blocks away. He'd heard reports of a storm, but it wasn't believed to be significant. A tropical anomaly, the local papers had called it. Nothing to cause too much concern.

Pocketing his find, he took off for the station. When he reached it fifteen minutes later, the man at the ticket counter explained that there were no trains heading south.

"The storm's picking up, so I hear," he explained. "Only train heading south is a relief train for the workers on Matecumbe."

He motioned toward the tracks. Old 447, a 160-ton locomotive, rested on the nearest railway with eleven cars attached behind it. A swarm of railroad workers were preparing to get underway.

McCabe stepped away from the ticket counter. Reaching into his pocket, he wrapped his right hand around the compass. In his other pocket, he had two dollars. That was all that was left, the only wealth to his name. With a wife and three kids at home, he had no choice.

I am a man of fortune, and I must seek my fortune, he thought, remembering the line from the famous pirate Henry Avery.

He looked around, then headed down the walkway alongside the tracks. When no one was looking, he darted behind an outbuilding, then eyed the rear train car. There was a fence between them, but it was nothing he couldn't handle with a running start. He looked around, then, just as he was about to make his move, a voice startled him.

"There you are, Douglas," a man said in a strong Irish accent.

McCabe turned around, saw his friend Caleb O'Reilly. He was shorter than McCabe but wide-shouldered and strong. In addition to the red hair they both had, O'Reilly had a matching thick beard.

"I've been looking everywhere for yuh," he continued. "John said he saw yuh headin' for the tracks. Yuh—" He paused when he saw the look in his friend's eyes. "What are yuh doin', Douglas?"

McCabe had no choice but to let his friend in on what he'd found. He reached into his pocket, pulled out the compass, and handed it to O'Reilly. The big Irishman froze in disbelief for a moment as he grabbed the antique and read the inscription. The story of Hastings and the hidden diamond was regarded as pure legend, but the two collectors knew that every legend usually had at least a little bit of truth to it.

O'Reilly paused a moment, collecting his thoughts.

"There's a storm comin', Douglas," he said. "Haven't you read the paper? We should wait until it passes."

A train whistle blew violently behind them, signaling the train's departure.

"You can wait. I'm going now."

McCabe grabbed the compass, pocketed it, then

turned back to look at the train.

"You're crazy. You'll get yourself killed. I received the latest word that the pressure's dropped to twenty-seven inches."

McCabe didn't care about the risks. When the coast was clear, he took off for the fence. O'Reilly hesitated, then followed right behind him. Without being seen, the two Irishmen boarded the rear car just as its wheels began to move. They hid in a cramped closet until the locomotive brought them up to speed, then ducked out into a row of seats.

After a ten-minute delay crossing the Miami river, the train barreled south toward the Keys. The veteran engineer, a man named J.J. Haycraft, decided to shift the locomotive from the front to the rear in Homestead. This would allow him to back his way down the island chain, then hightail it out of there once everyone was piled aboard.

McCabe and O'Reilly looked through the window panels at the menacing dark sky that they were heading toward. The winds were already roaring violently. Anything capable of movement began to shake and vibrate as they passed by.

By the time they reached Key Largo, visibility was near zero. Sheets of pelting rain slammed against the cars, winds in excess of 150 miles per hour pummeled into the cars, and massive swells crashed up to twenty feet above sea level. The two Irish collectors were quickly realizing the significance of their mistake as they rode into the jaws of the massive, terrifying beast.

They both felt their ears pop from the changes in pressure. O'Reilly had been wrong. The barometers in Islamorada had plunged from a typical 29.9 to 26.35 inches of mercury, the lowest reading ever recorded in US history.

The farther south they steamed, the closer they came to the eye of the most powerful storm ever to make landfall on US soil. Near its center, gusts exceeded two hundred miles per hour, winds stronger than most tornadoes. The islands were being stripped completely bare. Houses, trees, cars, roads, everything was being blown away in a horrific storm that left behind nothing but sand.

As the train muscled along at just twenty miles per hour through the category five behemoth, Haycraft spotted a group of refugees holding on for dear life beside the track right at the end of Plantation Key. Somehow he managed to see them through the chaotic, black bottomless pit surrounding them. The train was the last and only hope for the 650 World War I veterans living in mere shanties as they worked as part of FDR's New Deal, along with the hundreds of locals in the Matecumbes. But Haycraft couldn't leave these helpless people to die in the storm. He brought the train to a stop, and the crew helped them aboard.

McCabe and O'Reilly moved into the adjoining car to avoid being seen, then sat and remained hidden as the train struggled to accelerate. The wind and rain pounded the car, shaking it like a violent earthquake.

O'Reilly had been staring at McCabe's pocket, and he couldn't take it any longer. He reached for the compass, but McCabe slid sideways and shoved him away.

"What the hell are you doing?" McCabe said, staring angrily at his lifelong friend.

The storm outside was striking fear into both of them, but O'Reilly seemed to be doing a good job of avoiding it.

"You take me for a fool, Douglas," O'Reilly said. "You intended to find the diamond and take it for yourself. To leave me in the shadows. Twenty years, Douglas. Twenty years as partners and friends since childhood."

A loud gust of wind whipped the side of the car, causing it to shudder and shake like a terrified quarry.

McCabe snatched a switchblade from his coat pocket and pointed the blade at O'Reilly. O'Reilly laughed menacingly, then lunged for McCabe, grabbing him by his shirt and slamming him to the floor. The train accelerated suddenly, causing both men to roll back down the aisle as they struggled to subdue the other.

O'Reilly punched McCabe twice in the face while yelling out curses. McCabe managed to retaliate by slicing a gash in O'Reilly's cheek, causing blood to spill out.

Enraged, O'Reilly grabbed hold of his friend and slammed him into the side of a seat. Squeezing McCabe's wrists, he slammed the knife from his hands, sending it rattling to the deck. A subsequent punch sent McCabe staggering back into a seat.

O'Reilly shuffled as best he could in the shaking train. Grabbing the knife from the deck, he regained his balance, then lunged toward McCabe and stabbed the blade deep into his chest. The two men made sinister eye contact for a few seconds. Just as O'Reilly was about to finish off his friend, there was a sudden loud crashing sound as a palm tree was thrown through one of the windows. Glass shattered, and the massive projectile nearly killed them. A waterfall of rain pelted their faces. The wind was so strong that they had to bend down and cup their mouths to get even the smallest amount of air into their lungs.

McCabe crawled desperately toward the door. He managed to grab the handle, but the wind was howling too strong for him to push it open. During a short break in the relentless gusts, he managed to shove it open a few inches. O'Reilly staggered to his feet and ran after him, his body shifting left and right from the shaking car. He tackled his old friend out the door, sending both of them into the dark inferno of the terrifying hurricane.

The two men yelled and fought with everything they had before a powerful wind-fueled wave grabbed hold of them and pulled them into the storm like a monster ripping its prey from a hiding place.

O'Reilly's head slammed hard against the edge of a trestle, crushing his skull and killing him instantly. McCabe splashed into the surging swells, the torrent tossing him around like a feather in the merciless pitch-black hell. He managed to catch two short breaths before he was dragged deep into the vortex and his lungs filled with seawater. As nature took his life, the gold compass fell from his pocket and sank into the dark, thundering tempest.

TWO

Key West
October 2009

Walt Grissom stepped off the white bus with wavy green and blue stripes at the corner of Whitehead and Fleming Streets. He directed his gaze to the green sign with white letters across the street that read "MILE 0." It marked either the end or the beginning of US-1, depending on your direction. For Walt, it marked the end of the line. His last hope.

He was average height and weight but had an endurance and spring in his step that were unusual for a man in his seventies. His thick hair and scruffy beard were all salt and no pepper. His skin was leathery from a lifetime out on the ocean. He wore tan shorts, leather flip-flops, a dark blue long-sleeved shirt, and a pair of JFK-style sunglasses connected to a strap that hung loosely around his neck.

He turned to the west, stood stoic and breathed in the fresh sea air mixed with diesel fumes from the idling bus. Once the pale, wide-eyed visitors exited and the sunburned ones boarded, the bus's hydraulics engaged, lifting the end up off the curb.

If he walked ten blocks southeast on Whitehead Street, he'd come face-to-face with the oversized concrete buoy that marks the southernmost point of the continental United States.

Key West, the tropical paradise he'd called home for much of his life. It felt good to be back, but Walt didn't have time to reminisce. He wasn't there just for a visit. No, he had important, life-or-death business to attend to.

He turned around and looked down the long stretch of Fleming Street. His destination, and last hope for survival, was only a few blocks away. Just off the main hustling and bustling downtown area. He clutched his worn backpack tightly, then secured it over his shoulders. He didn't have much, but he'd always been a bit of a minimalist.

Once considered to be one of the greatest treasure hunters in the world, Walt had made a substantial living scouring the Caribbean for treasure. But after fifteen years of failed expeditions, he'd whittled his small fortune down to nothing but the little wad of cash in his front pocket. Needing to regain his former glory, he'd decided to go after a famous wreck in the Mediterranean. But he'd needed to borrow money to do it. A lot of money.

"Our institution doesn't approve loans for hobbies," managers told him at every bank he stepped into.

Desperate, Walt had turned to the wrong kind of

people. Illegal gamblers and lifelong criminals from Albania.

After four months of searching, the wreck had been found by a maritime survey team from Egypt. Walt had spent nearly everything and had nothing to show for it.

With no other options, Walt had snuck off the operation before his creditors had come to demand payment. He didn't know how much time he had before they figured out where he'd run off to, but he knew it wouldn't be long.

Stopping for a moment at the corner of Fleming and Duval, he reached behind him and made sure that the backpack's main compartment zipper was still secured. Its contents were his last chance. A Hail Mary like no other he'd tossed up before. But if he succeeded, he'd not only be able to pay off his debt, he'd also solve one of the world's greatest mysteries.

Walt kept his eyes forward and his gait rushed as he made his way through the busy downtown streets. Among the Conch Republic, Key West is often referred to as Key Weird. Never is that title more fitting than during the ten days at the end of October every year. The wild weirdness is amplified off the charts, with madness and parties filling the streets long into the night. This unique and unforgettable event is known as Fantasy Fest.

Since its inception in 1979, Fantasy Fest has become the biggest annual celebration in the Keys. Over sixty thousand people turn out every year, nearly tripling the city's population. The famous festival is known for its wild costumes, parades, fireworks, and boat races.

As the sun began to fall in front of him, he turned down Mangrove Street. Just a few quick blocks from the hustle and bustle of the main drags, he gazed upon his old friend's restaurant for the first time in nearly twenty years. He read the words "Salty Pete's Bar, Grill, and Museum," painted in white letters against a blue backdrop. He barely recognized the renovated structure. The colors had changed, the seashell parking lot had doubled in size, and he could see a large added balcony extending from the second floor out back.

He stepped up onto the front porch, past a few small groups standing idly, and pulled the door open. A bell rang out, signaling his entrance. The high-pitched sound was barely noticeable over the voices and chaos of the packed house. Every booth and table was filled with locals and tourists alike, filling their stomachs with some of the best seafood in the world.

The inside looked different but was similar to how he remembered it. The walls were covered with old photographs, fishing nets, an impressive marlin, a few wooden helms, and various other nautical memorabilia from around the island chain.

"Afraid the wait's half an hour for a table," a brunette waitress said. She was pretty and had a ready smile. "But you're in luck if it's just you." She motioned across the dining area and added, "Got one spot left at the bar."

Walt eyed her name tag, which was pinned to a light blue Salty Pete's tee shirt.

"Thank you, Mia, but I'm here to see the owner," he said in a high-pitched, crackling voice. "That crusty barnacle around?"

Mia quickly eyed the man up and down. She'd never seen him before but knew that Pete's list of acquaintances ran deeper than their beer kegs.

After a few seconds, she nodded. "Last I

checked, Pete was upstairs. I can get him for you, Mr....?"

"No need," Walt said, waving a hand at her. "I'll go up and find the old seadog myself."

"You hungry?"

Walt sniffed the air and smiled.

"For Pete's grub? Of course. What's the catch today?"

"Grouper."

Walt nodded. "I'll order a plate a little later. Got some business to attend to."

Mia told him to let her know, and he headed for the large wooden staircase at the back of the dining room. The second story of Salty Pete's was the museum part. Rows of glass cases displaying artifacts from around the islands covered the floor. A group of tourists stood admiring an old cannon and reading about its history.

Walt headed for a large sliding glass door that led out to a balcony just as packed as the main dining area below. The moment his hand wrapped around the handle, a familiar voice called out from behind him.

"Wally?" Pete Jameson said as he stepped toward Walt. "Who the hell let you in here?"

Walt turned around and smiled. Pete's low, pirate-like voice was unmistakable.

"Place looks nice, Petey," Walt replied, nodding at the glass cases surrounding them. "Looks like you've made a little dinero for a change."

Pete laughed and pulled his old friend in for a big hug.

"It's good to see you, old-timer," Pete said. "How the hell have you been? Haven't seen you in what, twenty years?"

They let go of each other, and Walt nodded.

"You always said the islands would call me back someday."

"Yeah, well, I figured it'd be a few years tops. Last I heard you were looking for a ship in the Mediterranean. Any luck?"

Walt's smile quickly vanished.

"Oh, that bad, huh?"

Walt looked over his old friend's shoulder.

"Your office still back in the corner? I could sure use a drink."

"That it is," Pete replied. "And I've got just the bottle." He turned and motioned toward the corner. "Come on, let's take a load off. You look terrible, old friend. Long travel day?"

"You have no idea."

THREE

The two old friends headed across the room, and Pete pushed open a creaky wooden door, welcoming Walt into his corner office. Like much of the restaurant, the walls were covered with pictures and old maps of the Keys. He had a few large bookshelves filled with everything from Cussler to the *Encyclopedia Britannica.* An old wooden desk rested in the far corner with a faded leather chair behind it. The desktop was covered in papers, a few open books, and various knickknacks.

Walt sat on a linen sofa, and Pete plopped down into the leather chair. Reaching into a small compartment under the desk, Pete pulled out an old, faded bottle of rum and two diamond whiskey glasses.

"Found these in a pirate treasure trove on Lignumvitae," he said. "Over three hundred years old.

The pride of the pirate Captain John Shadow's reserve."

Walt grinned as Pete poured the drinks and added a few chilled whiskey stones from a tiny freezer behind the desk. They each grabbed a glass, clinked them together, then took small sips to savor the flavor.

Both men leaned back and gave satisfied expressions.

"Not that I'm complaining," Walt said, "but I thought you'd decided to trade up your metal detector for a spatula?"

Pete took another sip, then leaned back into his chair.

"You remember what you said when I told you that I wanted to open a restaurant?"

Walt laughed. "Once you catch the treasure bug, it never goes away."

Pete nodded. "Lot of truth in that. Though the passion's not as overwhelming as it once was. I like to keep balance as well as I can. Plus, some new friends moved down here in the last few years who stumble into trouble and treasure a great deal more than most. I like to tag along on their adventures from time to time."

"Feel like tagging along on another one of mine?"

They fell silent for a moment. Walt's tone had shifted, and Pete narrowed his gaze as he looked over his old friend. The two had first met back in the seventies. Eighteen years old and fresh out of high school, Pete hadn't had the slightest clue what he wanted to do with his life, but he knew that he loved the ocean, and growing up in the islands meant he'd had a childhood and adolescence full of diving, fishing, and boating. But it was his knowledge of boat engines that had caught Walt's attention.

In his late twenties, Walt had already established himself as one of the most proficient treasure hunters in the Keys, having discovered a chest of Spanish gold and purchased his own fifty-foot salvage vessel. For fifteen years, Pete had worked alongside him, and the two had eventually become partners in their endeavors before parting ways in '89. Pete had opened his restaurant and focused more on business and fishing, while Walt had moved on to bigger and more lucrative treasure-hunting projects.

"It's been many years, Wally," Pete said. "But I'd know that look a mile away." He paused a moment, took another sip, then added, "What are you looking for now?"

Walt smiled. He and his old friend had always been straight and to the point with each other. No beating around any bushes. No wasted time.

"The Florentine Diamond," he said flatly.

They both paused a moment. Walt wanted his words to sink in.

After a few seconds of silence, Pete laughed, shook his head, and looked out the only window at the ever-darkening sky.

"Not this again," he said. When he saw Walt's face turn stone serious, he added, "You've been going on about that lost diamond for years. We've tried, again and again. Countless people have tried looking for it. The trail's dry, brother. That diamond's long gone. Hell, it was probably cut down to smaller diamonds and sold off years ago."

Walt leaned back into his chair and took another enjoyable sip of the aged pirate beverage.

"Maybe," he said. "Or maybe it's been right

under our noses all this time." He grabbed his backpack and unzipped the main compartment. "What if Hastings was telling the truth?"

"That guy was old and out of his mind."

"There was never any way of knowing for sure because the compass was lost. Without the clue Hastings etched into the back, no one could ever expect to find the diamond unless by dumb luck. But what if I told you I knew where it was?"

Pete fell quiet. "Please tell me you've got it in that bag of yours."

Walt reached into the bag and pulled out a leather-bound journal. Rising from the couch, he strode over toward Pete and set it on the desk. Leafing through to a bookmarked page, he turned it around and handed it to Pete. The handwriting was small, elegant, and covered all the pages, front and back.

"Read this part," Walt said, pointing to a few lines of text.

Pete grabbed his glasses from the desk and slid the temples over his ears.

"In the uproarious chaos just before Haycraft ordered us to stop on Windley, the dark outline of two men in suits appeared," Pete read aloud. "They struggled for dear life, trying to climb into the swinging open door, and vanished into the torrential storm as quickly as they'd appeared, swept over the bridge into the storm's relentless jaws."

Pete looked over at Walt, who was huddled beside him.

"Who wrote this?" Pete said, closing the journal on one of his fingers and flipping it over.

There was a stamp on the back that read: Property of the Henry Flagler Museum.

"Walt, you stole this?"

Walt shot his old friend a sly smile. "I prefer the word *borrowed*. Besides, those Boy Scouts that run that place don't know what they're looking at." He grabbed the journal and flipped to the back of the cover. "Look here, it belonged to G.R. Branch. He was a trainmaster for the FEC. Branch was sent with engine 447 the night of the Labor Day Hurricane. The train was sent down from Miami to save the people in the Matecumbes."

Pete paused a moment. He didn't get where his old friend was going with this, but it looked suspiciously like another one of his famous wild goose chases.

"Nearly five hundred souls perished that evening," Pete said solemnly. "Men. Women. Children. Mother Nature doesn't prioritize life as we do." He paused a moment, took in a deep breath, and sighed. "Looks like these two poor guys were struggling to survive with the others."

"But answer me this," Walt said. "Why would these guys be wearing suits? It was September in the Keys. Eighty degrees. No AC for hundreds of miles. If they'd been laborers or locals they wouldn't have been wearing suits. Also, if the series of events in this journal is accurate, they would have been chugging over the Snake Creek Bridge at the time. No, these two were on the train when it left Miami."

"Railroad workers, maybe?"

Walt shook his head.

"That's the thing," Walt said. "These two guys weren't supposed to be there." When Pete looked confused, Walt continued, "Caleb O'Reilly and Douglas McCabe disappeared that night. Both men were collectors and the owners of a small antique

31

shop in Miami. Neither man had any known reason for being in the islands. Their families both stated that they had no knowledge or explanation as to why they would be there, but McCabe's body was found washed ashore in the Crane Keys two days after the storm. O'Reilly's body was never found, but neither were hundreds of other corpses after that fateful night."

Pete raised a hand and shook his head.

"Back up a minute," he said. "I don't see the connection between these two and the diamond."

"I did a little research on McCabe. Apparently, he was obsessed with rare stones. A lifelong collector like him would've known the legend of the diamond and Hastings's story. My theory is he stumbled upon the compass somehow and took off first thing for the islands."

"Into the eye of the worst hurricane in American history?"

"You know as well as I do that the news underestimated it. I think the term used was 'tropical anomaly.' But given that Branch didn't recognize either of them, I'm guessing they snuck aboard."

Pete paused, finished off his rum, and squeezed the bridge of his nose.

"So, let me get this straight," Pete said. "You think that this compass is somewhere on the seafloor under the old train line?"

Walt shook his head, grabbing his glass and downing the remaining fluid.

"I don't think, I know, brother." He leaned over the desk and stared fiercely into Pete's eyes. "And I'm going to find it, one way or another. Then I'm gonna track down the diamond." He looked down at the desk, grabbed a gold doubloon in a plastic case, and plopped back down into the couch. "But I need your help."

"What do you need?"

"A boat and all the necessary equipment."

"You came all the way back home with nothing but that pack?" Pete said, raising his eyebrows.

"Which is why I'm willing to go in fifty-fifty," Walt said. "Look, I'm not gonna beat around the coral patch with you. I've fallen on some hard times, and I got nothing. So here's the deal: I help find the diamond, you supply the equipment, and we both get filthy rich."

Pete thought it over for a moment.

"And then you start acting your age," Pete replied. "Maybe buy a house and dig in your roots. We're not the same young, wild-eyed kids we once were."

Walt stood up and refilled both of their glasses.

"Maybe not. But I'm up for one more adventure."

Pete nodded. "Searching for a small compass in the ocean. I think I'd rather look for a needle in a whole barn of haystacks."

Walt smiled. Pete hadn't said yes yet, but he knew he'd successfully captured his old friend's interest.

"If there are two idiots who can do it, it's us," Walt said with a laugh, grabbing his glass and raising it. Pete thought for a moment while looking off into space.

"Come on, old friend," Walt said. "Once you catch the treasure bug," he added, raising the glass slowly.

Pete looked up at him, smiled, and grabbed his glass as well.

"It never goes away," he said, clanking their glasses together. "Alright. Let's go find ourselves a diamond."

FOUR

They spent two hours catching up, telling stories, and discussing where they'd start their search. Mia brought them a few plates of freshly grilled grouper and sweet potato fries, which they ate in the office.

"We're gonna need some young help if we're gonna pull this off," Pete said. "And I know just the people."

"Anyone I know?"

"Jack Rubio, for starters."

"Ruby! How's that kid doing these days?"

"Not a kid anymore," Pete said. "Owns the family diving and fishing charter business now. There's also a guy who just moved here a few years ago. Logan Dodge. He and his wife would be perfect for something like this, trust me."

"You're telling me they're landlubbers? What are a couple of—"

"They found that doubloon in your hands," Pete said. "Came from a Spanish galleon wreck over at Neptune's Table. The ship that carried the Aztec treasure."

"Shit, I read about that."

Walt's pocket suddenly vibrated. He reached in, pulled out a flip phone, and looked at the small LCD screen before silencing it.

"I'll give Logan a call in the morning and we'll meet up with him," Pete said.

Walt's expression had shifted noticeably. He looked uncomfortable as he nodded, then grabbed his bag and stood up.

"You got a place to stay?" Pete said. After a short hesitation, he added, "You'd have better luck finding that compass tonight than a vacant room. Fantasy Fest packs the island tighter than a can of sardines. The spare room in my house is yours if you want it."

Walt thanked him, and they both stepped out of the office.

Pete motioned toward the large sliding glass door. "Got live music playing all week. Logan and his wife, Angelina, were out here earlier. Come on, I'll introduce you."

"They left an hour ago," Mia said as she appeared up the stairs, balancing two trays of food. "But I've got a few seats at the bar if you two want to come out and enjoy the music."

"I'll be right out," Walt said. "I just need to step out for a sec and make a call."

Pete nodded and brought him in for another big hug.

"Good to have you back, brother," Pete said.

"It's good to be back."

Pete pulled the sliding door open for Mia, then

waved to Walt as he headed back down the stairs. Once through the throng of happy and intoxicated patrons, he headed out the front door and back down the steps to the shell driveway. Walt passed by a trio of smokers standing near a patch of grass to the left. He moved to the other side of the lot and looked around to make sure he was out of earshot. Seeing that he was in the clear, he grabbed his phone and called the most recent number in the phone's history.

After one ring, a low voice came over the line.

"Where the fuck are you, Grissom?" the angry guy on the other end said.

"There's been a change in plans," Walt said, trying to sound as calm and collected as possible. "The Phoenician wreck was found, but I've got a beat on another prize. One even more valu—"

"Shut the hell up, you stupid old American. I did not ask what you are doing. I asked where the fuck are you?"

Walt sighed. "I'm off Malta. We've got the ship and we're sending divers down twenty-four seven. Your money will be paid back soon. I promise."

"Wrong answer," the man replied, then went quiet for a moment. "I don't know what kind of financiers you're used to dealing with, but we will not tolerate liars."

Walt's eyes grew wide suddenly. He'd heard the man's angry voice clearly, but his words weren't coming from the phone. They were coming from right behind him.

The line went dead in an instant. Walt heard the crackling of shoes against the seashell driveway at his back. Before he could turn around, he felt something hard press between his shoulder blades. It was the barrel of a Beretta Px4 Storm.

The man had appeared from the shadows like a ghostly apparition. He was tall and lean. He was dressed in dark blue slacks and a black polo shirt. Two more men appeared from the darkness beside him as he dug the barrel of his handgun harder into Walt's back.

"What the—"

"Shut the fuck up, old man," the guy with the gun said.

His trigger finger began to press, then he looked around and saw groups of people making their way up and down along the busy well-lit sidewalks. There wasn't anyone within fifty feet of them, but he preferred to do his dirty work far from the eyes and ears of the general public.

He peered across Mangrove Street, eyeing a dark alleyway between a scooter rental pavilion and a fishing tackle shop. Both places were closed, and he even saw a few dumpsters they could use to conceal their violent work.

"Move it, old-timer," he barked. "Across the street. To that alley."

He motioned with his handgun.

The man kept his piece hidden from the lively passersby on the street as they led Walt across. When they reached the back of the ill-lit alley, he shoved Walt against a concrete wall behind a smelly dumpster.

"You should have never fucked with us," he barked. "Now, you'll find out what we do to people who double-cross us."

He slammed the grip of his handgun into the side of Walt's face, sending his head jerking sideways violently. Saliva sprayed out, and he grunted as his body lurched downward and he caught himself on the asphalt. The three goons took turns, laying into the old man with a series of kicks and punches until he was struggling on his knees.

Blood dripped out from his mouth. His body hurt so bad he could barely move. He was sure this was it. They were going to kill him, to end his life right there in that dark alley.

When Walt felt he was nearing the end of what he could bear, the men stopped suddenly.

The leader of the group wiped the sweat from his brow and pulled his cellphone out of his front pocket. He quickly dialed a number, then caught his breath and knelt down beside Walt.

"Doesn't feel so good, does it, old-timer?"

The phone rang twice before a woman's voice came over the line.

"We got him, boss," the kneeling man said. He paused a moment, listening, then added, "No, he's not dead. Not yet, anyway."

He listened a moment longer, then brought the phone away from his ear slightly and leaned over Walt as he struggled for breath.

"Boss wants to know if you have any last words?"

He waited for less than a second. When he heard nothing but Walt's gasps, he brought the phone back in close.

"Looks like the liar's speechless for once."

He listened, nodded, then was about to raise his weapon and put an end to the whole thing when Walt managed to get out a few desperate words.

"Stop," he said, his voice shaky. "I… I can repay double."

The man hovering over him grinned sadistically and shook his head.

"It's too late for that, American. You—"

"Tell your boss," Walt continued. He managed to lift his head and stared fiercely into the man's eyes. "I can repay double. Tell her I know where the Florentine Diamond is."

The man paused a moment. He took in a deep breath, then sighed. Tracking down the old man hadn't been easy, and he'd been looking forward to ending his life and flying back to his homeland as soon as possible. But he relayed the message to his boss.

For nearly thirty seconds, he waited impatiently, playing with his Beretta and occasionally aiming it at Walt. Finally, his boss replied.

He listened for a few seconds, then his eyes narrowed, and he gritted his teeth.

"Understood," was all he said, then he hung up the phone.

He slid it back into his pocket, then looked up at the night sky.

"You sly dog," he said. "Looks like you've managed to delay your death for a few more days." He grunted and rolled his eyes. "No matter. You'll fail, and I'll kill you with this gun when you do." He grabbed Walt by his bloody shirt collar and forced him up. Staring into his eyes, the man added, "You've got three days. Seventy-two hours. If you don't deliver us the diamond within that time, your ass is done. And if you think this beating was bad, wait until you see what I'm gonna do to you then."

He let go suddenly, letting Walt fall back to the concrete. Rising to his feet, he joined the other two guys and took a few steps back toward Mangrove Street.

Looking back over his shoulder, he said, "Don't

think for a second that I'm letting you out of my sight. We'll be right here, watching your every move. Make a run for it again, I beg you. Nothing would make me happier than beating you to a pulp and filling your empty skull with lead."

The three men vanished, leaving Walt alone with nothing but his throbbing pain and racing thoughts. After a minute, he managed to force his body up onto one knee. He'd always been strong, but the beating he'd just taken would incapacitate most men in their prime. And he was many years removed from his prime.

He thought about what the man had said, running his words over in his mind.

Some of the best treasure hunters in the world have been looking for that diamond for nearly a hundred years, he thought.

If he was going to save his skin, he'd have to find it in less than seventy-two hours. A daunting, nearly impossible task. And he was so banged up and battered that his assailants were long gone before he summoned the strength to struggle to his feet.

FIVE

Key West
Earlier that Evening

I stood right along the edge of Mallory Square, gazing to the west as the sun began its dramatic exit. It's a beautiful sight, and one that never grows old. I watched as the brilliant hues of yellows, reds, and deep purples shifted like an ever-changing masterpiece. The experience never ceases to amaze me. Never the same, and always awe-inspiring.

"Mother Nature sure is quite the artist," Ange said.

I couldn't have agreed more. Sliding my hand out of hers, I wrapped my arm around her and brought her body against mine.

Angelina and I have been married now for six months. Still, I wake up every morning and pinch myself, wondering how I managed to get so lucky. With the sun's dying light shining on her, I gazed at her tall, lean frame. I pushed aside a strand of her beautiful blond hair, then shifted to look into her perfect blue eyes.

"What is it, Logan?" she said, smiling back at me.

"Just very happy," I replied, then kissed her on the cheek.

Our bodies pressed tightly together, we looked out over the sparkling water. A few sailboats glided by, pelicans hovered in the ocean breeze overhead, and gulls cawed along the shoreline beside the soft crashing waves. Sunset Key sat a little over a quarter of a mile away and turned into a solid black outline as the glow drifted down behind it.

The last bits of light vanished to a loud chorus of conch-shell horns. The deep, ancient sounds boomed from all around us as the gathered crowd said goodbye to the day.

When the sun's exit was complete, most of the thousands of spectators let out loud cheers and claps. It was like a switch had been flicked. The relatively quiet group became wild and rowdy in an instant.

Kenny Chesney's "When the Sun Goes Down" played in my head as Ange and I kissed and turned around to face the crowd.

We'll be groovin', alright.

After dinner at Salty Pete's, we'd migrated down to the waterfront to take in the spectacle. Sunsets at Mallory Square are always a popular attraction, but during Fantasy Fest, the intensity of the end-of-day celebration is amplified astronomically.

We were surrounded by a sea of some the wildest and open-minded people you'll find anywhere. Many were decked out in costumes, everything from Crocodile Dundee to mermaids, along with handfuls of women wearing nothing but bikini bottoms and small stars over their nipples.

As we turned around, a jacked guy wearing a tiny thong and dressed up as Poseidon walked by. He was holding a brown Yorkshire terrier curled in one hand and a foam trident in the other.

"You could pull off that costume," Ange said, motioning toward him as he strolled past. "In fact, I think I'd like to see that."

I laughed. "Not sure even this city has enough alcohol for me to wear that in public."

"We'll see about that," she said with a smile.

In addition to the throngs of tourists and locals alike, the square was littered with rows of stands selling everything from local sea sponges to rainbow-colored Panama hats. There were food carts catering to lines of hungry people as well, serving up conch fritters, big pretzels, piña coladas, and coconut shrimp.

Along the water's edge beside us, there were numerous street performers, entertaining gathered spectators with their unique talents. A guy alongside us, covered in silver paint, kept motionless as stone, then occasionally spooked to life. A guy dressed as a genie hovered with his legs crossed over nothing but a small piece of wavy fabric.

Most of the performers I'd seen before, but there was a small handful of new arrivals. A group of acrobats on the other side of the square caught my attention. I reasoned that they traveled around the country, performing for crowds at various festivals and gatherings wherever they could.

"Hey, there's Jack!" Ange said, pointing into the

congested mass of bodies.

I spotted my old friend, and we both waved him over.

Jack Rubio was a real-deal beach bum conch and he was proud of it. He'd spent his whole life in the Keys and knew the beautiful islands as well as anyone. When his father had passed, he'd taken over Rubio Charters, and he'd been taking tourists out diving and fishing since he was a little kid.

A few inches shorter than my six foot two, Jack was a hundred and seventy pounds of pure wiry muscle. He had tanned skin, curly blond hair, and blue eyes. Usually, Jack walked with his patented unaffected gait, but today he had his head down and his shoulders hunched.

"What's wrong, man?" I said, patting my old friend on the back. "It's a party, and you look like you just cracked your favorite dive mask."

He shook his head. "Sorry, bro. Don't wanna put a damper on things." He paused a moment, greeted Ange, then added, "Just got word that the children's center is closing its doors at the end of the month."

The news caught me off guard. The children's shelter on Tavernier had been a landmark in the Keys since before I'd first moved here with my dad back in the late eighties, helping thousands of abused, neglected, and orphaned children over the years.

"What? Why?" Ange asked.

"Talked to Misty earlier today. Their expenses have gotten too high, and they're drowning in debt. Wish there was something we could do."

Ange and I had both found success in our careers before moving to the Keys, and getting a finder's fee from the Aztec treasure we'd stumbled upon had set us up well. But after buying my forty-eight-foot Baia

45

Flash and a house in Key West with cash, we didn't exactly have that kind of money just lying around. Like many people in the islands, we sent a check every month to give back to the community, but running an organization in the Keys is much more expensive than most places across the country.

"We'll figure something out, Jack," I said. "If anything, I could give Scott a call. See what he can do from the political side of things."

Scott Cooper was one of my best friends and just so happened to be a senator representing the state of Florida.

Just then, a shirtless hairy fat guy held two cans of beer in the air and started shaking them.

"Who's ready for lager rain?" he shouted at the top of his lungs.

We took that as our cue and decided to make our way along the waterfront to the Conch Harbor Marina, where Jack and I moored our boats. Though just a short walk from the hustle and bustle of downtown, the marina maintained a more relaxed and quiet vibe. Relatively speaking, of course.

"Let's wind down with a few drinks," I said, placing a hand on Jack's shoulder. "It's gonna be alright, man."

We moved past a solid group of people that had gathered around the acrobatic performers I'd spotted earlier. They wore nothing but speedos, putting their tanned, six-packed bodies on display. They had a thirty-foot pole set up with blue-ribbon-covered ropes extending down to where a few young women had been picked from the crowd to hold them in place. One of the guys was up top, balancing on one leg while doing Mr. Miyagi type moves.

"Who are these guys?" I asked.

Jack shrugged. "Never seen 'em before."

"They're the Soaring Modelos," an enthusiastic young dark-haired woman said beside us. She was wearing nothing but a pair of booty shorts, and red, white, and blue paint covered her upper body. I could smell the alcohol on her breath as she moved in close to me. "They're hot. Like you, mister?"

I took a step back. Ange slipped in between us and cordially informed the young woman that I wasn't on the market. I laughed and brought Ange in close.

We stood and watched the performers for a few minutes, mesmerized by their incredible feats of strength and acrobatics. Just as we were about to turn and continue our difficult journey through the crowd, I spotted something I couldn't ignore even if I wanted to.

One of the performers who was walking around the edge of their makeshift stage showing off his abs slid behind a drunk guy in the crowd. In a quick flash of movement, the performer reached into the unsuspecting guy's back pocket and snatched his leather wallet. Faster than a blink, the wallet was gone, hidden from view in the performer's fanny pack.

Daniel Ocean would've been impressed. He was good. Smooth, fast, and efficient. In the chaos of the gathered people, and with the feats on display behind him, I'd barely noticed the act.

In the heat of the acrobatic display, I leaned over and spoke into Ange's ear.

"Looks like we've got a pickpocket on our hands," I said, motioning toward the performer closest to us.

Ange nodded, keeping her gaze directed forward.

"That guy on the other side just snatched something from a woman's purse as well," she said.

I scanned over the scene with new eyes. Some kind of scheme they had going there. Pull into town, take advantage of drunk, wild, and distracted tourists, then make off with much more than the donation basket full of bills lying on the ground in front of them.

The normal thought of telling someone and keeping my hands clean of the situation didn't occupy any space in my mind. I'd always preferred the old handle-it-myself method.

I stared daggers at the closest performer as he navigated the edge of the crowd, heading toward us.

"I know that look," Ange said, tilting her head so her eyes met mine and giving a slight laugh. "You already know my stance on this kind of shit. So what's the play?"

"Somebody wanna fill me in here?" Jack said, noticing our expressions.

Ange and I were probably the only two people in a five-block radius without a happy-go-lucky look on our faces.

"These guys are crooks," Ange said, motioning toward the group.

Jack looked back and forth between us, then raised his hands in the air.

"Ah, bro," he said. "At least wait until the show's over to do your thing. Looks like he's about to do his finishing move."

No, Jack, I thought. *If these thieves aren't willing to play ball and own up to their actions, the show's just getting started.*

SIX

I spent a few seconds sizing up the situation. There were four performers in all. One guy high up on the pole, one at the bottom doing most of the talking, and two guys patrolling the edge of the crowd, taking prizes as they went like farmers picking apples. They had a few black bags and a gray case piled behind them. I was confident that they contained more than just extra supplies of spandex.

The most important thing was that none of them appeared to be armed. Though one of the guys could've had something small and deadly hidden away in their outfits.

"Alright," I said to Ange as one of the rovers moved toward us. I unzipped Ange's purse and added, "Time to act like a bunch of drunk party animals."

Ange and Jack were both more convincing actors

than I was, but I did my best to play the part. We raised our voices, wobbled side to side, and laughed our asses off. As I'd hoped, the closest performer zeroed in on us like a cat catching sight of an unsuspecting mouse.

The guy flexed his wiry zero-body-fat muscles and struck a few poses as he closed in. I intentionally looked the other way as he stepped toward Ange.

"Hey there, beautiful," he said in an Arabic accent. "Enjoying the show?"

In my peripherals, I saw that she was smiling back playfully.

"Every part of it," she replied in her drunk Valley girl voice. "You fellas are so hot I'm sweating."

I noticed Ange turn around slightly, putting her open purse right in front of the guy. With the bait in place, the thief couldn't resist. While looking one way and angling his body to cover his act, he slid his free hand quickly into her purse. When he pulled it back out, he froze and jerked his head around as my right hand clamped down hard around his wrist.

"Not quite fast enough," I said.

My tone and mannerisms shifted from so plastered I could barely stand to perfectly sober in an instant.

He locked eyes with me. For a brief moment, he looked like a kid trying to swipe a sugary treat from the cookie jar. His eyes twitched, and his mouth dropped open. As quickly as the *caught red-handed* expression appeared, it vanished, and the guy tried to relax as if nothing had happened.

"Easy, friend," he said, laughing it off. "Just having a little fun with her. Didn't know she was taken."

He tried to rip his hand free, but I squeezed

harder, holding it more secure than a vise.

Don't think there's a chance in hell that you're getting off that easy, bud.

"Hey, what the hell, man?" he said. He patted me on the shoulder with his free hand and added, "Why don't you just relax before you do something you'll regret, alri—"

"Which one of you dipshits is in charge?" I said, raising my voice.

The short-haired guy who'd been addressing the crowd stepped toward me.

"So much anger," he proclaimed. "Do we have a problem, friend?"

He was trying to embarrass me, to use his public speaking experience to try and get me to step back and retreat into a shell. But he had another thing coming.

"Yes," I said, raising my voice even louder than his and stepping forward into the open space. "We do have a problem." I turned to the crowd and added, "It's that these shirtless punks are crooks."

The crowd murmured, and the guy who was clearly in charge shook his head dramatically.

"Some people just don't know how to relax and have a good time," he said, shrugging and drawing a few laughs from the crowd. "We're just trying to entertain you all. If you don't like that, I suggest that you run off and be a bore someplace else." He stepped past me, lifted his hands in the air and added, "I'll even part this crowd like Moses, so even you won't have trouble leaving."

Most of the gathered crowd were tourists. Mainlanders who didn't know me from Adam. Naturally, they were mostly in the performers' corner and started to move so I'd have free rein to take a hike.

"Just trying to entertain, huh?" I said, unfazed. "Alright, well, if that's the case, why don't you have Tarzan here open up his fanny pack?" I motioned toward the guy who'd tried to steal from Ange's purse. The leader glared at me as I stepped toward the long-haired guy. "Go on," I added. "Open it up."

I stepped along the edge of the crowd, who were cursing and heckling me like an away team's star player as he stepped into the batter's box. I stopped in front of the drunk guy whose wallet had been snatched a few minutes earlier.

"'Cause I'm willing to bet that your wallet's in that pack and not in your back pocket."

The drunk guy looked angry, then confused as his right hand gravitated to the back pocket of his plaid shorts. His eyes grew wide when he felt nothing, and he looked up at me in shock.

"My wallet's gone," he said in a heavy Southern accent. "Somebody stole it!"

I crossed my arms and looked back at the long-haired guy.

"It's in there," I said, motioning toward the fanny pack. "Along with a whole lot more."

I stepped back toward the leader as he struggled to maintain control of the situation.

"Alright, that's all for tonight, folks," he said before whirling around and motioning for his boys to pack up.

Not so fast.

I strode back up beside him, getting right in his face.

"You're not going anywhere until you give back everything you stole tonight," I said sternly.

He gritted his teeth and furrowed his brow, his

cocky veneer cracking like a cheap vase.

"Listen to me, asshole," he said, lowering his voice so that only I could hear. "If you don't back off, we're gonna beat your snitching ass to a pulp."

Please try. Nothing would make me happier.

After eight years in Naval Special Forces, six years as a mercenary fighting around the world, and a few years of taking on bad guys here in the States, I'd learned a thing or two. I was confident that I could hold my own against even the most dangerous criminals. I wasn't about to back down or be intimidated by this clown and his gang of shirtless gymnasts. Just not the way I'm wired.

"No, you listen to me," I said, stepping even closer to him. "One way or another, you're giving back everything you stole tonight. Whether that happens while all four of you are strapped to stretchers or standing under your own strength is up to you."

He froze for a moment, then eyed me up and down angrily.

"You gonna let him talk to us like that, boss?" Tarzan said.

He was moving in alongside the other two performers. They'd started taking down their equipment, but stopped and closed in like sharks sensing blood in the water.

The gathered crowd was antsy as they watched the scene unfold. Some kept quiet, but most yelled out for the performers to open up their bags. I'd managed to sway the crowd; now it was time to put an end to their charade.

"Give everything back," I stated, my tone revealing my irritation. "Now."

"Who the hell's going to make us?" the leader

said, sticking his chest out in front of me.

"I am," I replied.

"You mean we are," Ange said, stepping toward me along with Jack. "You're not hogging all the fun."

The leader eyed the three of us, then tossed his hands in the air in submission.

"Fine," he said, clearly irritated.

He stepped toward me, unclipped his fanny pack, then threw a quick haymaker. His intended target was the left side of my jaw. The moment before his knuckles landed, I weaved sideways. He was fast, but not fast enough.

Grabbing his forearm just below the elbow, I pulled his arm back and twisted his body around. I jerked hard, flaring his elbow out in a chicken wing and wrapping my left arm around his upper body.

He groaned and yelled as he tried to escape from my grasp.

"I'll break it," I said matter-of-factly. Then I looked up at the guy's three buddies and raised my voice. "One more step and I'll break it."

His body relaxed slightly. Then, by way of an answer, he yelled out barbarically and slammed the back of his head into my face. I just managed to turn my head to the side and avoid a broken nose, but the force of his thick skull slamming into my cheek still hurt like hell.

I grunted, and my upper body lurched sideways. The angry acrobat used the brief distraction to whip his body around and pull his arm loose. I narrowed my gaze as he spun around and stared me down.

Okay, asshole, if this is the way you want it. Just don't say I didn't warn you.

He might have been incredibly fit, an experienced performer, and a decent thief, but he was about to find out that he was in way over his head.

He engaged me a second time, lunging toward me and gritting his teeth as he threw another punch my way. I took a step back, planted my left leg into the ground, and hit him with a strong side kick. My right heel smashed into his jaw. I heard bones crack as his head whipped sideways and his body spun, trying to keep up. He slammed hard into the pavement, his body motionless.

Without a moment's hesitation, I stormed toward the other performers, who were still coming at me confidently. Now in fight mode, my eyes scanned over each of them in a fraction of a second. None of them were armed.

I had my Sig Sauer P226 9mm handgun concealed in a holster under the right side of my waistband. Attached horizontally to the back of my leather belt was my razor-sharp titanium dive knife. I had options just in case things went south in a hurry but didn't plan on utilizing anything other than my fists.

Just as I stepped over the leader's unconscious body, a second guy came at me in a flying *Crouching Tiger, Hidden Dragon*–type kick. I slid to the side, grabbed hold of his body, then spun around and chucked him as hard as I could. A combination of his own momentum and my throw sent his short, lean body flying. He spun wildly before colliding hard into the pole they'd set up. The force caused the women holding the colorful stabilizing ropes to lose their grips, and the log slammed to the pavement like a fallen tree. His body collided hard with the ground, spun a few times, then disappeared over the edge. His water landing was signaled moments later by a loud splash.

Two down.

Next came the tallest of the group. He engaged me just as I took my eyes off the guy I'd just sent swimming.

Before I could react, he managed to strike me with a front kick, but I absorbed the blow as best I could and held his leg in place between my left arm and my chest. Gripping his thigh, I pulled him close, then jabbed my right fist square into his face. My knuckles shattered his sunglasses and cracked the fragile bones of his nose. Blood spewed out, and he gagged as I swept my right leg into his stabilizing leg. His body flew out from under him, and he nearly performed an unintentional backflip before gravity knocked him back to earth.

After watching me immobilize his three buddies, Tarzan came at me with reckless abandon. He threw a big, sweeping punch toward me. Dropping down, I grabbed the strap of his fanny pack and jerked him forward. With his body moving toward me, I hit him with a hard left, punching him right in the gut and knocking the air from his lungs. His upper body bent forward, his eyes grew wide, and his mouth shot open.

Releasing the strap of his fanny pack, I jammed my right hand forcefully up into his neck, crunching his trachea. He wobbled sideways, then collapsed onto the ground. He wrapped his hands around his neck and struggled for air. Wheezing and gasps filled the air. His face was pure panic as he rolled from side to side.

I took in a breath and let it out as I rose up onto one knee.

Looking up, I saw that the guy with the bleeding, broken nose was struggling to rise to his feet. Out of the four performers, he was the only one who seemingly hadn't had enough.

Before I could finish what I'd started, Ange swept in from behind me and kicked him across the face, knocking him out.

The crowd cheered, whistled, and clapped wildly as I rose to my feet. I felt like a professional boxer who'd just dethroned the heavyweight champion and claimed myself a shiny golden belt.

Ange turned around and placed her hands on her hips as she looked at me.

"So much for not hogging all of the fun," she said, shooting me a slight grin.

The truth was, it had all happened too fast for either her or Jack to make a move. The entire confrontation had lasted only a few seconds beginning the moment I'd sent their leader to sleep.

"Sorry," I said with a shrug. "Guess I got a little carried away."

"You're not sorry," Ange corrected me.

She was right. I wasn't. Something about witnessing injustice gets my blood boiling, and I take satisfaction in putting a stop to it, whether it requires the use of force or diplomacy.

"You're bleeding," she said, her tone shifting as she knelt down beside me and examined my left cheek.

"A lucky shot," I said, waving her off.

There was only a little bit of blood. My jaw was sore as I slid it side to side, but it didn't feel like anything was broken.

Suddenly, part of the crowd shifted from cheers to shouts of anger. I turned my head to look out over the water. At the edge of the square, the guy I'd sent swimming was climbing up into view. Water dripped down from his soaked body and his face contorted with rage as he staggered to his feet and eyed me angrily.

He took two steps toward me before a big-bellied tourist shattered a beer bottle on his head. He wobbled, then collapsed to the ground and joined his friends in their naptime.

The crowd cheered again, and the big-bellied guy yelled out victoriously as he waved what remained of the bottle high in the air. Jack appeared at my left, and the three of us laughed as we looked at each other and the surrounding chaos.

SEVEN

"Alright, everybody back!" Jane Verona shouted as she appeared through the crowd in her dark blue Key West Police Department uniform.

Jane was the temporary sheriff and had arrived just as the aftermath of the fight was beginning to get out of hand. With four unconscious thieves on the ground and a few bags of stolen goods, the highly intoxicated group surrounding us would've been nearly impossible for us to control.

Two other police officers showed up, helping Jane take command of the scene. Jane gives off a strong Michelle Rodriguez vibe. She's a tough-as-nails Hispanic woman with a pretty face and a take-control mentality. She's only about five and a half feet tall, but she's incredibly strong and carries herself in a way that makes her look much taller.

As the two other officers kept the crowd at bay,

she stepped toward us and looked over the scene.

"Well, if it isn't Key West's very own Batman," Jane said. She looked over at the four unconscious performers and added, "Nice to see you're dialing down your vigilante side."

"You're welcome," I replied with a smile. "And you sound more and more like Charles every day. Gotta talk to the mayor and have him make your title official."

She cracked a smile. Charles Wilkes had been the island's previous sheriff. A great lawman and a better friend, he'd been murdered by a ruthless and corrupt group of private military members six months earlier.

After a moment she said, "So, you guys gonna keep me in suspense here, or are you gonna tell me why you decided to put a unique exclamation point on this evening?"

We told her everything, and by the time the paramedics arrived, she was thanking us for intervening. She turned away from us only when a couple of college-aged kids grabbed hold of one of the fanny packs and started rummaging through it.

"Drop it!" Jane yelled in a spine-chilling, hell-hath-no-fury tone.

The young guy holding the pack froze, his face filled with terror. He wisely did as he was told, and Jane began the process of returning the stolen goods to their rightful owners.

"Nice moves, Logan," a familiar voice said from behind me.

I turned around and saw a middle-aged woman dressed up as a cat. Body paint, a mask, the works.

"Harper?" Ange said, raising her eyebrows.

The cat nodded, and she lifted the mask, revealing her pale face. Harper Ridley was a reporter for the *Keynoter*, Key West's local paper. She'd been working there forever and we'd become friends over the years. Not only was she a great writer, but she'd also helped us a lot in tracking down notorious serial killers who'd been killing across the Everglades.

"I always knew you were secretly a crazy cat lady," I said, "but I think you're taking it a bit too far."

She laughed.

"Who ever said it was a secret?" She grabbed a small notepad and pen that she always kept on her person someplace and added, "Who should I write saved the day this time? I'm running out of ideas for fake names."

It hadn't exactly been my first brush with danger since I'd moved to the Keys, and I've never liked attention. So naturally, I'd struck a bargain with Harper not to use my name in her editions of the *Keynoter*.

"Plain old good Samaritan always works," Ange said.

"Or you could listen to Jane and just start calling him Batman," Jack said with a grin.

"Already working on a custom spotlight," Jane called out, listening in on our conversation. "I'm thinking a Dodge logo, or maybe the Navy SEAL trident."

I chuckled and shook my head. Never really thought of myself as heroic. If I see evil taking place, I take action. Just that simple. Once Harper was content she had enough for her story, I thanked her for her discretion, and Jane for taking over the scene.

"Well, that was a fun little bit of danger," Ange said as we turned to leave.

"The only danger is gonna be getting out of here

without dying of alcohol poisoning," Jack said as a hundred rowdy people offered us drinks at the same time.

We managed to slip through the raging crowd of party animals. By the time we reached the Conch Harbor Marina just up the waterfront, Jack was the only one having a hard time staying on his feet. The fourth-generation conch embraced the islands and all of their traditions to his core.

We helped him onto his boat and made sure he crashed onto a bed. Then Ange and I strolled down the dock to where our forty-eight-foot Baia Flash was moored. It was a sleek, shiny blue-hulled boat that offered the perfect combination of speed and comfort. *Dodging Bullets* was painted in white letters on the transom.

I heard the sound of happy paws coming from below deck as I disengaged the security system, climbed aboard, and hinged open the main hatch. My yellow Lab, Atticus, jumped topside in a flash of energetic movement. He licked us both, acting as if he hadn't seen us in years, then I took him for a quick walk down along the wharf.

After a late-evening snack of leftover shrimp Alfredo, we sat up on the sunbed and drank a few Paradise Sunset beers while Ange tended my cheek. Even though it was nearly midnight, the marina and the downtown streets were buzzing with activity.

When she finished fixing me up, she grabbed two more beers from the saloon and nestled beside me. She kept her gaze drawn out over the dark, calm water of the marina.

"Something on your mind?" I asked.

She'd been unusually quiet, and I could tell her mind was busy at work.

"What are we going to do about the children's shelter?" she said.

I nodded. Jack's mention of it had crawled back into my mind a few times since the scuffle at the square.

I wrapped an arm around her.

"We'll figure something out, Ange."

She paused a moment, then cracked a slight smile.

"You know, I had fun tonight," she said, changing the subject.

"Me too," I said. "I think those guys are gonna think twice before stealing again."

"Or they're gonna swear revenge for the embarrassment and ass-kicking. Guess we should watch our backs."

I laughed. "Yeah, 'cause our list of bad guys we've crossed wasn't big enough already."

We stayed up another hour talking, then headed to the main cabin and made passionate love before passing out to the sound of distant music and lapping water against the hull.

EIGHT

I woke up to the bright sun as its light shone through the overhead hatch. It was open, allowing a refreshing breeze to sweep in. Gulls flew past, and I heard occasional splashes as fish swiped bugs from the water's surface.

Leaning onto my side, I grabbed my phone from the nightstand and saw that I'd received a message. It was from Pete. He wanted to meet with me later that morning. He said it was something important, though not an emergency.

I stepped barefoot into the galley, greeted Atticus, then filled his food and water bowls. Climbing topside, I looked around at the quiet marina while taking in deep breaths of fresh air. Ange met me in the saloon wearing nothing but one of my tee shirts.

I whipped up a quick mango banana smoothie

and some coffee for breakfast. After showering and getting dressed, we locked up the Baia and headed for the parking lot. My black Tacoma 4x4 was backed into a first-row parking spot. The three of us climbed in, and I started up the six-cylinder engine.

"Any idea what this is about?" Ange said.

I shrugged. "Not a clue. You never really know with Pete."

She laughed as I drove us out of the lot.

We pulled into the seashell lot in front of Salty Pete's just after 0900. While walking to the front door, Atticus trotted over to his usual spot in the shade of a gumbo-limbo tree. But instead of doing a few quick circles and plopping down, he caught a whiff of something and took off toward the backside of the restaurant.

"Atticus!" Ange yelled, but he'd already disappeared from view.

"I got him," I said, stopping Ange as she stepped toward my sometimes overly curious pooch. "Tell Pete I'll be right in," I added as she headed for the door, and I jogged after him.

I rounded a large snow bush at the corner. The backyard was small, just a patch of green surrounded by trees on two sides and a shed at the back that Pete used to work on old cars. Jack's nephew, Isaac, worked at Pete's part-time, and he did an excellent job mowing the grass and trimming the edges.

I spotted Atticus right away. He was playing in the middle of the yard and staring at a shirtless guy who looked like he was in his seventies and was striking a Lord of the Dance yoga pose. For a moment I thought I was seeing things, that maybe one of the jerk Cirque du Soleil wannabes had hit me a little too hard across the head.

Then the guy spoke.

"Easy, boy," he said to Atticus. "Sit."

To my amazement, Atticus relaxed and instantly did as he was told. He usually only took orders from myself or Ange.

"Thanks," I said, walking toward them. "He's still a puppy at heart."

"Aren't we all," the guy replied without looking up at me.

I wasn't sure how to reply to that, so I just bent down and petted my curious pooch. The guy looked even more unorthodox up close. He had a strange build. He looked strong but had a lot of loose skin. He was incredibly tan and had more scars than I could count to go along with two visible tattoos, a lighthouse on his right arm and an anchor on the other. He had thick white hair and a matching scruffy beard.

"Come on, Atticus," I said sternly. When he hopped back toward the front of the restaurant, I turned back to the guy, "Sorry for disturbing your workout."

He waved me off.

"Just finishing up," he said, planting his raised foot to the grass.

"That's a tough move."

He smiled. "Been doing yoga for a few years now. Back in '87, my doctor told me that I needed to ease back on the booze and fried foods and recommended that I start doing yoga every day." He laughed and added, "One out of three ain't bad. Hell, that'd get me into the Hall of Fame if I was a ballplayer."

I laughed.

"Well, you're not dead, so I guess it's working,"

I said. "Never seen you around before. You friends with Pete?"

He nodded. "Used to live here. Just visiting for a few days."

He turned to face me for the first time. His face was tanned and covered in sunspots, but the first thing I noticed was the impressive fresh shiner around his right eye. He also had a few cuts to his forehead and bruised cheeks.

"Jeez, are you alright?"

He looked at me for a moment, confused, then lifted a hand to his eye and nodded.

"Just had a little too much fun last night, if you know what I mean." He stepped over and extended his hand. "Walt."

"Logan," I said.

A little too much fun? More like he got hammered and lost a fight with a staircase by the looks of it.

He had a firm grip despite his lean frame. He paused a moment as we shook hands, then raised his eyebrows.

"Logan Dodge?"

I nodded slowly, then narrowed my gaze and tilted my head, confused how he knew me.

"Pete says you might be able to help us with something," he explained.

"Something?"

He grabbed his shirt from the grass, wiping the sweat from his brow. Atticus barked from the side of the restaurant. I looked up and saw Ange leaning over the second-floor balcony.

"You coming, babe?" she said.

"Be right up."

I turned back to Walt and was about to ask what

he and Pete needed help with when he beat me to it.

"We'll explain everything," he said as he slid his blue shirt on. "See if you're interested. Let's go get something cold to drink."

Atticus plopped down in his usual spot while we headed inside. Pete's didn't open until noon, so the dining area was empty. We met Ange and Pete up on the balcony. It was covered with umbrella-shaded tables, with a bar on one side and, a small stage on another, and had a beautiful view of the ocean.

"I see you two have already met," Pete said.

He stood from a table near the railing and patted me on the back when I reached him. Ange stayed seated and took a drink of her Key limeade.

"Wow, are you alright?" Ange asked when she saw Walt's face.

He waved her off. "Just took a tumble down some steps, Miss…?"

Stairs. I figured as much.

"Walt, this is my wife Angelina," I said. "Ange, this is—"

"Walt Grissom," he said, stepping toward Ange and offering a hand.

"Wait a second," I said, "you're Walt Grissom? Like *the* Walt Grissom?"

"Yep," Pete said, answering for him. "The one and only. Famous treasure hunter extraordinaire."

I was impressed. Walt Grissom was one of the best-known treasure hunters in the world. He'd made headlines years ago for his extensive research and salvage work throughout the Caribbean.

"I liked your book on the Spanish galleons off Jamaica," I said as I sat down and filled a glass from the pitcher of fresh juice.

He laughed. "Well, I hope you did. Writing the

damn thing took even longer than finding and salvaging the wrecks."

I took a sip and leaned back into my chair.

Suddenly, Jack appeared through the glass. He slid open the door, stepped out, and strode toward our table.

"Figured you'd be out at least until this evening," I joked as he pulled out a chair and sat down.

He looked like he'd just woken up and the word *hungover* just didn't do justice to how he was feeling.

Jack was notorious for his impressive sleeping in. That, combined with the fact that he didn't wear a watch, meant that he fully embraced the island time mentality.

"Coffee?" was all he said, and I grabbed the pot and handed it to him after filling my mug.

There was a short moment of silence, then Pete said, "I heard you had a little excitement last night."

I smiled. The coconut telegraph was working even faster than usual.

I eyed both Pete and Walt. "I'm guessing you two didn't have us meet you so we could talk about a little brawl."

Pete laughed. "Logan here isn't one for beating around the bush."

"Neither am I," Walt said.

Pete and Walt then explained the situation, beginning with the history of the Florentine Diamond, a rare stone that had been lost for over a hundred years. I'd heard the local legend before but never thought there was much truth to it.

In an animated tone, Walt explained how the diamond had been secretly purchased by Henry Flagler, the oil baron co-founder of Standard Oil and one of the richest men of his time. He explained how

Flagler had purchased it while planning his railroad down to Key West, then it was stolen and fell into the hands of a famous archeologist.

"Alfred Hastings hid the diamond and gave a clue to its whereabouts on his deathbed," Walt explained. "He also spoke the famous last words you all may have read before: 'Of all the secrets in my life, I hid the greatest at the bottom and in the center.' Of course, these words are meaningless without the proper clues."

"Exactly," Pete said. "And when one of the clues vanished, the trail quickly turned cold."

"Let me guess," Ange said. "You found the clue."

"Well, not yet," Walt said. "But we have a good idea of where it could be."

He continued, telling us about a pair of antique dealers from Miami and their unfortunate falling-out during the Labor Day Hurricane of 1935. He explained how he had good reason to believe that the key to finding the diamond, a custom gold compass, lay somewhere on the seafloor in Snake Creek, a channel that cuts between Windley Key and Plantation Key.

"Wait a second," Jack said. "Even if one of these guys had the compass on them, it could be anywhere. Bodies from that monster 'cane washed up all the way as far as Cape Coral."

Walt nodded. "We've thought about that. If the compass is as big and heavy as we're expecting, there's a good chance it fell and sank. Based on Pete's and my combined salvaging experience, we're both confident that the compass is still somewhere in the channel."

We paused a moment, thinking it over.

"Say somehow we do manage to find this thing," Ange said. "What then? That look in your eye tells me you're not interested in going the Indiana Jones route and donating it to a museum."

"I've given more treasure to governments and paid more taxes than just about anyone alive," Walt said. "No, this one's ours. This one's my retirement fund, and whatever you all want your half for." He closed his eyes and continued, "I'm talking white beaches, tropical drinks with those little umbrellas, and a few beautiful women for the rest of whatever time I got left."

The table fell silent for a moment as we let his words marinate. I glanced over at Pete, and we exchanged quick smiles. This guy was quite the character. Regardless, it was clear that when it came to treasure and salvage, he was everything I'd read about him and more.

"So, just out of curiosity," Jack said, "how much dinero are we talking about here, man?"

Walt paused a moment.

"The Florentine is a one-hundred-and-thirty-seven-carat yellow diamond. Based on pure weight alone and not taking the historical significance into question, we're looking at about ten mil. But I'm willing to bet we can easily secure closer to twenty, given how rare it is."

Twenty million dollars.

The immense figure rolled around in my head. My mind instantly shot back to what Jack had told me the previous evening at Mallory Square. That kind of money could set up an organization like the children's shelter for decades, and it could help to fund similar programs around the state. If we did find it, it would be fitting that a good portion would go toward helping the young and neglected children of southern Florida.

"But we need to move fast," Walt said. "Like *today* fast. Been hunting treasure around the world for years, and it's always the same. Once people catch the scent of treasure, it's every man's game. The prospect of sudden immense wealth drives many men mad. It leads to betrayals among good friends. It even leads to murder."

His words made me think of Benjamin Kincade, a former Key West police officer and friend who'd handed me over to Black Venom for far less than this diamond was worth. The notorious Mexican drug cartel had put a bounty on my capture after we'd fought off their attempt to steal the Aztec treasure.

We asked politely if we could have a moment to speak with Pete in private. Walt was happy to oblige.

"Take all the time you need," he said, rising to his feet. "I'm gonna go raid the kitchen."

Pete laughed and told him he'd be opening a tab.

"You can take it out of my cut for the diamond," he replied with a wink as he entered through the sliding glass door.

He disappeared from sight, heading downstairs. I hoped his hangover had dwindled enough for him to be up to the task of stairs this time.

"Quite the character," Ange said.

"He's old-school Florida Keys," Pete said.

"Funny," Jack said, "I thought you were old-school."

"Even older, boyo, believe it or not. Grissom's been roaming the islands since the fifties."

There was a brief silence, and the three of us exchanged dubious glances.

"I can see you're skeptical," Pete said. He shook

his head and added, "We can make other arrangements. I just wanted to run it all by you guys first. Now that I'm getting up there in age, you're the best folks around for a job like this."

"You know we trust you," I said. "Like family we trust you. But this guy, something seems off about him. Seems like there's something he's not telling us. I mean, why is he in such a hurry? Doesn't strike me as someone who's got a lot of places to be and things to do."

"He's an alcoholic," Pete said. "Been there myself at one point. It's not an easy road to travel. He's also broke. I'd be in a hurry to strike it big myself if I had his lot."

"But you trust him, though?" Ange said.

"The Walt Grissom I used to know was one of the best friends I ever had. He was the real deal. He is the real deal. If he says we can find this diamond, come hell or high water, there's a good chance that he's right."

We paused a moment. I looked over at Ange. She locked eyes with me for a few seconds, then nodded.

"Alright," I said. "Let's go for it."

NINE

It was 0900 when we arrived back at the Conch Harbor Marina. We assembled at the stern of Jack's forty-five-foot Sea Ray at slip forty-seven, just down the dock from where I moored the Baia. He'd named it *Calypso* when he'd purchased it years earlier. It was a traditional name for his family's boats and served as the flagship for Rubio Charters.

It was a beautiful boat, with gleaming white hulls, plenty of deck space, and a flybridge above. Flapping in the calm morning breeze high overhead were two flags: a black Jolly Roger pirate flag and a dive flag.

We loaded up the cooler, then Ange and I headed down to the Baia to grab our gear. We zipped open a few black duffels and packed up our wetsuits, BCDs, fins, and masks. Jack had plenty of tanks and dive weights, so we left ours.

74

I already had my Sig concealed under the right side of my waistband with a fully loaded fifteen-round magazine. I didn't have to ask Ange to know that she was armed as well with her go-to Glock 26. We had plenty of firepower to defend ourselves, just in case we ran into trouble. Not that we were expecting any. We just both liked to be on the prepared side of things when shit hit the fan unexpectedly.

With our dive gear in order, I grabbed a large heavy-duty plastic hard case from the guest cabin, then ran through a checklist in my mind. Confident that we had everything we'd need, we hauled our gear topside, then locked the Baia and activated the security system.

Pete and Walt showed up just in time to help us carry the gear over to the *Calypso*. Pete had filled a large cooler of food and drinks from the kitchen. It was clear that we had a long day ahead of us, and we wanted to spend as much time as we could out on the water.

Before heading out for the day, I walked over to the office to look for Gus Henderson, the owner of the marina. When not helping customers, I usually found him watching television while snacking on potato chips and lounging on a giant beanbag chair. Today, however, he was working on an old Evinrude outboard engine he had up on wooden blocks.

"Hey, Logan. You guys looking to buy some raffle tickets?" he said, rising to his feet upon seeing me. "We're giving away a hundred-dollar gift certificate to the Greasy Pelican."

"Not at the moment, Gus," I said. "Just need to get into storage."

"Goin' kayaking?"

"Not this time."

He unlocked the large shed and pulled open the double doors. The big metal object I was after was right where Jack and I had left it.

I strode into the shed, then looked back at Gus.

He smiled.

"Taking the mailbox out, huh?" he said.

I nodded.

A mailbox is a giant metal shroud that's shaped to form a ninety-degree angle. When mounted to the stern, it's used to redirect a boat's prop wash to the seafloor. Credited to being invented by the famous salvager, Mel Fisher, mailboxes have become one of the primary ways to clear away sediment and debris from the seafloor when searching for wrecks or other artifacts.

Gus helped me load it up onto a flat metal cart.

"After another pirate ship, Logan?" he asked enthusiastically.

I laughed. "Not quite. But I'll be sure to let you know if we happen to find anything out of the ordinary."

I rolled the cart out of the shed and down the dock toward the *Calypso*, the wheels thudding rhythmically with every gap in the mahogany planks. Jack didn't usually keep it aboard. Having adequate space for patrons and all of their gear during dive charters is vital, so the bulky piece of equipment spent most of its time in storage. Jack helped me lift it up onto the deck, then I wheeled the cart back to Gus.

Once everything was aboard the *Calypso* and we were ready to make way, Jack started up the twin 300-hp engines.

"Topped off the main tanks and the spares, bro," he said as he motored us slowly out of the marina.

"We're set for a long day of mowing."

I smiled and nodded. *Mowing the lawn* is a term used by salvagers and treasure hunters around the world. It's used to describe the process of surveying a large area of the ocean floor by performing back-and-forth scans, just like when cutting your grass.

Once past the white no-wake-zone buoys, Jack hit the throttles, bringing us up on plane and motoring us out of Key West Bight at our cruising speed of twenty knots. It was a beautiful October morning. Not too hot, not too cold. A calm four-knot breeze coming in from the east. A hell of a day to spend out on the water.

We lounged on the cushioned seats up in the flybridge and opened a few bottled waters. Jack piloted us around Fort Zachary Taylor, then turned east. We had roughly seventy miles of ocean and islands to cover to reach our destination.

Walt had his leather bag open and pulled out a journal, a few old books, charts, and sketches. He shuffled closer to us and showed us a few pictures.

"This is how the Florida East Coast Railroad's emergency relief train looked after the Labor Day Hurricane," he said, holding a black-and-white photo out in front of us.

I gazed upon the jagged line of train cars lying on their sides off the track. The scene was bleak, devoid of any structures or even trees. Only scattered, broken remnants littered the flat, sandy landscape. It looked like a scene straight out of a postapocalyptic movie.

"That looks horrible," Ange said.

Walt nodded. "It was a bloody nightmare. Winds in excess of two hundred miles per hour completely leveled the Matecumbes. The hundred-and-sixty-ton locomotive was the only thing that remained

77

standing."

Ange and I stared in awe as Walt showed us a few more images of the train and the surrounding destruction caused by Mother Nature's wrath. Pete and Jack kept quiet and looked either out over the water or down to the deck. The Labor Day Hurricane of 1935 was a hard subject for many conchs to talk about. It had been without question the most devastating loss the islands had ever experienced.

I bent down and petted Atticus, who was resting on the deck at my feet. He'd enjoyed the breeze for most of the trip but had gotten hot and was now enjoying the shade. After taking a swig of water, I cleared my throat and grabbed one of the charts.

"You're saying that these two dealers fell off the tracks here," I said, pointing at the Snake Creek Bridge.

Walt nodded. "That's right." He opened the leather-bound journal and turned to the entry he'd showed Pete the previous evening. "According to G.R. Branch, the trainmaster, he spotted two well-dressed men quarrel and disappear into the relentless surging sea while crossing a bridge just before they reached Windley."

Snake Creek Bridge is located at mile marker 86 on US-1 and connects Plantation Key and Windley Key just northeast of Islamorada. The bridge traverses a body of water roughly four hundred feet wide at its narrowest. The channel is called Snake Creek, and it runs from Florida Bay to the Atlantic.

"Looks like the channel's about two miles long," Jack said. He'd moved closer and was gazing at the chart. "We can rule out the Atlantic side."

"That's right," Walt said. "That 'cane traveled north and took just about everything with it."

Jack nodded, keeping his eyes glued to the chart.

"Gonna be only about eight feet deep," I said, moving my head close alongside my old friend's. "Little deeper near the bridge."

Using the calculator on my smartphone, Jack went to work punching in numbers. A moment later, he had our search area.

"Fifty acres, bro," he said.

"Not even a tenth of a square mile," Ange added.

"Sure as hell isn't the biggest lawn we've ever had to mow," Jack said, eyeing Ange and me.

He wasn't kidding. During our search for the *Valiant*, a famous pirate shipwreck, our search area had been one and a quarter square miles, or eight hundred acres. Needless to say, it had taken us weeks before we'd found the main remnants of the wreck.

"But if the compass managed to stay in his pocket," Ange said, "the search area could grow a lot bigger very quickly."

Walt smiled. "I always like to foresee on the side of hopeful."

Ange and I looked at each other. That kind of thinking was dangerous in our previous occupations. It was the kind of thinking that got people killed.

Roughly three hours later, just before noon, Jack eased back on the throttles and motored us into the narrow opening into Snake Creek. Compared to our usual relatively remote search areas, the channel was bustling with boat traffic. We passed two powerboats and a sailboat, both heading out for an afternoon on the water.

Jack piloted us under the sixty-foot-tall bridge, then put the engines in idle as we all took in the scene. To the west was a small marina. Right beside us to the east was the Islamorada Coast Guard

Station. To the north, the channel cut to the right, then eventually split before reaching Florida Bay. A large catamaran was moored in the center of the channel, and a group of paddleboarders were laughing and occasionally losing balance and splashing into the water.

"This could be problematic," Pete said, rising to his feet as he looked out over the starboard bow.

He wasn't looking at the passing boats, however. He was looking at row after row of housing communities, separated by channels along the eastern side of the channel.

"All that dredging of silt and soil over the years could very well make this venture of ours hopeless," he added.

It was a good point. We could spend a lifetime searching, but if the compass was buried thirty feet under a house's foundation, it wouldn't matter.

If Pete's words swayed Walt's resolve in the slightest, he didn't show it. He rose to his feet, took in a deep breath of fresh air, then pointed toward the shaded line of water under the bridge.

"I think it's high time we get the fish in the water," he said confidently. He was referring to the magnetometer, which is often referred to as a towfish. He removed his sunglasses and added, "See what we can find."

TEN

Jack stayed up in the flybridge to have a better view, but the rest of us migrated down to the main deck. I grabbed the hard case from where it rested against the starboard gunwale, then unclasped its hinges and lifted it open. The cigar-shaped yellow device looked more like a futuristic torpedo than a piece of salvage equipment.

Walt let out an impressive whistle as he laid eyes upon the advanced piece of equipment.

"Man, Pete," he said, "you weren't kidding about them being the right people for the job." He patted me on the back and added, "She's a Proton, right?"

"Yeah," I said. "Their newest model."

Ange helped me lift it out, and we ran a few quick diagnostics before hooking it up to my laptop.

When looking for a wreck, it's usually good practice to begin your search by creating a digital replication of the seafloor using sonar. Then, once you have a good idea of what the bottom looks like, you can go back over with a magnetometer and place metallic hot spots on your survey. But since we were only looking for one relatively small metallic object, it made sense to jump right into using the mag.

Once the mag was ready, I carried it over the transom.

"Gonna drop it in the water, Jack," I said, raising my voice so he could hear me over the low hum of the idling engines.

"Alright," he replied. "Bringing her up to three knots."

He slowly accelerated us, then turned around to face the bridge.

While waiting for Jack to finish the turn, I looked up at the cars passing on US-1, then closed my eyes and tried to imagine a train forcing its way across the old bridge as the most powerful storm in United States history roared into it. My eyes gravitated from the bridge down to the water below.

Could it be possible that a gold compass, and the only clue to the lost Florentine Diamond's whereabouts, has been sitting here all this time?

"All clear for now," he said. "Let her go!"

"Aye-aye!" I yelled. I stepped my bare feet to the edge of the swim platform, then bent down and splashed the forty-pound device into the water. I paid out about twenty feet of cable and watched for a few seconds to make sure that it was cutting through the water properly. Since the water was so shallow, I kept her gliding along just a few feet beneath the surface.

Once in place and swimming properly, I gave a thumbs-up to Jack.

"All set," I said, then stepped back over the

transom.

Ange sat on the padded stern bench seat with the computer in her lap while Pete and Walt sat on either side of her and peered at the monitor. Ange quickly adjusted the settings for the size of the object we were looking for. Again, Walt was impressed.

"Guess I can just sit back and relax for this one," he said with a smile. "You kids got it covered."

I stepped inside with Atticus right on my heels. After filling his food and water bowls, I moved back out into the warm tropical air. Having spent a good portion of his young life on the water, Atticus was comfortable on a boat and could spend the entire day sprawled out in the shade without showing any signs of unhappiness.

I moved to the stern and looked back and forth between the towfish and the laptop monitor. It appeared to be working perfectly, having already located a small handful of objects. The Proton has a total swath detection range of three thousand feet. That range is also unaffected by the medium between the mag and the metal target. Performance isn't affected whether detecting through air, water, silt, sand, or even solid coral. With those things in mind, there was no way we could pass over a compass without it being detected.

Once past the bridge, Jack idled us for a few minutes as we waited for a pleasure boat to motor out, then turned us around beside a small trolling fishing boat. Within five minutes, we were back where we'd started, and Jack brought us along an uninhabited part of the channel's eastern shoreline.

"This might be a little trickier than we thought," Ange said as I leaned over to look at the screen again.

Even with the narrow detection range that she'd

83

implemented to filter out objects that were either too big or too small, we still had over thirty hits already.

"Not surprised," Pete said. "This waterway's been used extensively for a hundred years. That's a lot of accumulated garbage, tools, and everything else that somehow finds its way into the ocean."

"Well, I think it's time we hook up the mailbox and take a proper look around," I said.

"That's the spirit," Walt said, patting me on the back.

Some of the objects detected were indicated at over five feet beneath the seabed, so unless we wanted to dive down and shovel our way through endless silt and rocks, the mailbox was our best option to see if one of the thirty-some-odd pieces of metal were our winner, winner, chicken dinner.

"Not that I'm a sucker for the rules or anything," I said. "But just out of curiosity, aren't we supposed to have a permit to do something like this?"

I was just playing devil's advocate, knowing that setting up the mailbox and turning the seafloor into a dirty storm was going to draw more than one set of suspicious eyes.

"Sometimes it's easier to beg for forgiveness than ask for permission," Pete said.

"Spoken like someone who's never served hard time before," Walt said. We all eyed him skeptically, which caused him to smile and add, "Not that I have, of course."

Since Pete knew most of the police officers and Coast Guardsman in the Keys, we figured we could get ourselves out of trouble if need be.

Jack brought us back around, then idled once we were over our first set of targets. We quickly installed the mailbox. Seeing that there was a break in the boat traffic, we looked up and gave Jack a thumbs-up.

"Here we go," he said excitedly.

He punched the throttles, causing the props to spin violently and send a surge of bubbling water straight toward the seafloor below. The water turned dark in an instant as a swirl of sediment quickly spread outward like a thick dust storm. Jack kept the engines running at nearly full throttle for thirty seconds before easing them back.

We watched as the clouds of dirt settled and were slowly carried off by the shifting tide.

Reaching into my gear bag, I grabbed my mask, snorkel, and fins. I slid off my tee shirt and tightened a weight belt with three pounds around my waist. The plan was to scuba, but I wanted to get into the water and see what kind of current and visibility we were dealing with before I donned my gear. I was also sweating from all the time out under the sun and was anxious to get cooled off.

Before diving in, I grabbed a waterproof handheld metal detector and an aluminum prospector scoop to dig up anything I found. I took one more look at the laptop screen, and Ange pointed out a few clustered targets below us.

"We'll get the gear ready while you're down," Jack said from up in the flybridge.

I nodded to him, then stepped down to the swim platform. After a quick rinse of my mask, I spit in both lenses, swooshed the saliva around with my finger, then gave it a quick dip in the seawater. Tightening it around my neck, I slid into my fins and dove headfirst into the water.

The water felt amazing and gave me newfound energy. The lead weight allowed me to sink to the bottom easily. The seafloor looked like a crater from being cleared away by the prop wash, and just as my stomach hit the remaining hard sediment, I powered on the metal detector and began my search.

The LED on the detector's controls was out and would illuminate when the device detected anything metal. It lit up either red, green, or white, depending on how close the metal object was. White meant it was within an inch of the device, green meant you'd have to do a little bit of digging, and red meant it was over six inches down. Jack had a more sophisticated detector aboard, but I preferred to use the wand when freediving.

After just a few seconds of scanning, the light illuminated. It was white.

I dug the scoop a few inches into the bottom and scooped out a small pile of sand and rocks. Reaching into the little basket, I grabbed our first catch of the day: a rusted old dock cleat.

I shrugged and dropped the worthless remnant into my mesh bag. At least we knew the mag was working.

I finned and watched as the green light came on. Another scoop, another grab. No dice again. This time it was a rusty broken fork.

I came up empty two more times, then surfaced.

"Anything?" Ange said as I caught my breath and looked over at the *Calypso*.

"Oh for four on that dive," I replied.

I kicked over to the stern and set the mesh bag on the swim platform. Ange had brought over a plastic bucket, and I emptied the contents so that we wouldn't waste our time with the same hits over and over again.

"You part fish or something?" Walt asked, raising his sunglasses to his forehead. He'd removed his shirt and had one foot up on the transom. "You were down there forever."

I laughed, then glanced at my dive watch.

"Just three minutes," I said, reading the LCD screen.

My Suunto dive computer allowed me to track both scuba and freediving.

Ange had the laptop in her hands. She sat on the transom and turned the screen around to face me.

"Got another group of hits right here," she said.

I pulled myself up to get a better view, and she pointed to a spot on the channel floor. I nodded, then performed a few more fruitless free dives before Ange and I decided to don our scuba gear.

We slid into our 3mm wetsuits, then tightened our nitrogen-enriched tanks to our BCDs and strapped them on. Using nitrogen-enriched air, commonly referred to as nitrox, would allow us to stay down longer. Once geared up and ready to go, we stepped off the swim platform and splashed into the water.

We got into a routine of wash away the sediment, dive and dig up the hits, repeat. Since there were a decent amount of shallow rocky areas at the edge of the channel under the bridge, Walt slipped into a pair of knee-high boots, and we dropped him off. Using the other metal detector, he walked back and forth along the mud and barnacle-encrusted rocks, scanning and digging as he went.

After an hour and a half of diving, Ange and I switched places with Jack and Pete. By 1300 we were just about finished digging up the first sweep of hits. So far we'd found a D battery, a flip phone, an old pair of glasses, a railroad spike, and a handful of various other random pieces of discarded metal. We'd manage to fill and remove three buckets worth of junk, but no compass.

I glanced over at Atticus, who was lounging just inside the sliding glass door. He was looking a little bored and antsy, so I grabbed a tennis ball from inside and tossed it far out over the water. Without a moment's hesitation, he sprang to his feet and dove with reckless abandon over the port gunwale. When it comes to dogs, Labs are about as good of swimmers as they come, and Atticus never turned down an opportunity to go for a dip, especially on a hot day.

After twenty minutes of playtime and with just a few hits left until Pete and Jack would surface, I stepped into the galley and came back out fifteen minutes later.

"Lunch's ready," I said.

I whipped up some lobster rolls to fuel an afternoon of searching. Just as I told Ange, I looked toward the opening of the channel as the sound of heavy metal music filled the air. It was the fishing boat we'd seen earlier, motoring back into the channel after a half day's charter.

"Anything?" I added, motioning toward the water and the rising bubbles.

Ange shook her head.

She directed her gaze to the eastern shoreline and said, "Looks like we might have trouble, though."

I looked over and saw Walt standing in knee-deep water. He had his back to us and was talking to a group of three guys about fifty feet away from him on a grassy bank. From where Ange and I stood at the stern of the *Calypso*, it was impossible to hear what they were saying, but judging by their body language, it didn't look friendly. That was putting it mildly. The truth was, the three guys looked beyond pissed off. They were young, well built, and sure as hell didn't look like locals.

It appeared as though their little chat was growing more and more heated by the second. I couldn't tell for sure what he had, but the guy in the middle was hovering his right hand at an unusual position near the back of his waistband. It didn't take a psychic to predict what he was likely reaching for.

"Ange," I said as I stepped to the port gunwale.

"I see it," she said, reaching for her holstered Glock.

We were far off for an accurate pistol shot, but I wanted to at least have Walt's back in case something bad was about to go down.

"Walt!" I called out.

He didn't turn around, but the three guys tilted their heads up in unison to look my way. They each wore dark sunglasses, button-up dress shirts, and tight slacks.

The music I'd heard earlier grew louder and louder as the fishing boat motored toward us in the narrow channel. I kept my eyes glued to the situation on the shore, however.

Who the hell are these guys, and what do they want?

I thought back to what Walt had said earlier—how once people catch a whiff of treasure, they tend to go mad.

How could anyone possibly know about it already? Unless... unless we weren't the first ones Walt told.

"Logan!" Ange called out.

I snapped my head back to look at her and, to my surprise, she was no longer eyeing the suspicious activity on the shore. Instead, she was pointing over the starboard side of the *Calypso* at the passing fishing boat. Their music was loud, so loud I could barely think. But I realized that she was pointing at one of the large fishing poles that were secured in a holder at the stern, its line still out.

My eyes followed the line, and I realized that the lure at the end was heading straight for Jack. In an instant, the shiny hook stabbed into his body and dragged him through the water.

The line went taut, the pole bowed dramatically, and the bail zipped.

ELEVEN

As if a switch had gone off in my mind, my adrenaline surged, and everything around me was instantly in slow motion.

Ange calls it SEAL mode, and it's a trait I've had since I was a kid. It's like in that movie *For Love of the Game*, when Kevin Costner's on the mound and he says, "Clear the mechanism." Or when Spider-Man's Spidey sense tingles. Everything around me goes quiet. Everything slows.

"Hey!" I yelled out at the top of my lungs, trying desperately to get the attention of anyone on the fishing boat.

It was useless. The wild group couldn't hear me over the roar of their speakers, blaring out "Highway to Hell."

With time running out and my friend in serious trouble, I lunged up to the starboard gunwale and dove as far as I could out into the water. I cut cleanly through the surface and kept my body streamlined as I transitioned in the most intense freestyle stroke of my life.

My pulse skyrocketed as I forced my way through the water, trying desperately to reach Jack before he was dragged past. I forced my eyes to stay open under the salty water, pushing through the burn and focusing my blurry gaze on Jack as he was pulled backward.

He struggled to get free of the hook and yelled out bubbles from the pain, leaving a trail of red in the water as he moved.

If he'd been tangled in something less dangerous, I could have grabbed hold of him and held on for the ride as I cut him free. But the cloud of blood indicated that the hook was secured to his body and not the BCD. If I grabbed him, my extra weight would cause the sharp tip to dig in even deeper, or it could rip off a chunk of his flesh.

No, I need to cut him loose. I need to go straight for the line.

I took in a deep breath, then kicked with everything I had and took one final stroke, pulling the water back and propelling my body forward and down. When my hand reached the end of the stroke, I snatched my dive knife from its sheath at the back of my waistband.

Extending it forward, I reached as far as I could. I continued to kick and slashed the sharpened titanium blade against the taut line just inches above Jack's struggling body. In a heart-pounding instant, the line snapped, and Jack's body quickly slowed to a stop.

I grabbed hold of his BCD and turned him

around to face me. Somehow, he'd managed to keep his second stage in his mouth. He was squinting through the dive mask and yelling out bubbles as he placed a hand over his left shoulder.

Maintaining composure as best I could, I held the power inflator button on the end of the inflator hose, causing air to be transferred from his dive tank into his BCD. A moment later, we broke the surface. Keeping my body behind his, I wrapped an arm around his chest, and we both kicked for the stern of the *Calypso*.

Pete surfaced just as we reached the swim platform. He removed Jack's fins while I unclipped and slid off his BCD.

"Shit, this hurts, bro," he said, wincing as he looked at the five-inch-long hook that was burrowed deep under the left side of his collarbone.

Blood continued to drip out. A dangerous amount of blood.

Once free of his equipment, I climbed up onto the swim platform and grabbed him under his armpits. Ange stepped over and helped me lift him up out of the water, over the transom, and onto the deck. Drops of deep red splattered against the white deck as we quickly examined the wound.

"Ange, first aid kit," I said, but before the words were off my lips, she was already grabbing the large red hard case Jack kept bungee-strapped under the flybridge stairs.

She popped it open, and I snatched a pair of scissors to cut part of his wetsuit off.

"Wait!" Jack said, raising a hand to stop me before using the neoprene for arts and crafts. He winced as he rolled over and struggled to unzip the back of it. "This is my favorite wetsuit, bro."

93

I shook my head and helped him loosen it.

"You crazy conch."

The hook was so big, it completely wrapped around his collarbone and the tip stuck out from the neoprene on the other side. Ange grabbed a pair of needle-nose pliers and flattened the pointy barb. Trying to pull the hook out with it still in place would make his wounds a hell of a lot worse.

As carefully and delicately as she could, Ange grabbed hold of the hook and pulled it out. Jack let out a grunt and a few rounds of curses as the bloody point came free.

With the hook removed, I rolled down his wetsuit, allowing us to see the extent of the damage for the first time.

"You're lucky," Ange said. "Looks like it didn't hit your cephalic vein. Just muscle tissue."

He took in a few breaths, then nodded.

"Alright, patch me up," he said, ignoring the pain. "I think we're getting close."

"I think you should stay on the boat from now on," I said. "First that .45-caliber to your side a few months ago and now this?" I shook my head. "You're either the luckiest or unluckiest guy alive."

"Or maybe I'm on the grim reaper's most wanted list," he fired back. "Ever seen *Final Destination*?"

After removing his gear, Pete climbed over and lent a hand. Just as we were finishing patching him up, Walt climbed up onto the swim platform, having swum over with his hands raised, carrying his boots and metal detector.

"Holy crap!" he said. "Is he alright?"

"Just a scratch," Jack said as Ange pressed the outer bandage down. "I gotta say, I've been running charters for a long time and I've never seen that one

94

before."

Seeing that my friend was just fine, I laughed and said, "You might've been a record catch had they been able to pull you in."

I helped Jack up onto the padded bench, then washed off the blood with the freshwater hose.

"The fishing boat took off," Walt said, pointing over the bow. "Not sure if they even realized what happened."

"I didn't recognize the boat," Pete said as he glared out over the channel. "Some people just don't belong out on the water."

I grabbed a towel from inside and dried off while taking a swig of water, then offered the bottle to Ange. When I reached into the cooler to grab a bottle for Jack, he said that given the situation, he'd prefer something a little stronger. I exchanged the water for a bottle of tequila, handed it to him, then looked over at Walt.

"Who were those guys you were talking to?" I asked, after taking a moment to collect my thoughts.

Walt tilted his head, then fell silent for a moment. His demeanor shifted in an instant. I could tell that he was suddenly uncomfortable and also that he was trying his best to hide it.

"Those three on the shore?" he said. "Just a few old acquaintances."

"You sure you don't wanna try answering that again?" Ange said in her no-bullshit voice. "Because that looked like anything but a friendly chat between old friends. We were far off, but we know pissed off when we see it."

"Yeah," I said. "Anything you want to tell us? Like that maybe we aren't the only ones you've told about this search?"

He looked back and forth between Ange and me, his expression revealing what appeared to be genuine confusion.

"I don't know what to say," he began. "They're a couple of young men I used to know. They were eating over at Island Grill and saw me prospecting the shoreline."

Ange and I gave each other a look. Neither of us were buying it.

"They didn't look like locals," I said.

"Well, they aren't exactly," Walt clarified without skipping a beat. "They're visiting from St. Petersburg."

"And how do you explain their demeanors?" Ange said. "They looked like they wanted to rip off your head."

Walt shrugged. "Can't explain that. Just the way some folks are, I guess. We like to jab and make fun. They invited me to dinner, but I said I had other plans. I headed over as soon as I saw that Jack was about to become the catch of the day."

Jack laughed, then took a few long pulls from the bottle of tequila.

"Hey, what's with the twenty questions?" Pete said, confused by the sudden line of questioning.

I kept my gaze zeroed in on Walt, trying to read him as best I could. Having spent a significant amount of time in the Navy, I'd experienced a lot of those "friendly" interactions. Jabbing and attacking guys with friendly banter was a constant. He appeared to believe what he was saying, but still, something about the interaction had seemed off.

I looked at Ange, who gave a slight shrug, letting me know that maybe for now it wasn't worth it. She was right. But gut feelings are there for a reason.

They stem from our primal survival instincts, which have helped humans stay alive and avoid trouble for all of history. And I trusted both Ange and my instincts. We'd be keeping a sharp eye on this guy.

"Nothing," I said, waving a hand to finally respond to Pete's question. Stepping toward the saloon door, I added, "Alright, who's hungry?"

TWELVE

After lunch, we dove right back into the search. Within a few hours, we'd sifted through the entire channel under and within three hundred feet of the bridge. We directed our efforts north, where the channel widened to roughly six hundred feet. I kept focused on the task at hand but glanced every now and then at the nearest shoreline. The three guys Walt had been talking to were still lingering in my mind. I wasn't certain whether Walt was telling the truth about them or not, but I knew one thing: there were things he was keeping close to the chest.

We got into a routine of search with the mag, blow sediment away with the mailbox, dive the hits, repeat. Though our spirits were high, even after Jack's fishing incident, it was quickly becoming apparent how daunting our task could prove to be.

I looked around at our search site, the structures,

and the shape of the seafloor. Mankind, in general, doesn't like to leave nature be. We build, we destroy, we manipulate and change landscapes. The Snake Creek we were looking at was much different than the Snake Creek of 1935. Even in just seventy-four years, mankind had made drastic changes. Those projects, combined with storms and the shifting of the tides, made the odds of finding the compass bleak.

By the time the sun began to sink into the islands and distant ocean beyond, we'd searched over five of the most promising acres and had yet to discover anything remotely valuable, let alone the compass.

We ate a quick dinner up on the flybridge and watched the beautiful display of colors. I've made it a habit in my life to watch the sunset whenever I can. To take at least a few minutes and enjoy nature's art show that marks the ceremonious end to each day. My dad used to say that you only get to watch so many in your life, and you never know which one will be your last. I miss him every day, but especially when I'm out on the water. If he were still around, he'd have found the compass before lunch and had us back at the marina in Key West in time for happy hour.

Using high-powered dive flashlights, we continued long into the night. It was a calm evening, with little wind and just a few sporadic clouds. In the darkness above, we could see a brilliant display of stars and a nearly full moon that reflected off the channel. Traffic had died off, making us the only boat still in the channel aside from a tied-off catamaran.

By 0200, Jack and Pete were dozing off. They decided to call it a night just after that.

"I'm gonna keep at it," Walt said. "You all go off to bed if you want."

I enjoyed the quiet and the cool air of the evening, so I decided to stay at it longer too. Ange stuck with us for another hour, then passed out on the bench while gazing at the computer screen. I carried her into one of the guest cabins, then filled a thermos with coffee for what felt like the tenth time that evening before stepping back out to rejoin Walt.

The man was a machine. We'd been at it all day, but he hadn't slowed. I had to force myself to keep up with him, even though he was over twice my age.

He took a rare break and sat down beside me on the transom to refill his thermos with coffee.

"Some woman you got there," he said. "You're a lucky man."

I nodded.

"I kept waiting for her to come to her senses and ditch me, but it never happened."

I grinned, but Walt kept his face stuck in a serious expression.

"I once had a woman like her," he added.

I was about to correct him and state that there was no one like Angelina, but I let it slide.

"What happened?" I asked. "If you don't mind me asking."

"Not at all," he said, shaking his head. "Unfortunately, I messed everything up. Then after she left, I messed everything up with my son as well." He paused a moment, looking out over the water. "Haven't seen him in years. He took his mother's maiden name and eventually moved to Memphis and got married. I've never even met my grandchildren."

I took a sip of coffee and thought over his words. I never liked to give advice unless it was asked for, but I felt the need to speak my mind.

"Well, you aren't dead yet," I said. "Maybe

you'll meet them someday."

I wanted to add that he needed to man up and do some serious apologizing for whatever it was he had done. But I'd just met the guy and didn't want to delve too much into his personal life.

"Maybe so," was all he said.

He took a few more sips of coffee, then we went right back to work.

At 0400, we were finishing up our digs of the most recent mag search when Walt surfaced after just a few minutes beneath the waves. He ripped out his regulator and took a few struggled breaths.

"You alright?" I said, leaning over the starboard gunwale.

He coughed twice, then nodded unconvincingly.

"Think there's a crack in the mouthpiece," he said. "It's letting in water." He turned around and finned for the swim platform. "Be a hero and grab me a replacement, will ya?"

I nodded and stepped toward one of the gear bags. Before reaching inside to snatch another regulator, I glanced at my dive watch and shook my head.

"It's getting kinda late, Walt," I said. "We should call it a night and get back after it in the morning."

He lowered his mask, letting it hang around his neck, then smiled.

"Didn't peg you as a quitter," he said, taking a friendly jab at me.

"Look, Walt, I'm an advocate for being determined. But there's a fine line between tenacious and crazy, and you're flirting with it. There's no reason for us to be running ourselves to the bone like this."

I'd fought and trained all over the world. I'd been

pushed to the limit and beyond time and time again. My body and mind have been acclimated to perform even under heavy stress and severe sleep deprivation. But there was always a reason for the rhyme. A method to the madness. We went to the lengths that we did out of necessity, not for the hell of it.

"Those hits aren't gonna dig up themselves," he replied.

"Those hits will still be there in the morning."

Walt sighed and wiped the dripping water from his forehead.

"Alright," he said. "We'll turn in. But not yet." He turned and nodded toward the seafloor. "Let's just finish up these hits. I've got a good gut feeling."

I shook my head. He'd been saying stuff like that since we'd started our search over eighteen hours earlier. He was optimistic, there was no debating that. But optimism without common sense is like having the greatest ship in the world without... well, a compass. A fitting analogy to our present situation.

In the end, curiosity got the better of me. I relented, looked down at the water, and said, "Alright, Walt. Just these hits. Then we're hitting the sack."

I handed him the extra mouthpiece, and he quickly switched it out, then dropped back down into the dark water. He dug up a few more promising hits, but none of them turned out to be the compass.

"Your turn," he said, climbing up onto the swim platform and sliding off his BCD. "I'm all out of air."

He was finally starting to show signs of fatigue and disappointment. I think all of the crunched-up soda cans and rusted chain links had finally taken their toll on him.

I glanced over at the computer screen. We still had a few hits left, but they were small and scattered along the outskirts of the area we'd cleared. I figured I could drop in, knock them out, and be back on the boat in twenty minutes. By the time we stowed our gear, we might even make it to the rack before the morning glows of the rising sun appeared.

I slid into my wetsuit, then strapped on a fresh tank and tightened my BCD in place. Sitting on the transom, I donned my mask and fins, then checked to make sure my dive light was working.

"Good luck," Walt said.

He was blinking, and his head was bobbing a little.

I laughed and told him not to pass out.

"The day I fall asleep while in the middle of a treasure hunt," he said, "is the day the Keys freeze over."

After one last glance at the laptop screen, I grabbed the metal detector and took a big step out into the water. The dark world engulfed me as I entered negatively buoyant, sinking quickly to the bottom just nine feet down. I adjusted the bright beam of my flashlight, secured it to my left shoulder, then finned toward my first target.

Even though I'd been awake for coming up on twenty-four hours, my pulse still quickened as I dug into the hard-packed remaining sediment. Treasure hunting is quite a rush. There's nothing like digging for an unknown object and the excitement that comes with grabbing it for the first time. It's an old and romantic feeling that entrances those who dare to venture out and look.

I lifted the scoop of muck and reached inside. Pulling out an object, I wiped away the dirt and tilted my head as I tried to figure out what it was. I adjusted the light and shook it a few times to clean it off more.

When the small cloud of dark settled, I realized that it was a Hot Wheels car. I smiled and shook my head as I dropped the tiny blue Volkswagen bug into the black mesh bag.

My optimism waning and fatigue setting in, I finished off the remaining hits one by one. Nothing.

Okay, Logan, I thought at I glanced at my dive watch and saw that it was almost 0500. *Now it's time to get some shut-eye.*

I finned past the edge of our search site and reached to power off the detector. Just as my finger pressed the button, a green light illuminated.

I paused a moment and briefly thought it through. The logical thing would've been to call it a night. We'd investigated hundreds of hits already that day. The chances of this one being anything other than a worthless piece of junk were slim to none. But again, curiosity got the best of me.

I reached over, powered back on the detector, and hovered it over the seafloor. Again the green light illuminated, signaling that there was a metal object just a few inches down.

The tide was shifting, and the current was steady at about two knots. I held the detector steady with my left hand and dug with my right. It wasn't easy. The sediment was even harder than usual, and it took me nearly five minutes of work to make it four inches down.

I took a break, shifted over my detector, and checked again. This time I was roughly three inches from my metal target.

I took a few calming breaths through my regulator and pressed on.

"You find something?" Walt said through the face mask speaker.

"Yeah," I said. "Trying to figure out what exactly."

"You finished up all the hits, right?"

I forced the edge of the scoop into the silt, pulling out a baseball-sized rock.

"Going off the game plan here," I said.

I could tell he was smiling at me even through the radio.

"Now you're getting the buzz."

Two more strong scrapes. Then another. On the fourth, I heard the familiar and beautiful sound of metal on metal. I didn't know what I was about to find, but I knew for sure that at least I wouldn't have to dig anymore.

I let go of the scoop, reached my hands into the deep hole I'd created, and felt a hard edge. Reaching beside it, I dug my fingers into the hard sediment and scraped away as best I could. Moments later, the object began to take shape.

My eyes widened in shock.

Holy shit.

I could feel it. It was round and flat on two sides, whatever it was.

Thin clouds of dirt blocked my view as I shimmied and pried the object free.

Could still be anything, I reminded myself. There are a lot of metal things that are shaped like this. Tobacco cans, valves, small containers, and... compasses.

It's a compass!

My heart raced as I aimed the bright beam of light through the loose dirt that was gradually being carried away with the tide. There was no denying it. I was holding an old gold compass.

THIRTEEN

"Logan, are you alright?" Walt said frantically through the radio.

I'd let out a few ecstatic cheers and hooyahs since realizing what I'd found—sounds that are easily mistaken for cries for help.

"Yeah, I'm fine," I said, my voice unable to mask the excitement I felt. After hours of scrounging the ocean floor, we'd somehow managed to find it. "You sitting down?" I added. "The last thing I want is for you to have a heart attack on me."

The line went quiet for a few seconds as I inspected the compass in the light.

"You tell me right now, Dodge," he said. "I swear to God if you're messing with me—"

I tuned him out as I quickly filled my BCD with air and rocketed up to the surface like a submarine that just blew its ballast tanks. After breaking free into the night air, I bobbed a few times, then slid off my face mask.

Turning around, I saw Walt standing on the deck and leaning over the side like an excited puppy. He was staring straight at me, and after a moment, he threw his hands in the air. I decided that I'd let the suspense build up enough and lifted my right hand up out of the water. The compass glimmered in the silver moonlight.

In an instant, Walt's eyes lit up like a forest fire.

"Hot fucking damn!" he yelled, then jumped up and down like an old prospector who'd just found a large nugget in his gold pan.

Smiling, I kicked over to the swim platform and handed it to him. He held it up and admired it like it was the most precious artifact on the planet. Part of me couldn't believe we'd actually just found it. It felt more like a dream than reality.

Walt helped me up out of the water, and I quickly removed my gear. After stowing everything, we motored the *Calypso* over to the edge of the channel, then dropped and set the anchor. Once the busy work was all done, we moved into the saloon with all of the excitement of two kids on Christmas morning.

Lethargic and struggling to keep his eyes open, Atticus followed right at our heels and dropped down onto a shaggy rug across from us.

We flipped on the galley light and sat across from each other at the dinette. Holding the compass out in front of Walt, he wiped it down, and we both examined it.

It was a simple design, clearly constructed for functionality as well as fashion. It had a sturdy gold outer shell, gold backing, and a loop above the north point to secure a chain that had long ago gone missing. The glass front was scratched to hell, but the inside and the gold were unaffected.

"Still works," Walt said with a smile as he held it out in front of him. "The worst storm in American history, then over seventy years at the bottom of the ocean. They just don't make things like they used to."

He wasn't kidding. The compass still looked pretty good all things considered and didn't require any cleaning other than a quick wipe-down with the cloth. There was no doubt in either of our minds that it was pure gold. Gold is such a stable metal that it rarely if ever oxidizes. Unlike most metals, which corrode and tarnish over time, especially in saltwater, gold usually remains shiny and new.

"There's an inscription here," Walt said after flipping it over and examining the back. "But it's small. You got a magnifying glass?"

I grabbed one from the navigation drawer that I used to look at charts. After handing it to him, he focused it and read the words aloud.

"Buried at the base of the city's undying sun, the secret deed was done. Facing the ten score, eleven paces more."

He read the words, then his eyes narrowed as he looked up at me. He handed it to me while thinking it over.

I ran the words over and over in my mind as I read them. The back was just as unassuming as the front. Just flat gold with the inscription in the middle. Looking closer at the back, I grabbed a rag and wiped underneath the inscription. There was something else, a symbol etched into the gold.

"Hey, check this out," I said, pointing at the symbol.

Walt leaned over.

"What is that?"

I shrugged. But after staring at it for a few seconds, I grabbed my phone and performed a quick search. I smiled and held out a displayed image to Walt.

"It's the Florentine Diamond," I said.

The symbol had the same irregular double-rose-cut nine-sided shape as the lost jewel. He smiled and patted me on the back. Once we knew what it was, the symbol was clear.

We thought over the inscription for a few more minutes. Even with the excitement of having found the compass, I still felt more tired than I had in a long time.

With my eyes growing heavier by the second, I said, "We'll have a better time figuring out what it means if we're well-rested."

He gave a reluctant nod, then rose to his feet and patted me on the back.

"Wait till we show the others," he said.

I headed straight for the starboard guest cabin and crashed softly on the full-sized bed beside Ange. I was out before my head hit the pillow.

I woke up to the sound of the door swinging open and bare feet against the teak floor. As I opened my eyes, I could see light peering in through the cracks of the pillows burying my head. I turned around and caught a whiff of freshly brewed coffee.

I blinked a few times to clear the morning haze and watched as Ange sat down beside me. She was wearing a pair of workout shorts, a tank top, and a big smile on her beautiful face. In her hands were two steaming mugs.

"Good morning, Captain Dodge," she said in her sexy accent. "You guys did good. Though I'm

109

disappointed I wasn't there to see your reaction when you found it."

I laughed as I rose up out of the pillows and leaned back against the headboard.

"It wasn't half as entertaining as Walt's."

She handed me the mug, and I took a sip. It was good. Jack's Colombian medium roast. Black, just the way I liked it.

"What time is it?"

"Nearly ten."

Damn, I thought, unable to remember the last time I'd slept in so late. I guess staying up past five will do that.

"You guys make any headway on the inscription?"

"Not really," she said. "But we've only been up half an hour or so. They're all looking at it now."

I could hear the animated chatter coming from the saloon. Sliding my feet to the deck, I rose just as Atticus came storming through the open door. He practically tackled me back onto the bed in excitement. He licked my face, wagged his tail violently, and breathed heavily.

"Come on out," Ange said with a wink before turning around. "I just finished up some eggs."

Still dressed in the same shorts and tee shirt from the previous evening, I joined the others out in the saloon.

"There's Indiana Jones now," Walt said as he raised his mug to me. "I was just telling Pete how you managed to strike it rich on the last hit of the early morning."

"That was real?" I said while jokingly rubbing my eyes. "I thought I'd dreamed that."

The group laughed and greeted me as I joined

110

them around the dinette. Jack and Ange plated the food, then brought it over. We scarfed it down quickly while taking turns looking over the compass.

"It's incredible, bro," Jack said, holding it like it was a genie's lamp.

"It really is something," Pete said. "And an artifact that I hope will end up on display at my place."

"Of course," I said. "Once we're through figuring out what the words mean, of course."

Walt shook his head. "I dreamt about it all night. Can't seem to make heads or tails of it."

"Well, let's break it apart," Pete said after finishing off his eggs and washing them down with a swig of coffee. "First, 'Buried at the base of the city's undying sun.'"

We sat in silence for about a minute, then Jack beat a fist on the table.

"I got it!" he exclaimed. "Maybe it's referring to the Sun Sun Restaurant over at the Waldorf."

Pete shook his head. "A good guess. But the Waldorf Astoria didn't open its doors until New Year's Eve of 1920. Long after Hastings's time."

After a few more minutes of far-out-of-left-field guesses, Ange took her first shot at it.

"It sounds like he was being poetic," she said. "I mean, this guy Hastings did say on his deathbed that it was a scavenger hunt after all."

We looked over at her, our expressions welcoming her to elaborate.

"Let's look up synonyms for sun," she said, grabbing her phone off the counter.

After a few seconds, she sat down beside me and began at the top of the list.

"What about star?" she said. "After all, the sun is

just a star."

"Buried at the base of the undying star?" I said.

"Could be referring to constellations," Pete said. "Though I wouldn't have the first idea where to start digging."

"A constellation would explain the use of the word *base*," I said. "What else you got?" I added, looking at her cellphone screen.

"Sunlight, sol, shine, light, sunshine—"

"That's it!" I said. The word *light* caught my attention and completely changed the way I was thinking about the riddle. I grabbed the compass and read the words slowly. "Buried at the base of the city's undying light."

I looked around the galley at nothing but confused faces. Then, I saw a switch turn on in Jack's head.

"Undying light," he said, his lips contorting into a big smile. "The lighthouse, bro."

I nodded. "Exactly."

"That makes sense," Walt said. "The Key West Lighthouse was built back in the 1830s. And it's a big enough landmark to ensure that it would still be around long after Hastings's death."

"And it helps tie in the rest of it," Pete said, his voice filled with excitement. "The secret deed was done. Looks like the next clue was buried near the base of the lighthouse."

"Eleven paces is simple enough," I said. "But what about 'facing the ten score'?"

Walt jumped to life this time and grabbed hold of the compass, looking closely at the front of it. His face grew into a big smile.

"Facing the ten score," he said quietly. He looked up at us, then pointed at the compass. "He's talking about the degrees. Ten score is two hundred. So all we have to do is go to the lighthouse and—"

"Face the two-hundred-degree position," Ange said, completing his sentence.

"Right," Walt said.

"And then walk eleven paces and voilà!" Jack said.

We all smiled as we looked at each other, then raised our mugs into an enthusiastic cheer. With breakfast finished, Pete and I took care of the dishes while the others prepared to make way.

Atticus, sensing that we were getting ready to leave, jumped up and down excitedly. Once the anchor chain was coiled up and the anchor secure, Jack started up the *Calypso*'s engines. We brought the cooler up to the flybridge with fresh ice and a refill on beverages for the trip back.

"I think it's time we head back to Key West and dig ourselves up a secret deed," Walt said, placing a hand on Jack's shoulder as he accelerated the *Calypso* north, heading out of the channel toward the Atlantic.

FOURTEEN

We passed under the Snake Creek Bridge, and just as we were about to reach the end of the channel, a boat caught my eye behind us. It looked like a twenty-foot bowrider, and it had a pristine hull and a black Bimini top. The boat itself was nothing unusual, with watercraft of all types coming and going in the channel. The issue was that it was moving fast. Way too fast for a no-wake zone.

"Get a load of this," I said, motioning toward the quickly approaching boat.

I grabbed my binoculars while the others peeked back to see what I was looking at. Atticus jumped up onto the flybridge bench beside me and growled at the boat.

"First those plastered city slicker fishermen yesterday and now this?" Pete said.

Ange gave a piercing whistle to get their

attention. She and Jack also waved, trying to get them to slow down, but it didn't work. There were kayakers and paddleboarders right at the edge of the channel. There's a reason why no-wake zones exist. Incidents involving reckless boaters are far too common and rarely end well for anyone.

I peered through my binos and focused on the approaching boat. Within seconds, I realized that this wasn't a case of an ignorant captain.

Through the lenses, I gazed upon the same three guys Ange and I had seen on the shore the previous day. All three of them were staring at our boat as they thundered toward us at well over thirty knots. Judging by their expressions, they weren't looking for a friendly chat.

I lowered the binos and looked straight over at Walt, who was standing at the edge of the flybridge.

"Looks like your friends are back," I said sternly.

"No fucking way," Ange said, snatching the binos from my hand and taking a look for herself.

"Walt, what's going—" Pete started, but I interrupted him.

"You've got one chance to tell us who these guys really are and what they want or I swear to God I'll throw you overboard," I said, stepping toward him and staring fiercely into his eyes.

Walt looked back at me with wide eyes. He stood in shock for a moment at how fast my persona had shifted from friendly to serious.

"They're..." He closed his eyes and looked down.

"No time to talk now," Ange said as she lowered the binos. "These guys are packing and coming in hot."

Shit, I thought, my mind racing through potential

scenarios.

After a moment, I had an idea. It wasn't perfect, but it was the best I could do on short notice.

"Walt," I said sternly, "you get below deck." Before he could protest, I turned my attention to the others. "Jack, you keep motoring us along at this speed. Pete and Ange, you two cover me."

They didn't know we were armed. For all they knew, we were just harmless locals trying to help out an old friend looking for treasure. I wanted to keep it that way, to play the innocent card as long as we could.

If we engaged them right off the bat, we could very well find ourselves in an old-fashioned gunfight back and forth between our boats. It would be easier to catch them by surprise up close and personal.

I headed down to the main deck, whistling for Atticus to follow and practically forcing Walt along.

"Be careful, Logan," he said.

Once he and Atticus were through the saloon door, I slid it shut behind them without a reply. By the time I turned around, the approaching bowrider was within a few hundred yards of our stern. I felt my Sig at the side of my waistband. It was hidden from view by my shorts and tee shirt. I didn't need to grab and inspect it to know that the safety was off and that it was loaded up with fifteen 9mm rounds.

Thirty seconds later, the bowrider slowed along the *Calypso*'s starboard side. Two of the guys were standing and eyeing me suspiciously. The third seated at the small helm station, smoking a cigarette and lowering his sunglasses to get a better look at me.

"Going a little fast for the channel, aren't you?" I said.

If any of them heard me, they didn't show it.

In lieu of a reply, the pilot rose to his feet and said something I couldn't hear to the two guys. The pilot was shorter than the other two and had long black hair tied back in a ponytail. The two other guys were bigger than my six-two and looked like they knew how to carry themselves. They each wore black tank tops that showed off their bulging muscles, while Ponytail wore a sweat-stained silk button-up.

Suddenly, Ponytail grabbed a handgun from the dash. Without a moment's thought, my right hand hovered casually over my Sig. I could have it out, aimed, and fired in half a second.

With a quick wave of a hand, Ponytail ordered the two guys to climb over to our boat. We were still moving at about five knots, but Ponytail kept their boat even with ours.

"Where the fuck is Walt?" Ponytail shouted as the first big guy jumped over.

I shrugged.

"He's in the head," I said casually. "Hey, you can't just come aboard without asking."

I tried to sound as innocent as possible.

"We'll do whatever the hell we please," the big guy grunted in a low, husky voice.

Once both men were aboard, they eyed me, then glanced back at Ponytail. Again he spoke in a language I couldn't understand. Sounded like Albanian, but I couldn't be sure. What I could understand was the statement big guy number two was making when he reached over to the bow of their boat, grabbed a shotgun, and angled it toward me. He had a look in his eyes I'd seen many times before. It was the look of a man who was about to take a life. No sign of potential remorse. Just cold, hard, deadly, and straight down to business. The look of an experienced killer.

Before he had the barrel leveled on me, I heard an explosion from just over my head. In an instant, blood and bone exploded out the back of the guy's skull, and he fell backward over the starboard gunwale and collapsed back into their boat.

While the report of the weapon still filled the air, I lunged after the other big guy before he could react. I intended to take him down and use the gunwale for cover as we engaged Ponytail, but I slipped on the wet deck. Just as I grabbed hold of him, my momentum caused us both to go tumbling over the side and crash into the stern of the bowrider.

We hit hard, but I spun him around and tried my best to keep control. Looking up, I watched as Ange fired off a few rounds at the pilot. Seeing that they were outnumbered and that we weren't as innocent as we appeared, he managed to hit the throttles and duck from view as her bullets shattered the windscreen and rattled against their exposed hull. He turned sharply, causing me and my newfound friend to roll hard to port as Ponytail tried desperately to put as much distance between himself and his new enemies as possible.

The big guy woke me up and rattled my brain with a strong jab to the side of my face. But I got him back with a quick elbow to his left eye and a chop to the throat. He gasped and struggled for air as I rose to one knee, struggling to remain balanced as the boat bounced up and down.

Just as Ponytail had her up on plane, he looked back at me over his shoulder. We were too far away for me to engage him hand to hand, so I reached for my Sig. Just as his eyes met mine, he turned to level his weapon at me. But I beat him to the trigger.

With a rapid squeeze, I sent a 9mm round into the back of his left shoulder. His body jerked and his hand let go of his weapon, which fell to the deck and bounced a few times before settling against the side behind him. He lurched forward and grunted in pain as he placed his right hand over the wound.

I was just about to send another round through his chest when the big wheezing guy on the deck swiped his right leg, causing my body to jolt forward and slam into the deck. He grabbed me forcefully, threw me against the gunwale, and staggered to his feet just forward of the transom.

He yelled out barbarically and reached for something at the back of his waistband. Not wanting to figure out what it was, I rolled over, snatched my Sig from the deck, and fired two rounds through his chest. His body shook with the blows and blood splattered out his back. He staggered for a second before I kicked him in the chest as hard as I could. He grunted as his body flew back, his legs slamming into the transom, causing his upper body to whip over the side.

His head hit the small swim platform as his body tumbled and splashed into the water, disappearing in an instant in the boat's torrential wake.

Flipping onto my chest, I rose to my feet and locked eyes with Ponytail once again. I could see his dropped gun in my peripherals, but it was still lodged against the edge of the boat. I had him. He was done for, and I kept the sights locked on him as I yelled for him to freeze and shut off the boat.

He glanced back at me, and for a moment I thought he was going to dive for his dropped weapon. But Ponytail had other ideas. Just as I was about to finish him off, he turned the helm sharply. The quick turn at such a high speed caused the deck to fly out from under me. In the blink of an eye, my body was in the air, crashing into the gunwale, tumbling over the side, and splashing into the water.

My body spun and flipped in the turbulent haze of white bubbles. For a moment, there was only confusion as I couldn't tell up from down. Then the wake subsided, and I saw the brilliant morning sun piercing down through the ever-clearing water to my right. I kicked and tore at the water, reaching the surface and welcoming a lungful of air.

Blinking and gazing through blurry eyes from the saltwater, I spotted the bowrider motoring full throttle away from me. It had turned even more and was now heading northeast, back toward Snake Creek Channel. Turning around, I spotted the big guy I'd filled with lead floating face down on the surface. Clouds of red were already spreading around him.

I shook the water from my ears and heard the *Calypso* approach from the south. Jack brought her around, and I climbed up onto the swim platform.

"Are you alright?" Ange said, inspecting me from head to toe for damage, then wrapping her arms around me and squeezing me tight. "They didn't get you, did they?"

"Not even close," I said, stretching the truth just a little. I shook my head and added, "But you sure got them."

Jack leaned over from up in the flybridge.

"That last guy's making a break back for the islands!" he shouted. "I've got a bead on him. You want me to call in the police?"

Pete walked over and offered me a hand and a towel as I stepped up to the main deck. If we had the Baia, I'd simply put the throttle to the fiberglass and let the engines go wild. With a top speed of over fifty knots, there aren't many boats anywhere that can keep up with her on the open ocean. But we couldn't chase down the bowrider in Jack's *Calypso* even if we wanted to.

"Everyone heard those gunshots for miles, so we kind of have to," I said. "Call Jane. Let her know what happened."

He nodded and disappeared from view. I patted myself down and made brief eye contact with Pete. Neither of us said anything. Neither of us had to. The first order of business for us wasn't to go after the guy who'd managed to get lucky and escape. No, the first order of business was to have a little chat with Walt.

FIFTEEN

Jack motored us out to deeper water, then put us on a southwesterly course and switched on the autopilot. I took a moment to dry off and change into a fresh tee shirt. Atticus followed me as I moved aft, then stepped up to the flybridge. Walt was standing near the aft bench, and the others were eyeing him suspiciously.

"Old friends, huh?" I said, raising my eyebrows at him.

He paused a moment, and Ange chimed in.

"Now's the time where you answer," she said sternly.

"Alright, alright," Walt said, raising his hands in the air to try and deflate the situation. He took in a deep breath and let out a big sigh. "They are old friends, in a way. I can explain." He took a swig of water and sat on the cushioned bench. "Those three guys who just attacked us, they're from Albania."

I eyed Ange. We sure as hell weren't expecting that answer, but I guess I was right about what language they were speaking.

"I just got back from the Med," he added. "We were working together to find a wreck. The partnership turned sour, and I took off before all hell broke loose." He shrugged. "Then they followed me here and are trying to find out what I'm looking for."

"Just out of curiosity," Ange said without skipping a beat, "what line of work are these old friends of yours in?"

He paused again, which I took as a bad sign.

"They dabble… here and there…"

"Dammit, Wally, just spit it out, man," Pete said, growing irritated as well.

"Alright," he said. "They're part of the Albanian mafia."

I closed my eyes, threw my left hand into my face, and massaged my forehead while shaking my head back and forth.

"You don't think that's something you should've told us about?" I said, genuinely bewildered by what he was saying.

He shrugged. "I didn't think they'd find me. Yesterday was the first I've seen them in a while." He paused a moment and cleared his throat. "But they're no concern of ours. They couldn't find treasure in Midas's castle, and those three aren't exactly the top brass. You seemed to have no trouble fighting them off."

I genuinely had a hard time believing what I was hearing.

"You asshole!" Ange said. "You realize you'd be mincemeat right now if it weren't for Logan. Those guys weren't here to talk or to make threats. They were here to kill all of us."

"Look, I'm sorry," he said. "I thought they'd be all threats and no action."

"You should've told us, Walt," Pete said. "What did they say to you yesterday when you talked to them on the shore?" Pete turned to me and added, "Logan, you said they were the same guys, right?"

I nodded.

"They were just showing face yesterday," he said casually. "They just wanted me to know that they're here." He paused a moment. "Look, I know how bad this looks. But they came and now they're running. Clearly, we don't gotta worry about them. We just need to focus on finding the diamond."

"Yeah, why the hell should we be worried?" Jack said sarcastically. "A few criminal enemies of yours track you down all the way from Albania. Yeah, after what just happened, it's obvious they're just here for the views and the Key lime pie."

"Jack's right," I said. "Give us one good reason why we should trust you and bother continuing with this search."

He paused a moment. Reaching into his pocket, he pulled out the compass and held it out in front of him.

"Here's a damn good reason," he said.

It was like he was completely oblivious to the magnitude of what had just happened. A group of Albanian mafia guys were hot on his trail, wanting him dead and clearly us along with him, and all he could think about was the diamond. He was a treasure hunter, through and through. But I had a hard time figuring out whose side he was on—whether he was the villain or the misunderstood hero. Because at that moment, he was looking a hell of a lot more like Long John Silver than Jim Hawkins.

"You drag us into your shitty business with lies, then expect us to continue on like blind idiots?" I said. "You're a real piece of work."

I turned away from him and hit the stairs. Ange and Jack followed me, leaving Pete and Walt alone up in the flybridge. I couldn't talk to him anymore. It seemed like the more I did, the more upset I got.

We headed into the saloon and sat around the dinette. Atticus curled onto the carpet beside us. I grabbed a few coconut waters from the fridge and handed them out.

"You believe the nerve of that guy?" Ange said. "He seems completely oblivious to what just happened. He's either certifiable, a filthy liar, or both."

"All I know is once he steps off, he's not welcome back on my boat," Jack said. "I don't care if he's got the coordinates to the damn Aztec treasure 2.0."

We kept talking for half an hour. Jack piloted from the main deck cockpit, checking to make sure that our path was clear and making occasional adjustments to our course. There'd been no sign of the others until Pete finally stepped down from the flybridge and entered through the sliding glass door.

Without a word, he grabbed a beer from the fridge and plopped down beside us on the dinette couch. Popping the cap, he took a few long pulls before clearing his throat and eyeing each of us.

"I'm sorry for getting you three into this mess," he said. Glancing out a crack in the starboard porthole curtains, he added, "If you guys want out of this, I understand. But the two of us are gonna continue the search."

We eyed him like he was crazy.

"You can't be serious, man," Jack said.

"How can you work alongside someone who flat out lied to us?" Ange added.

It was a good and important question.

"He and I go way back," he said calmly. "Longer than any of you have been alive. Look, I believe we can find this thing, and I want to see it through."

"And when those Albanians come back?" Jack said.

"Then we'll deal with them," he said. "You three aren't the only ones who've dealt with bad guys, you know."

I sighed. "Pete, you—"

"Look, guys," he said, cutting me off. "Walt's in serious trouble."

"Yeah, that much is pretty clear," Jack said.

"These Albanians want him dead," Pete continued. "If they get him, they'll force him to find the diamond, and then they'll kill him. So the way I see it is we have two options here: we can either walk away and let these criminals sweep in, kill him, and make off with the diamond, or we can do something about it."

We fell quiet for a moment as we let his words marinate.

"And if he's lying again?" I slid out from the seat and rose to my feet slowly. "Pete, I know he was a close friend of yours. But how well do you really know him now? You said it's been what, nearly twenty years? Who knows what he's been up to all this time? Hell, he could be part of the Albanian mafia himself for all we know."

"I don't believe that for a second," Pete said. "All

I know is that he's fallen on hard times and he came to me for help." He paused a moment to clear his throat. "He's family, son. A thoroughbred conch, through and through. He's my brother and I'll have his back through thick and thin."

I took a swig of coconut water and leaned back into the cushion, thinking back to earlier that year, when an old Navy friend of mine who was supposed to be dead had shown up out of the blue. A convicted traitor to the United States, I'd been mad as hell at him at first and hesitant to help him salvage his life. But I'd helped him nonetheless. Despite the danger and the many risks it had posed to me, I'd helped him. I wasn't certain what Pete was feeling, but I figured it was similar to how I'd felt—conflicted, but genuinely wanting what was best for someone I'd once called my brother.

"If you're pressing on, man, then I am too," Jack said, catching me off guard. "I can't sit here and pretend I'm not itching to go and check out this next clue. I haven't been this excited since we found that pirate shipwreck."

I glanced over at Ange. She was shooting me a look I'd seen a few times before. It was her *this is crazy and stupid but I support you* look. Pete's words on family had hit home the hardest. With my mom and dad gone, Ange was the only legal family I had left. But I had my island family, and I wasn't about to let them dive headlong into danger without tagging along.

"You guys are both nuts," I said flatly.

And I'm nuts too for not leaving it at that and walking out of the room.

Instead, I smiled and added, "Alright. With all of the close calls you've had lately?" I said, raising my eyebrows at Jack. "Someone's gotta keep you from getting yourself killed."

But after the smiles, I explained that the entire dynamic of the endeavor had changed drastically. We were no longer just looking for a diamond. We were looking for a diamond with a group of criminals breathing down our necks. We had to keep our eyes on the prize while also watching our backs.

And we had to keep a sharp eye on Walt. In light of everything, I couldn't help feeling like there was a lot more that he still wasn't telling us.

SIXTEEN

Two and a half hours later, just after 1300, we motored back into the Conch Harbor Marina. We'd used the journey to shower, gather our gear, and eat. We'd also talked to Jane again, letting her know what had happened, and authorities were notified up and down the islands. When the hull pressed against the fenders at slip forty-seven, Ange and I carted our gear to the Baia, then left Atticus with Gus at the marina office.

"You guys missed a lot of festivities yesterday," Gus said as he greeted my happy Lab. "They lost control of the pirate float. It took off full speed straight into the side of the Tiki Bar." He laughed hysterically. "I think the mainlanders thought it was part of the act, but you should have seen Bert's face when he saw the spanking new entrance through the south wall. No one got hurt, but maybe he can add a

129

new patio or something."

I laughed and petted Atticus.

"That would've been a sight to see."

"Yep. You guys do anything exciting out on the water? Word on the water is that the blackfin tuna are early this year."

"Not really," I said, choosing to withhold the truth for the time being. "And we'll have to go out on the *Calypso* and get a haul."

"After the fest, I'll be free as a bird. You guys going to watch the fireworks tonight? You can see them from the marina, but the view's much better over at Mallory."

My mind was too busy thinking about Walt, the diamond, and the Albanian mafia to take in much else.

"Maybe," I said. "If we do, we'll call and meet up."

"Alrighty."

I thanked him for watching Atticus, then joined the others and headed down the dock toward the parking lot. The five of us crammed into my Tacoma four-door, and I pulled us out onto Caroline Street.

The city was already abuzz. After pulling onto Duval Street, I remarked that it might have been quicker to walk the roughly three-quarters of a mile as people crossed the streets in seemingly never-ending clusters.

We passed Jimmy Buffet's first Margaritaville, then headed down a cross street, turned onto Whitehead and passed the Green Parrot Bar. Three slow blocks later, we somehow managed to find a parking space right down the road from the Lighthouse and Keeper's Quarters Museum.

Stepping out into the warm afternoon air, I

glanced across the street and saw a large crowd of people standing in a line just outside the entrance to the Ernest Hemingway Home and Museum. I smiled as I spotted a white-and-orange cat sitting in the shade on top of the brick wall surrounding the renowned novelist's compound. I thought back to the first time I'd visited the house as a kid. The tour guide had told me that Hemingway had favored the six-toed cats since they were regarded as better mouse hunters and were able to keep their balance better while out on the water. Unfortunately, I was too far away to count its toes.

I joined the others, and we walked down the sidewalk to the lighthouse. After standing in line for a few minutes, we greeted the woman at the counter and paid the entrance fee, then she handed us a brochure.

Most everything on the well-kept ground was painted brilliant white, the only outliers being a few sections of the picket fences and the shutters of the keeper's house, which were painted in a fresh coat of dark green.

We walked along the concrete path that cut between short, manicured lawns. Rising up at the back was the eighty-six-foot lighthouse. It towered over the coconut palms and the large mahogany beside it.

We walked the grounds slowly, trying to fit in with all of the other people who were just enjoying one of the island's many historic sites. But we weren't like the others. We were there to perform reconnaissance.

The Albanian mafia was ever-present in my mind, and I constantly looked around and over my shoulder for any sign that they might be following us.

131

Ange held out the information pamphlet we'd been given at the entrance. She had it unfolded and was looking over old pictures and small lines of text.

"She was built in 1825," Walt said, not bothering to look at the pamphlet.

"Actually, this lighthouse wasn't constructed until 1848," a voice said from behind us. We turned around and saw a short chubby guy wearing a polo shirt that said Staff, plaid shorts, and a gray ball cap. "You're thinking of the first lighthouse that was built close to the water." He nodded toward the towering lighthouse and added, "This one was also only fifty feet back when it was built. It's seen many improvements and has been built higher over the years." He paused a moment, then waved at us and added, "I'm Marty. I'm a tour guide here. Any of you interested in the tour? We run it every hour on the hour from nine until five."

The five of us looked at each other. We were all hoping for someone else to answer.

After a few seconds, I said, "We're not interested."

Marty shrugged.

"Suit yourself."

He walked past us and raised his voice, speaking to a group of people who'd gathered under a tour starts here sign. We waited for Marty to finish his welcoming spiel, complete with the usual touch of corny jokes guides like to throw in now and then. When he led the group past us and into the lighthouse, we had the courtyard mostly to ourselves.

"Alright," Walt said, grabbing the compass from his pocket.

"Buried at the base of the city's undying sun," Ange said, having memorized the riddle.

We were standing right beside the lighthouse, keeping cool under the shade of a gumbo-limbo tree.

"The secret deed was done," Pete said, completing the first line.

"Facing the ten score," Jack said.

Walt took a quick look around, then stepped right against the lighthouse and held out the compass. Generally, when using a compass, in order to gauge your proper direction on a map, you need to account for magnetic declination. This refers to the angle of difference between magnetic north and true north. Due to Key West's location, these two are essentially equal, making the declination close enough to zero not to be a factor.

"Two hundred degrees," Walt said, still holding out the compass.

We walked around the base of the lighthouse until we reached the two-hundred-degree mark on the compass. Turning around, we faced the southeast part of the courtyard.

"Eleven paces more," Ange said.

Not wanting to look too suspicious, we walked casually beside Walt as he counted off the paces. He walked in a straight line and whispered the numbers to himself.

"One... two... three..."

When he got to six, I looked ahead and realized that we were heading for trouble. Not the Albanian criminal variety, but the man-made treasure-hunting-hinderance kind. In this case, it was in the form of a hardened concrete-powder-and-water mixture.

"Eleven," Walt said quietly.

We stood in silence for a moment as we gazed down at the ground. We'd reached the supposed site where Hastings had buried the next clue. The only problem was that the ground was covered by a paved walkway. We were standing right at the point where three paths converged, making it even wider than most areas.

"Well, that's some shitty luck," Jack said.

Pete wandered off to the edge of the path and bent over.

"It's gotta be at least four inches thick," he said.

We had a new and unexpected problem on our hands.

"How are we gonna break through four inches of concrete in the middle of a popular downtown historic site without anyone noticing?" I said, putting into words what all five of us were thinking.

SEVENTEEN

Valmira Gallani stepped out from her private jet and into the warm afternoon air. She hit the steps quickly, followed closely behind by two big guys.

She had smooth olive skin and short raven-black hair that she kept straight. She was six feet tall, wide-shouldered, and strong. She wore black pants and a gray tee shirt. Her arms and neck were covered in tattoos. Sparkling diamond studs littered her ears. She had a pronounced, narrow jawline and fierce dark eyes.

She strode with a commanding presence down the steps, onto the tarmac, and into the air-conditioned backseat of a blacked-out SUV. Without a word, the two big guys entered, one in the passenger seat and the other in the back beside her. The guy who'd opened the door for her slammed it shut, then plopped down in the driver's seat and drove them off the Miami International Airport tarmac.

From the moment she'd learned about the Florentine Diamond, she'd decided to drop what she was doing and take off from Albania. She had two objectives: find the gem, then kill Walt Grissom. It was a task she was all too happy to perform after the old treasure hunter had cheated her out of what had amounted to over a million US dollars.

He thought he could run away from us, she thought with a sly smile as she kept her gaze forward.

Twenty minutes later, the driver pulled the SUV into Crandon Park Marina on Key Biscayne. Stopping right at the curb, he opened the door for Val, and the group walked down the dock to where a fifty-nine-foot-long Sealine T60 yacht was moored.

After boarding, she headed straight for the elegant saloon, where three men were waiting for her. Two stood as soon as she entered, but the third remained seated. He was wearing a silk button-up that was drenched in sweat. He looked exhausted but straightened up when Val entered the room.

She stood still for a moment, then narrowed her gaze.

"Where's Arven and Lesh?" she asked in her strong Albanian accent.

The seated guy swallowed hard.

"They're dead. I barely made it out myself."

"And Grissom?"

"He got away. Headed back to Key West far as I know."

She paused a moment. Her anger was masked by a stone-cold expression that rarely changed, a trait she'd learned from her father. As the daughter of a ruthless mafia leader, she'd been raised more like a boy than a girl.

"You look terrible, Jorik, and you smell worse," she said. She motioned aft and added, "Go shower and change."

He hesitated a moment, then rose to his feet and did as he was told. Val gave a cold smile as he disappeared.

"Take us out," she said to one of the guys beside her.

"Where are we going?" he asked back.

"You heard him. Key West."

As the man strode out of the room and into the cockpit, Val thought about Jorik. The coward was most likely concluding that her reputation was worse than her reality. In the criminal circles of the Balkan Peninsula, she was known as the Angel of Death. But he probably was thinking that she merely had a façade of evil. That in reality, she was just a young girl trying and failing at what most believed was a man's business.

Val liked to play mind games with her subordinates. To make them think that they were getting off easy, then strike like a vicious cobra when they least expected it.

When Jorik finished showering, he changed into fresh clothes, then was told to meet Val at the stern. It'd been half an hour, and the yacht was now fifteen miles southeast of Miami.

She looked out over the surrounding water. The horizon was littered with boats of all types, but none were within a mile of them. She'd told the pilot to make sure and keep distance between them and other vessels—at least until she was done teaching a lesson.

"You sent for me, ma'am?" Jorik said.

Val wasn't one for dragging things out. Instead of a verbal reply, she turned around and quickly

137

slapped Jorik across his face. Her long black-painted nails sliced deep, leaving rows of gashes that quickly seeped out blood. Jorik yelled from the pain and lurched forward.

"What the—" The words barely made it out of his mouth before Val planted her right leg and hit him with a strong roundhouse kick that knocked him hard on his ass.

Filled with rage and wailing from the pain, Jorik staggered to his feet. Just as he lifted his fists into a fighting stance, Val's two personal bodyguards and the two other mafia members that were on board stepped out casually and stood idly by. They eyed Jorik with narrowed gazes, and he lowered his fists.

Val grabbed an Albanian jambiya dagger. The rare knife had a razor-sharp steel blade and an ivory handle.

Clenching Jorik's blood-soaked shirt collar, she lifted him up and pressed the tip to his neck.

"You failed a simple task," she said. "And you ran away like a little girl." She paused a moment, then pressed the tip in deep enough to draw blood and added, "Is there anything useful that you can tell me? Anything that might persuade me from ending your life?"

He winced, breathed frantically, then coughed to clear his throat.

"They found something," he said, rushing the words out. "Near that bridge they were at. Snake Bridge, I think. Whatever they were looking for, they found it."

Val paused a moment, focusing her terrifying dark eyes.

"They?"

Jorik nodded. "Walt isn't alone. He's got others

with him. At least three others that I saw. And they know how to fight."

"What did they find?" she said.

"I... I don't know," he exclaimed. "Please believe me, I don't know!"

Val nodded slowly. Turning around, she looked at her nearest thug. She raised her right hand and slid her index finger dramatically across her neck. The two big guys smiled sinisterly, then closed in on Jorik.

"What's happening?" Jorik asked, looking desperately at the two guys. "You said if I told you—"

Val interrupted his vehement pleading with a quick twist of her body and a thrust of her knife. The sharp point sliced effortlessly through Jorik's abdomen, sticking out the other side. Jorik gasped and yelled horrifically as blood flowed out and dripped to the deck.

As quickly and mercilessly as she'd stabbed, Val jerked her knife free and grabbed Jorik by his shirt.

"You're a worthless coward," she said. "Nothing you say can change that."

She let go and stepped back. Her two henchmen moved in swiftly and held him down against the transom while the other two guys tied a nylon rope around his shoulders. The knife wound wasn't to kill him. It was only the beginning of Jorik's painful, life-ending lesson.

They tied the other end of the rope to the stern, then forced Jorik into a lifejacket, securing it with tight knots. This was to keep him from sinking and drowning his way out of his due torture. This wasn't the first time Val had utilized her father's unique method of sending a message.

With a remorseless heave, the two big guys tossed Jorik into the yacht's wake. They were traveling at twenty-five knots, so the rope quickly went taut. Jorik yelled as his bloodied body was dragged behind them. It was only a matter of time before the ocean's predators made their violent move.

"Video this shit," Val ordered one of her men. "I want to watch this show later."

"Yes, ma'am," he replied in a low, smooth voice.

She headed back into the saloon. Taking her mind off the incident, she thought about what she would do when they reached Key West. Jorik and her two other men had proved useless.

Sometimes, if you want a job done right, you have to do it yourself.

She climbed up onto the bow and looked out at the faraway island-littered horizon. In the distance behind her, she heard Jorik's frantic screams, and her lips contorted into an evil smile.

"Enjoy the fresh air of life while you can, Walt," she said to herself as she kept her eyes cast forward. "For soon, your life, and the lives of those helping you, will be mine."

EIGHTEEN

We followed the instructions on the compass two more times. Each time we found the two-hundred-degree point, then checked the paces just to make sure. Each yielded the same results as the first. It looked like our next clue was buried under the concrete path in the middle of the historic site.

On our way out, we ran into Marty the tour guide again. He reminded us of the hours, then tried to detour us into the gift shop. Instead, we exited the way we had come, climbed back into the Tacoma, and drove over to Pete's place for lunch.

We kept a sharp eye out for any bad guys, but it looked as though we were still in the clear when we pulled into the seashell driveway and headed inside. We claimed a table out on the balcony that was off in the corner, just out of earshot from the small bands of people that had shown up for Pete's famous happy hour.

When you're starving, everything looks good. And after the boat ride back from Snake Creek and the reconnaissance at the lighthouse, we were all ordering food rapid-fire. It wasn't long before the table was covered with trays of raw oysters on ice, steamed shrimp doused in Old Bay seasoning, steamed clams swimming in melted butter, conch fritters, and stuffed mushrooms.

We ate to our heart's content and washed it all down with glass after chilled glass of Key limeade.

Many of the people we passed in the restaurant were locals that we saw on a recurring basis. Conchs who made an effort to watch each other's backs. We were among friends at Pete's, and that made it one of the safest places we could be in the island chain. Regardless, I had my Sig just a quick arm's reach away and my head on a constant swivel. We'd killed two of their guys. One had barely managed to tuck tail and run. There wasn't a doubt in my mind that they'd be back. The only questions were when and how many.

"Jackhammer," Walt said after dropping two mignonette-and-lemon-juice-covered oysters down the hatch back to back. "We need to get ahold of a jackhammer." He turned to Pete. "Does Jensen Palmer still own that hardware store on Ashby Street?"

"He passed away a few years back," Pete said. "Son runs the place now."

Walt stared blankly for a moment, then said, "That's a shame. He was a good man. Well, after we have our fill, let's head over there and rent one of the bad boys."

"And then what, man?" Jack said. "We walk

142

back to the lighthouse and hammer that path to kingdom come?"

"You think of a better way to break through concrete?" Walt said.

Ange cleared her throat dramatically.

"And you don't think," she said, "that using a jackhammer in the middle of a crowded downtown is going to raise any eyebrows?"

Ange was right. Anyone who's ever operated or been anywhere near an operating jackhammer can tell you that the sound is brutally loud. But Walt was also right—there isn't exactly an extensive list of options when challenged with breaking through concrete. It was either a jackhammer or a sledgehammer. Both options would be loud, but at least using a jackhammer would prevent a few months of weekly chiropractor visits.

It was clear that our progress had hit a bit of a roadblock, or in this case, a concrete path. Sure, we had friends in law enforcement and the local military, but using a jackhammer on a historical site would be difficult to explain.

As we were finishing up our food, Jack's nephew, Isaac, began clearing our table. At sixteen years old, Isaac was incredibly smart for his age and even took classes at the local community college while finishing up the few remaining credits he needed to get his high school diploma.

Jack believed, however, that his young, pale-faced, skin-and-bones nephew spent too much time in front of computers and books and not enough out in the real world. So he'd insisted a while back that Isaac take a part-time job at Pete's. He only worked a few hours here and there, but it had succeeded in getting the shy kid out of his shell a little bit.

After a quick greeting, Isaac asked enthusiastically what we were doing this evening.

"The fireworks are gonna be the best ever this year," he said. "A friend and I were riding our bikes over by City Hall and peeked into the storage room where they're keeping the fireworks." He paused a moment for dramatic effect. "They've got a stack of Thor's Hammers and a crate of Demon's Revenge this year. They're some of the biggest and loudest fireworks money can buy."

I thought over his words for a moment while leaning back into my chair and killing the rest of my chilled drink. Fireworks. Gus had mentioned them as well earlier at the marina. Loud explosions in the night sky. A good way to spend an evening. Few things distract and grab attention like fireworks.

I smiled at Isaac. The bright young man had just given us our window of opportunity.

"Isaac, you're a genius," I said.

He looked over at me like I was crazy, then shrugged and continued filling the big gray plastic container with dirty dishes.

"Does that mean I'm getting a big tip, Logan?" he said as he walked past me.

I grabbed my wallet, slid out a twenty, and pinned it to the table beneath my empty glass. Thanks to the idea he'd just given me, there was a good chance that we were all in for a big tip.

When Isaac walked off, I turned back and saw that everyone was staring at me, waiting for me to explain my seemingly random proclamation.

"Something you want to share with the rest of us, babe?" Ange said.

"Yeah, bro," Jack said. "You can't just go around tossing the genius praise for no reason like that. It gives the kid a big head."

I smiled.

Turning to Walt, I said, "I think it's time we drive over and pick ourselves up a jackhammer."

Pete shook his head.

"You gone mad, boyo? We were just talking about how it'll be impossible to pull off without drawing half the island's attention to what we're doing."

I nodded.

"Unless their attentions are already fixed elsewhere." I paused a moment, then added, "Unless there was something even louder and more distracting than a jackhammer."

Ange was the first to catch on. I wasn't surprised. Her sharp wit was one of the first things that had drawn me to her when we first met years ago. Usually, it was her figuring things out first and explaining them to me. For once, at least, I'd beaten her to it.

She looked in Isaac's direction and said, "Something like a fireworks show?"

Walt's lips contorted into a big smile. Jack grinned as well and looked over at his nephew proudly.

Pete laughed and reached into his wallet.

"The kid deserves another Jackson for that one," he said.

NINETEEN

We finished up our lunch, then cruised over to Ashby Street to pick up our required tool of the trade. As with many of the island locals, the guy in charge knew Walt and gave him a special discount given his old relationship with his father. When asked what we were working on, Pete said that there was an old slab at his house that was in serious need of renovating.

He gave us an overview of how to use it and the required safety gear. After paying a deposit and signing on the dotted line, we carted the sixty-five-pound beast out and loaded it into the bed of my Tacoma.

"Jackhammer for a treasure hunt," Walt said, stroking his big white beard after plopping down into the backseat. "Now that's a new one for me."

It was 1700, so we still had two hours until sundown and another hour after that until the fireworks were scheduled to start. We passed the time over at Pete's house and went over the details of the plan. The idea was to be as quick as possible, to be in and out of the lighthouse property before anyone noticed we were there.

At 1930, half an hour after the red sun sank into the Gulf of Mexico, we made our move. After driving around the block twice to see if there was any activity in the compound, we pulled up to a no-parking zone along the curb.

"Empty as a tomb," Pete said, looking out through the back open window.

"Remember what that guy Marty said," Ange said. "They closed at six. Place should be cleared out by now. He also said that nobody lives in the keeper's house anymore."

I looked up and down the street. Whitehead had a few people walking about, most heading toward the waterfront at a hurried pace. Compared to earlier that day, the place was cleared out. The fireworks show and the rest of the festivities near Mallory were drawing everyone on the island like ants to a picnic.

I glanced down at my dive watch.

"Fifteen minutes until showtime," I said.

Just moments after the words left my lips, we heard a distant boom, followed seconds later by a loud explosion. Trails of small shooting stars exploded out in all directions like a bright blossoming flower. I peered out through the windows as the firework lit up the dark sky beneath a blanket of looming dark clouds overhead.

"Looks like they started early on account of the weather," Jack said.

Great, I thought. *The evening just started, and we've already got a wrench in our plans.*

But we'd planned for the unexpected. According to the city's statement in the Fantasy Fest event flyer, the evening's show was scheduled to last for approximately thirteen minutes. That meant we'd have to kick it into gear if we were going to break through the concrete in time.

"Jack—" I turned back to tell my friend to hop out and open the gate, but he was already on it.

Using a pair of bolt cutters, he made quick work of the chain holding the wooden gate shut, then hinged it open. During our recon earlier that day, I'd eyed the path into the compound from the road and estimated that there was just enough room to back in my Tacoma.

I put the truck in drive, pulled into the street, then shifted to reverse and backed us smoothly onto the grass. It was a tight fit between the two walls and up a narrow grassy ramp, but the truck made it. I was able to back us right up to the spot where the three paths converged beside the lighthouse.

"Walt, do the orientation and paces again," I said as I jumped out, leaving the engine running. "We'll grab the hammer and get it ready."

An orchestra of explosions filled the evening air to the northwest. Plumes of brilliant bright streaks lit up the darkness in a beautiful and colorful display. But I merely glanced up every now and then to catch a glimpse of the show. We had work to do.

While Walt reverified the dig site, we carried the jackhammer from the bed and set it on the sidewalk. I quickly surveyed the grounds, paying particular attention to the entrances. The last thing we needed was for law enforcement to catch us in the act, or worse, more of the Albanian criminals.

Seeing that the coast was clear, I turned my full

attention back to the task at hand.

Most jackhammers are pneumatic and therefore require an air compressor to operate. Fortunately, Walt's old friend had just upgraded to a few newer models that were electric instead, saving us from having to get a compressor as well. Unsure if the outdoor outlets on the grounds would be working or not, we'd brought Jack's generator just in case.

"Looks like they're hot," Jack said after plugging in the jackhammer's power cord to one of the place's outdoor outlets.

Finally, some good news.

Once Walt had the site located, I powered up the heavy piece of machinery. With an 1800-watt motor and a five-pound striker, the guy at the rental place was adamant that it would make quick work of any concrete slab.

Pete handed me a pair of safety glasses, and I slid them over my eyes. I quickly checked my watch, then glanced up at the frenzy of explosions continuing relentlessly overhead. We still had seven minutes.

Squeezing tight to the handles on either side, I put the striker in place and started it up. In an instant, the metal tip pounded up and down, cracking the concrete as effortlessly as a rock breaking through a barely frozen lake.

The guy at the store had said that the new models had vibration reduction technology, which minimizes the trembling felt by the operator. Regardless, I could still feel my teeth chatter and shock waves travel down my spine as the heavy metal pounded over and over again at an unrelenting pace.

In less than a minute, I transformed a good portion of the section of sidewalk into small manageable chunks. I gave us some margin for error in our search before powering off the machine and setting it aside.

The others quickly moved in with shovels and crowbars, throwing the broken shards of concrete into a pile on the grass beside us. In no time we managed to remove most of the concrete and started shoveling dirt one small pile at a time. The clue on the compass hadn't given any indication as to how deep Hastings had buried whatever it was we were looking for. Being in his late seventies when he'd stumbled upon the diamond, I imagined that he wouldn't have buried it too deep.

Soon the fireworks show grew in intensity. More and more exploding fireballs illuminated the night sky as the display drew closer to its grand finale.

I turned around, scanned the grounds yet again, then dug the shovel hard into the dirt. We were three feet down when Ange's shovel hit something hard, causing the rest of us to freeze in an instant. She looked up at us and smiled.

A few more shovels of dirt revealed what looked like a small box. As if to put an exclamation point on our find, the finale of fireworks began just as Ange bent down and grabbed hold of the unknown object. A chaotic crescendo of booms and streaks and crackles filled the darkness above. The lights, sounds, and intensity put the earlier part of the show to shame. It was so bright it was as if the sun had resurrected itself like a phoenix and rocketed back up into the evening sky.

We didn't need a flashlight to see what it was that Ange was holding. It was a small, intricately designed metal chest.

The five of us exchanged ecstatic glances, high fives, and back slaps. We didn't know what was inside of it, but we knew that there was a good chance that it was the lost Florentine Diamond. Whether it was or not, we were one step closer to finding it, and we could all feel it. We were all high on the treasure buzz.

Ange lifted the chest so we could look it over. She tried to raise the lid, but it wouldn't budge. That was strange because there was no visible lock. There were, however, unique shapes intricately ornamenting each of the chest's four vertical surfaces. The five of us admired it and tried to figure out how to open it as the final fireworks exploded.

The lit-up sky turned dark in an instant, the awe-inspiring bursts of flames leaving a massive blanket of smoke behind. We could hear the loud cheers from the thousands of gathered spectators voicing their enthusiastic approval.

Moments after the final explosion went off, I heard Atticus shuffling uncomfortably in the cab of my truck. Many animals get scared when fireworks go off, but I'd brought him to a few shows before and he'd been just fine—which led me to assume that something else was bothering him.

At first, I thought he might have to relieve himself. I'd let him out just before heading to the lighthouse, but maybe he had to go again. Then he barked while staring forward through the windshield. I directed my gaze to where he was looking. Seconds later, a big guy dressed in all black walked into view on the sidewalk. From the moment I laid eyes on him, it was clear that he was trouble.

His build. The way he carried himself. The way he was dressed. The fact that he was alone.

I observed him for a fraction of a second before he locked eyes with me and froze instantly mid-step.

If I'd had any doubts as to whether or not this guy was hostile, they were extinguished when he reached for an earpiece and spoke quickly in a low tone.

The others had heard Atticus barking and had been startled as well. Ange said something, but I couldn't make out what it was as my body and mind took over, leaping into action.

I strode to the edge of the sidewalk, my eyes watching the guy's each and every move. With his right hand on the earpiece, he glared at me, then reached for the handgun on his waistband with his left.

I bent down and grabbed hold of a jagged shard of concrete that was covered in dust residue. It was about the size of a baseball, though a little heavier. Without a moment's hesitation, I lunged forward with my left foot, then fired off a fastball.

I don't watch a lot of sports on TV, but I've always loved watching highlights. Especially the web gems on ESPN. Some of my favorite top plays are when an outfielder guns a runner out at home plate. From the moment the player gloves the ball until he lets it fly, it looks as though he's operating in a fast meditative trance.

That's how I felt as I hurled the jagged concrete slab with everything I had. Just as the guy's hand gripped his weapon, the frozen rope smashed into his chest. He grunted as his body jerked back. He lost balance and tumbled onto the hood of a parked Honda Civic and let go of his gun, letting it fall to the ground, where it settled uselessly on the road between the Civic's front right tire and the curb.

Just as the concrete shard hit home, I took off in a full sprint toward our new unknown enemy. I wasn't about to give him any form of leniency, not even a second to collect himself for a retaliation.

We'd been about a hundred feet away from each other, and just as he lifted himself from the hood of the car, I finished cutting the distance. I grabbed him forcefully and threw him hard onto the sidewalk. He was even bigger than I'd pegged him, at least two hundred and fifty pounds of densely packed muscle. He was still wheezing heavily from the impact. Blood dripped out through tears in his black button-up shirt.

There was a steady stream of muffled indiscernible chatter coming from his earpiece. Ange appeared right on my heels and had her Glock aimed straight at him. Jack moved in, tore off the earpiece, then snatched his radio and turned the volume up full blast.

"What the hell is going on?" a woman's voice said through the speaker. She had a stern tone and an Eastern European accent. "Come in, dammit!"

Jack didn't skip a beat. He lifted the radio to his mouth and pressed down on the talk button.

"Sorry, Fatso can't come to the phone right now," he said.

There was a short pause as the woman on the other end realized that her buddy was immobilized.

"Who the hell is this?" the voice replied, louder and even angrier than before.

Ange grabbed the radio. "We're the people that you shouldn't have messed with."

The woman said something we couldn't hear, then gave a loud, sinister laugh.

"You obviously have no clue who you're talking to, bitch," she said.

Ange's mouth dropped open. She glanced over at me, then shook her head. Whoever this mysterious woman was, she'd sure pissed off Ange in a hurry.

"You know, the last person to call me that died in a fiery explosion," Ange said flatly. "Why don't you show your face and maybe we can give you a similar fate?"

The woman on the other end didn't skip a beat.

"Oh, don't you worry, hun," she snarled. "We'll be there before you know it."

The moment after the last word came over the speaker, the line turned to static.

TWENTY

The big guy on the ground suddenly gained a newfound surge of energy. He jerked his body up, trying to jump to his feet and engage us. In the blink of an eye, Ange kicked him in the face. His head snapped back, and he fell out of consciousness, his body contorted awkwardly on the edge of the sidewalk.

A moment later, a loud engine roared from down the street to the south. I knew it wasn't a coincidence. Whoever that woman was, she was about to make her introduction.

"Get the chest out of here," I said to the group. "I'll draw them away and deal with them. Whatever happens, we can't let them get it."

The sound of the engine grew louder, and I looked up just in time to see a blacked-out SUV fly around the corner and into view. Its tires screeched as it skidded across the intersection and jerked to a stop less than a hundred yards in front of us.

We needed to make sure that they didn't get the chest. We needed to split up.

"Get in the truck and go!" I said.

Walt looked at the truck, which was still parked in the middle of the lighthouse compound, and said, "How? These guys are blocking the road."

"It's a four-by-four," I said, motioning toward the other side of the grounds. I handed Jack the keys. "I'll make a generous donation," I added. "Just punch right through."

"What are you gonna do, bro?" Jack said with wide eyes.

The SUV's engine roared again, then the vehicle peeled out and took off down the road straight for us.

"I'm gonna draw their attention," I said, grabbing my Sig.

"Not if I draw it first," Ange said confidently as she stepped into the street in front of me.

Before I could try and stop her or change her mind, she raised her Glock and fired at the rapidly accelerating SUV. A succession of rounds exploded from the barrel and slammed into the SUV's grille. One bullet struck the front right tire, which exploded in a loud boom. The SUV jolted down, shot up sparks from the tire well, and spun out of control.

I'd moved alongside Ange, and we both barely managed to dive out of the furious vehicle's path as it flew past us. Just down the street, it jerked hard to the right, nearly flipping over before barreling over the sidewalk and crashing through the brick wall beside the entrance to the Hemingway House.

I glanced to my right, watching as Jack, Pete, and Walt climbed into my Tacoma. Jack started up the engine right away and floored it, sending the truck across the grounds and out of view.

Ange and I ran across the street, our weapons raised as we closed in on the SUV. After crashing through the wall and nearly flipping over, it came to a stop beside a cluster of banana trees.

A symphony of gunfire suddenly exploded from behind the wall. We took cover behind an old Volkswagen, the glass shattering just over our heads as the relentless barrage continued for a few stretched-out seconds.

When it stopped, we quickly popped around the backside of the car and took aim in the direction the gunshots had come from.

Stepping over the broken, scattered bricks, we gazed upon the battered vehicle. All four doors were open, the engine was still running, and the headlights were still on. But there was no sign of the former occupants.

"Looks like these guys wanna play a little hide-and-seek," Ange said.

I glanced over my shoulder, listening as I heard the sounds of my Tacoma accelerating in the distance and crashing through a metal fence.

Seeing the others making their successful escape, I turned my attention back to the bad guys, who'd disappeared into Hemingway's old backyard. The fact that they'd run off for a better strategic vantage point told me that they weren't just your average run-of-the-mill criminals with no experience and nothing to lose. These guys at least had some idea what they were doing.

"Let's move in," I said, raising my Sig.

We kept our distance from the wrecked SUV, moved over the wall beside us and into the tree-riddled grounds. The foliage provided sufficient cover, blocking most of the moon's glow. It made our approach easier but would also enhance our assailants' ability to hide.

We crept across a well-manicured lawn and took cover in the second row of trees. Moving toward the main house, we caught our first glimpse of our enemies.

There were five of them. A woman and four men. The woman looked like she could be a bouncer in one of those classic Hollywood movies. She was tall, wide-shouldered, and had short straight jet-black hair.

We moved in slowly and watched as she said something we couldn't make out into a radio, then addressed the others.

"Split up," she said harshly. "Time to teach these assholes a lesson."

Doing as they were told, the four guys dispersed. One headed for the back of the house, one climbed up to the roof, and one headed for Hemingway's writing cottage over by the swimming pool. The third held a stockless AK-47 with both hands and moved in our direction with his head on a swivel. The woman seemed to vanish into thin air, disappearing behind a garden of various flowers.

Moving silently, we crept to the side and took cover behind a thick cocoplum bush. He was heading toward us with long strides and would be beside us in seconds.

I gave Ange a nod, then shifted around to her left side. She nodded back. Just as the guy was in front of us, she popped out from the right side of the bush.

Spooked, the guy was just raising his weapon toward Ange when I pounced on him from behind. I forced my left arm around his chest while simultaneously wrapping my right around his neck. Digging my right knee into his back, I jolted him backward and crunched his airway. He was neutralized and unconscious in less than ten seconds.

One down.

I dragged him behind the bush, leaving him in the cover and dark shadows. Ange and I raised our weapons and moved in to deal with the rest.

With no other bad guys in sight, we decided to head up onto the roof to take down the guy above. I moved in toward the main house, then glanced left and right before quickly holstering my Sig.

Lunging forward and bending my knees, I jumped as high as I could, propelling myself upward like a basketball player going for a breakaway dunk. Though my vertical isn't nearly NBA-worthy, I managed to extend my arms and grab hold of the second-story balcony with my fingers.

Holding tight, I twisted my body and brought my right foot up onto the ledge. I kept silent as I climbed up the decorative metal railing, then slid over the top and landed softly on the deck. Turning back around, I stepped up onto the rail and grabbed a metal support pillar. Reaching overhead, I gripped the edge of the roof and pulled myself up slowly to take a look.

The roof was double-layered, with a square, flat section in the middle that rose above the outer part of the angled roof. From my vantage point, I couldn't see any sign of the guy. I heaved myself up, grabbed my Sig, and scanned the roof. Still no sign of him.

Turning around, I looked down at Ange, who was standing on the ground with her hands on her hips. She shot me a look I knew all too well. It was her *that was impressive, but wait until you see what I do* look. The facial equivalent to "hold my beer."

She took a short step back and eyed the challenge in front of her. But before she could make a move, footsteps approached from the corner of the house. Without a moment's hesitation or even a glance at me, she moved out of my view toward the approaching enemy.

Shit, I thought, not liking the idea of splitting up.

For half a second, I debated dropping back down and helping her. Then I spotted movement. The guy who'd climbed up to the roof appeared from the other side of the large AC unit. He said something that sounded like "all clear" into his radio, then froze when he saw me.

Fortunately, I'd spotted him first and had my Sig locked on him before he could level his own weapon on me. I fired off two quick rounds, but with a level of agility I hadn't expected, he managed to drop back out of view behind the metal box of groaning spinning fans.

I took off. Moving as fast as I could with my Sig raised chest height, I ran straight for him. As I rounded the corner of the AC unit, I was welcomed by a blindingly fast snapping kick that lurched me sideways and knocked my Sig out of my hands. It rattled and tumbled to the edge of the roof as he hit me with a rapid punch to the side of my head.

My head jerked sideways as the powerful blow shot pain through my skull. He came at me with another attack, this time a wide haymaker that I just managed to avoid.

With my enemy off-balance, I hit him with a quick slide kick that sent him flying backward. His head hit the side of the AC unit, and his back hit the roof hard. But he managed to grab hold of me at the last moment, pull me down, and force his hands into a chokehold.

I gripped him hard and spun my body, causing us both to roll toward the edge of the roof. I reached for my Sig, but he kicked it, sending it flying over the edge and out of view.

He grabbed a Beretta from his waistband and grunted as he tried to put me in the barrel's view. He fired off a few rounds that shook my eardrums and whizzed right passed me.

I grabbed his wrist, forced it up, then slammed it down until the weapon fell free. Enraged and in pain, he punched me in the chest and tried a second time to strangle the life out of me. I retaliated by sticking my thumbs into his eyes, forcing them deep into the squishy corneas. He yelled maniacally and loosened his grip enough for me to jump to my feet. But he wasn't out yet. He staggered to his feet as well, then let out a barbaric yell. He blinked a few times, fighting to see with his damaged eyes.

He came at me again, but this time I slid my dive knife from its sheath and stabbed it into the center of his chest. His yelling turned to gasps, and he stopped, then took a few slow steps back with my knife still sticking out.

Forcing his bleeding eyes to work, he yelled out again, then reached for the knife's handle. I lunged at him and hit him with a powerful front kick. My right heel slammed into the handle just as he wrapped his fingers around it, burying the sharp titanium blade even deeper in his chest.

The force of the blow caused his body to fall back and tumble off the roof. His yelling continued as his body free-fell the thirty feet down, then stopped in an instant as he hit the grass with a loud thud.

Holy shit.

I'd fought tough, trained, hardened men before. That guy was right there with the best of them, and I knew at that moment that this Albanian mafia wasn't messing around. They wanted Walt, they wanted the diamond, and they wanted us dead. And judging by the way the guy had carried himself, they usually got what they wanted.

My mind shifted instantly to Ange and the guy she'd gone off to engage at the back of the house. I spun around to look for the guy's dropped Beretta and was taken aback by what I saw.

The tall, muscular woman we'd seen earlier was just thirty feet away from me at the center of the roof. She was standing stoically, eyeing me up and down.

"You are a good fighter," she said in a strong Albanian accent. "It is a shame you have chosen to fight for the wrong side."

She slowly raised a revolver with her right hand. I only had a fraction of a second to make a move. Any kind of move.

My Sig was long gone, but the guy I'd just impaled had dropped his Beretta less than ten feet from me, where it rested with part of its barrel sticking out over the edge of the roof.

I dove for it but lost my footing on the wet metal roof and slipped. Instead of going for the gun, I rolled to my side and fell over the edge of the roof just as the woman sent a bullet my way. It slammed into the metal, shooting up a spark as I fell to the ground.

I landed about as athletically as could be expected given the circumstances, doing my best to roll and ease the downward momentum. My hip hit hard and caused me to grunt, but I got off easy. A broken or sprained ankle or a cracked bone would've been understandable given the height of the unplanned fall.

I quickly got my bearings and scanned for my Sig, which I knew had fallen somewhere close by. It was nowhere in sight, however. The only thing I could see in the darkness was the dead guy right beside me.

Suddenly, I heard sounds coming from up on the roof—a few gunshots, followed by a struggle. It was Ange. She'd engaged the mysterious woman, and my every instinct pleaded for me to do something. Anything to help her.

I lunged over to the dead guy and ripped my knife from his bloodied chest. It was at that moment that the fourth and final guy decided to make his appearance. Having gone to the far side of the compound, he was now moving tactically around from Hemingway's writing studio beside the pool to join the party.

Without thinking and with no other option of engaging him from such a distance, I reared my knife back, lunged forward, and fired it through the air. This time my aim wasn't as good as earlier with the shard of concrete. Instead of striking him through the heart, I barely managed to slice a gash in his left shoulder.

It wasn't a neutralizing blow, but it allowed me to distract him long enough to sprint straight over and close the distance between us. While he winced in pain and pulled the knife free, I dove at him, tackling him hard and sending us both flying into Hemingway's swimming pool.

We splashed and grappled for a few seconds, clawing at each other in a frenzy of bubbles and muffled voices as we sank to the bottom. He jabbed me with an elbow to my forehead while I struggled for a better grip to try and choke him out.

We were at the shallow end, and we managed to break through the surface of the five-foot-deep water and take quick gasps of air before going back at it. I managed to take intermittent blurry glances through the palm trees at the fistfight that Ange and the mysterious woman were engaged in.

Wanting to put my enemy down and help her as fast as I could, I punched him in the nose, then twisted him around and grabbed hold of him forcefully from behind. Splashing us both down to the bottom, I kicked as hard as I could, propelling us toward the deep end. It was clear from the fight that I was far more comfortable in the water than he was, so I knew I could take him easily in deeper water.

He managed to strike me a few more times before I pinned us both to the bottom, holding him tight and waiting him out. It wasn't long before his desperately struggling body went limp in my arms. I waited a few more seconds, just to be sure, then checked him over. He was gone.

Letting go of him, I kicked for the edge of the pool. In one quick motion, I surfaced and jumped out of the water while taking in a much-needed lungful of air.

I made a break straight for the guy's Beretta at the edge of the pool. Grabbing it, I took aim toward the roof of the house.

Ange and the woman were still engaged in a brutal fistfight, each blocking and barely avoiding strike after strike.

In the heat of the moment, the woman managed to grab Ange from behind. Her eyes diverted to mine for a moment, then grew wide. Holding Ange as a human shield, she whispered something to her, then threw her to the roof and disappeared from view.

I ran across the grounds, sprinting around the house in the direction she'd vanished. I heard only a distant shuffling of palm fronds and then utter silence.

"Ange, are you alright?" I asked, redirecting my attention up toward the roof.

"You see where she went?" Ange said, leaning over the edge.

I let out a sigh of relief upon seeing that she appeared unscathed and shook my head.

"No," I replied. I spent a few seconds catching my breath from the ordeal and added, "Who the hell was that girl?"

"That was no girl," she replied. "That was a beast."

She climbed down to the second story, motioned for me to get into position, then leapt like Buttercup into Fezzik's arms at the end of *The Princess Bride*. I caught her, though not with as much ease as the giant. After a quick kiss, I let her down to her feet softly.

"That bad, huh?"

"Imagine if Rhonda Rousey and the Undertaker had a daughter. Then pump her full of steroids and teach her martial arts."

I laughed, and she pushed me into the light of the moon, then examined my face.

"Jeez, babe," she said. "Are you alright?"

"Those guys weren't amateurs," I said. "Had to bring my A-game and still took more than a few hits. I've also had much better landings."

"Should we go after her?"

I stared at the dark edge of the compound for a few seconds, then turned to face her.

"I think she's long gone." I motioned toward the road. "Come on. Let's call Jack and get him to pick us up someplace downtown."

I slid my phone from my pocket and dialed his number. Without a single ring, the robotic woman's voice came over the line, letting me know that the number wasn't available.

"What is it?" Ange said, seeing the blank expression on my face.

"Jack's phone's off," I said.

Her face matched mine. It was strange for Jack not to answer and even stranger for him to turn off his phone, especially given our present circumstances.

Ange's face went from blank to worried in an instant.

"You don't think…?" she said.

Maybe. Maybe there's more than one group of bad guys cruising downtown tonight.

"Come on," I said, raising my voice. "Let's go!"

I holstered my Sig and took off in a run with Ange right beside me.

TWENTY-ONE

Jack wasted no time climbing into the driver's seat and starting up the Tacoma's six-cylinder engine. Shifting to drive, he U-turned and accelerated over the bumpy pile of concrete tossed aside during their dig, thundering onto a small patch of grass. Weaving in and out of trees, he looked ahead at a long white fence that blocked the way in front of them. There was no opening, so he was forced to make one.

"Hold on," he said as he accelerated and crashed through the fence posts, sending cracked pieces of wood flying around them.

He reached a small parking lot on the other side and cut a sharp left. Rumbling through the exit, he turned right onto Truman Avenue, then onto Thomas Street, heading northwest.

The streets were electric. Music played on every corner, and the sidewalks grew more and more busy with foot traffic the farther they drove downtown. They had to stop for a group of shirtless Spartan warriors as they crossed the street while engaged in a plastic sword battle. A group of women wearing nothing but paint followed beside them.

The three guys kept a sharp eye out for danger. Jack had watched the fight break out through his rearview mirror. He was pretty sure that Logan and Ange had been successful at drawing the SUV's attention away from them, allowing them to make an escape with the chest.

Jack glanced back and saw the artifact they'd dug up clutched in Walt's hands. Pete sat in the passenger seat beside him. He had the window rolled down and was looking back, making sure that they weren't being followed.

"We should go back and help them," Walt said, shaking his head.

"Logan told us to split up," Pete said. "So that's what we're gonna do."

After a few blocks, Jack turned to Pete and asked, "Where should we go?"

He thought it over for a moment. "Let's head over to the restaurant. I want to be relatively close so we can swing back and pick them up."

"I'm not sure you two understand how dangerous these mafia guys are," Walt said. "That woman we heard is their leader. These aren't the bottom of the barrel like the others were. They'll need all the help they can get. Trust me."

"Walt, you don't know them like we do," Jack said. "Even if there are ten bad guys crammed into that vehicle, it's still an unfair fight."

A woman wearing a skimpy bikini and a vibrant orange feathered headpiece walked in front of them.

They looked past her at the oncoming traffic across the intersection.

"Holy crap," Pete said.

"What?" Jack said, looking to his right.

He didn't have to wait for a reply to see what was wrong. A black SUV, identical to the one they'd seen earlier, was flying with reckless abandon straight toward them.

"More of your old friends, Wally?" Pete said.

Jack watched as the crowds of people scrambled to barely get out of the way as the SUV roared toward them. They yelled and cursed for the big vehicle to slow down, but the driver was on a mission. A mission to kill them and take the chest.

Jack didn't hesitate. He floored the Tacoma, causing the tires to screech and generate smoke as he jerked the wheel hard to the left. Once the treads gained traction, they accelerated down Southard Street. He just managed to avoid being struck by the incoming SUV, their grille just a few feet away from hitting the Tacoma's tailgate.

Southard quickly ended at a roundabout beside Truman Waterfront Park. Hitting the wide turn as fast as he could, Jack nearly brought the inner tires off the ground as he whirled them around and swiftly stabilized the truck onto Angela Street, heading south along the waterfront.

There were much fewer cars and pedestrians, so Jack was able to accelerate them to up over seventy miles per hour on the long straightaway. Glancing at his rearview mirror, he saw that his pursuers were still right behind them, breathing down their necks.

"What's the plan here, Ruby?" Walt said.

Jack's mind was running wild. They were flying down the dark waterfront street, but the SUV was still getting closer and closer with each passing second.

He reached to his waist and pulled his compact Desert Eagle from its concealed holster. Setting it on the front of the center console, he turned over at Pete.

"You got your—"

"Of course," he said, grabbing his silver Taurus Raging Bull .44 Magnum revolver from his waistband. He glanced back at their pursuers and added, "But something tells me these guys have probably got us outgunned."

Pete was right. These were hardened mafia criminals on their tail. Walt was the only one who'd dealt with them before, and he'd warned them of just how dangerous they were.

Jack's heart pounded in his chest. He needed a plan. He needed to do something.

We can't beat them in a gunfight, he thought. *But what if we...*

With the end of the road drawing near, something caught his eye far out over to the water to his right. It was the long stretch of the Fort Zachary Cruise Pier. The only cruise ship currently in town was tied off over near Mallory Square, leaving the one beside them empty and dark. He'd just barely noticed it due to the silver glow of moonlight.

With the road seconds away from ending in front of him, he eased off the gas and turned the wheel to the right.

"What the hell are you—" Pete managed to say before Jack drove right through a metal gate and a sign that said No Motor Vehicles Beyond This Point.

The truck shuddered as the chain broke free, and the thick bars of the gate burst open. He spun a hard right and hit the gas again, and moments later there was nothing but water on both sides of them.

"What's gotten into that crazy conch head of yours?" Walt said from the backseat.

Jack pressed the pedal harder, accelerating them up over eighty and making the dark world around them into little more than a blur.

As he approached the end of the quarter-mile-long pier, he eased off the gas pedal. Just enough for the SUV to move right up on them.

"You know the road ends up here, boyo!" Pete said.

His confidence in his friend's decision-making skills was waning beyond belief. He was either insane or suicidal.

"Just hold on!" Jack said, keeping his eyes focused ahead of him.

When the end was less than a few hundred feet in front of them, he switched off the headlights, braked, and spun the wheel hard to the right. Their bodies lurched sideways with the sudden change of direction. A chorus of screeching tires rang out as the truck skidded sideways, struggling to complete the turn.

As Jack had hoped, the pursuing vehicle's driver was paying too much attention to their quarry and not enough attention to his surroundings.

The SUV was moving too fast to stop. It thundered toward the edge, the front tires turning but failing to successfully redirect the vehicle's momentum to keep them from going over. The front bumper of the big SUV managed to clip the Tacoma's tailgate just before it flew over the edge and splashed far out into the dark water below.

Jack tried to keep the wheel steady as the Tacoma spun frantically out of control. His right foot still had the brake pedal glued to the floor. In a chaotic blur of activity, the truck slid slowly toward the edge, causing the back right tire to jut out over nothing but air.

Jack looked at his wide-eyed friends. For a moment, he thought it was over. That the truck would stay in place, and they'd make it out dry and unscathed. Then he felt an uncomfortable shudder, followed by a groaning chassis.

It had been a battle between the truck's balance and gravity. Gravity won. The truck suddenly began to slide. The three of them were barely able to make a sound, let alone speak as they quickly accelerated backward and down. Once over the edge, the truck immediately flipped over, spinning and free-falling toward the water.

They yelled out and braced themselves. The truck hit the water on its side with a big splash that tossed the guys inside around more than a jerky old roller coaster. Water shattered the windows and flowed in rapidly. Within seconds, the interior was filled with seawater, and they started to sink.

It was a miracle that none of them lost consciousness. Seeing the others were alright in the blurry darkness, Jack moved back and grabbed hold of the chest. The three of them managed to slip out through the broken windows and swim up through a sea of bubbles toward the surface. When they broke free into the night air, they took big gulps of air and looked at each other in amazement.

"Did that really just happen?" Jack said, managing to come up with words first.

He was working hard to stay above water. Born and bred in the Keys and having spent much of his life out on the water, Jack could tread on the surface until he died of thirst. But the chest was heavy, and it felt even heavier as he worked to keep it afloat while fully dressed and with shoes on.

Pete and Walt quickly swam over to help him. The three of them were amazed that they'd made it out of the ordeal relatively unscathed. Jack's head hurt like hell from being slammed against the wheel. He knew he most likely had a concussion. Blood dripped down from a cut above Pete's right eyebrow. And Walt was wincing and groaning from the bones he'd clearly broken in his left forearm. But they were all three of them still alive and able.

"Any sign of movement?" Pete said, motioning toward where the SUV rested thirty feet down at the bottom.

Jack shook his head.

"Looks like we're in the clear for now."

"I can't wait to see the look on Logan's face when you tell him that you've donated his truck to the artificial reef program," Pete added.

Jack laughed.

"He was in need of an American-made upgrade anyway," he replied jokingly. "Never understood how a guy named Dodge could drive a Yota."

The three guys treaded water and quickly decided that the best course of action would be to swim across the man-made inlet to the downtown cruise pier and promenade. Climbing up the end of the Zachary Taylor Pier would mean a long hike in wet clothes back to the main road to hail a cab.

It only took them five minutes to traverse the six hundred feet of dark tropical water. As they swam past one of the branches of the downtown pier, heading for the prom, a woman called out to them from a tied-off catamaran.

"Jack?" the woman said in a heavy Southern drawl.

173

Jack looked up, narrowing his gaze for a better look.

"Aren't you a sight for sore eyes," Jack said with a big smile. "How are you, Sweetie?"

She shrugged.

"Same old," she replied. Then she looked over the three of them and chuckled. "Ya know, I'd say this is a strange situation, but for you it's almost normal."

Lauren Sweetin was the owner and operator of a snorkeling charter. Her sailboat, *Sweet Dreams*, was a thirty-four-foot catamaran. She'd been standing on the port pontoon, coiling a rope, when she'd spotted the three guys swim over. She was pretty, with long auburn hair, tanned skin, and a voluptuous figure. In her mid-thirties, she'd migrated to the Keys from Tennessee after a nasty divorce with her cheating lawyer husband a year earlier.

"It felt like I was watching an old episode of *The Dukes of Hazzard*," she said with another contagious laugh. "Sure put an interesting exclamation point on this strange Key Weird evening. You guys aren't hurt, are you?"

"Nothing a little do-it-yourself first aid won't fix," Jack said. "The other guys weren't so lucky."

She nodded.

"Should I even bother asking what you guys are up to now, or should I just wait for the *Keynoter* article?"

"I'm sure Harper Ridley will make it sound more entertaining than I could."

"Alright, I won't prod. You know me, Jack. I'm pretty laid-back. Not really the proddin' type. You guys just be careful, alright? Key West needs its resident top dive aficionado and best restaurant owner. Not sure who you are, but I'm sure you're unique too if you got caught up in their mess."

"This is Walt Grissom," Pete said. That caused her eyes to go wide in amazement. "And he kind of caught us up in his."

She raised her eyebrows. "That so? Well, come on back and get out of the water already. Jack, you look like you're about to get a hernia keeping whatever that is in your hands afloat."

Jack grinned but felt slightly embarrassed. He'd been doing his best to hide his struggling. Over the years, he and Lauren had shared an interesting relationship. No intimacy had ever come of it, but Jack had developed a crush on her and planned to make a move soon.

Lauren helped them up onto the swim platform, then handed each of them a towel.

"Should really get that looked at," she said, motioning toward Pete's forearm. "Those guys that chased you off the pier," she added, looking over her shoulder toward the scene of the incident, "any chance there's more of them nearby?"

The three guys exchanged glances, not knowing how to respond.

"I'll take that as a probably yes," she said. "Well, I haven't called the Guard yet. I saw you guys swimming over and was gonna wait until I talked to you. But I can't speak for anyone else who might've seen what happened."

She glanced over at the people walking along the nearby promenade.

"Don't worry," Pete said. "We'll get ahold of Jane and let her know what happened. You got your phone, Jack?"

Working in and around the water, Jack kept his

phone in a waterproof sleeve most of the time. He reached into his pockets, patted them down, then looked up in surprise.

"Ah shit," he said. "Looks like my phone went to Davy Jones' Locker." Turning to Lauren, he added, "You mind if I use your phone, Sweetie? We'll probably need to call for a cab too with the streets so busy tonight."

She waved a hand.

"No need," she replied. "I'll give you a ride. I was just finishing up anyway. Plus I'd like to hear a little more about what you three have been up to tonight."

TWENTY-TWO

I tried Jack's number two more times. Nothing. It was still off, and Ange and I were unable to get ahold of Pete either.

We headed past the wrecked SUV, which was still resting halfway through the brick wall, and crossed the street back to the lighthouse grounds. Small clusters of people had gathered, the noise from the wreck and gunshots sparking their fear and curiosity. We heard sirens in the distance that were growing louder and louder with each passing second.

We detoured around the lighthouse and headed for downtown. We didn't know where they'd headed but figured that Pete's restaurant or the marina would be our two best bets for finding them.

We moved with a purpose. Not too fast to draw suspicion, but fast enough to traverse the distance quickly. Not only were we worried about what had happened to them, but we were also mindful of the fact that the bad guys could return to try and finish us off at any moment. It was clear that the big woman had been their leader, and she'd managed to slip through our fingers and get away.

Halfway to Pete's restaurant, my phone vibrated to life. I slid it from my pocket and read the screen. It was a local south Florida number. A 786 area code, but I didn't recognize it. I let out a sigh of relief when I answered and heard Jack on the other end.

"Are you guys alright?" I asked.

"We're fine, bro," he said. "Ran into a little trouble but managed to get away. What about you two?"

"A little beat up, but we've made off worse before. We're heading over to Pete's now."

"We'll see you there," he replied. "Anxious to take a good look at this chest."

We hung up, hailed a bike taxi, and were at the front door of the restaurant five minutes later. Needless to say, we were anxious to take a look at the relic we'd dug up as well. It'd been buried in secret and had remained hidden in underground obscurity for over a hundred years. Whether it contained the lost diamond or not, we were certain that we were in for one hell of a surprise.

"Logan!" I heard a voice call out just as I reached for the brass doorknob.

I turned around and saw Jack leaning out the passenger window of a yellow Suzuki Samurai. I smiled when I saw the group of four adults crammed into the small off-road vehicle.

They thanked Lauren for the ride, and I waved to her as she drove off. Ange and I looked them over from head to toe.

"You guys decided to go for a little swim, huh?" Ange said.

"More of a quick improvise to take down the bad guys on our tail," Jack said.

"Do I even want to ask why you guys needed to hitch a ride in Lauren's Samurai and not my truck?"

The three of them looked at each other. They were smiling but trying not to.

"No," Jack said. "You don't want to ask that, bro."

I shook my head and sighed dramatically.

He went on to explain how he might have kind of, sort of driven it off a pier. I raised my eyebrows and laughed.

"Sorry, Jack," I said. "But it sounded like you just said that you drove my truck off a pier."

Pete laughed. "That's what happens when you give Jack the keys. You know he got a ticket during his driving test, right?"

Jack shrugged. "Stop sign came out of nowhere. But what's important is that we made it out alive. All of us. Don't know how, but we did."

"And that you've got good insurance," Walt said. "I hope, anyway."

I'd bought the truck over a year ago. While cruising through Marathon in a rental car, I'd spotted it parked with a for sale sign at the corner of a small used car place. It was the first thing I'd bought after moving back to the islands, and I'd been driving it ever since.

There would be a time and place for giving Jack crap. But for now, he was right. We were alive. And we all had two major things on our minds: watching out for more Albanian mafia, and the mysterious chest.

Not wanting to draw too much attention or raised eyebrows, we entered through the kitchen. The place was packed, but we managed to slip through the back door and up the wooden staircase with just a few people noticing. The three of them were still pretty wet, and their shoes left faint wet marks on each step.

We went straight for Pete's office, crammed inside, and shut the door behind us. For the first time since bringing it out from the dirt, we took a good look at what we'd found. It was fascinating. The chest had captured all of our interests when we'd first laid eyes on it by the light of the fireworks. Now, in Pete's well-lit office, our excitement was amplified even more.

The chest was small, only about a foot long, six inches wide, and six inches deep. It was incredibly intricate. Every inch seemed to be customized with unique patterns. It was sturdy, built of what we suspected was steel. Unlike most chests, it had no locking mechanism at the middle of the front seam.

One of the first things I noticed was a symbol etched into the top. It was the same irregular double-rose-shaped symbol that I'd first seen on the compass. A symbol representing the Florentine Diamond.

The most unique aspect of it was the four round metal dials situated in the middle of each of the four vertical sides. The dials were similar to those of combination locks. They each spun smoothly, but instead of numbers, there were unique symbols marking the various positions.

"I've never seen anything like it," Pete said, shaking his head.

We examined it on his old oak desk, then took turns passing it around and looking over its elaborate details. I paid particular attention to the dials and was fascinated by the fact that each dial had an array of different symbols. I recognized a few of them from books I'd read or images I'd seen over the years.

"Some of them look like family crests," I said, pointing at the different etched images.

Ange nodded and leaned over me.

"Wait a second," she said, then snatched a magnifying glass from the top drawer. She examined the edge of one of the sides and added, "There are words here." Looking closer and focusing the magnifying glass, she added, "It's French." She cleared her throat, then read the words aloud in English. "I couldn't talk. I couldn't walk. Life had only just begun."

She looked up at us with raised eyebrows. I stroked my chin, mulling the words over.

"Why couldn't this Hastings guy have just been like, 'Hey, future treasure hunters, the diamond is buried at so-and-so location?'" Jack said, shaking his head.

Because he was having too much fun with it, I thought. *He was knocking on death's door. The money didn't interest him. He wanted to leave behind something fascinating.*

The others moved in closer, nodded their agreement as they peered through the magnifying glass, then looked over the other sides.

"This side's Italian," Walt said, pointing to the right vertical side.

The two remaining sides each had words etched as well, one in Devanagari, a nearly two-thousand-year-old script that's used widely in and around India, and the other in German. None of us were familiar enough with the other three languages to attempt a translation. Ange had been born in Sweden and had spent much of her childhood there. Even though German is a common foreign language spoken in the Scandinavian nation, she'd never learned it, instead becoming fluent in Swedish, English, and French.

We thought over the translation Ange had made but couldn't make heads or tails of it. It was clear, however, that the words somehow corresponded to the symbols around the dial. Each of the four dials had twelve possible positions, which meant that it would take forever to try all of the combinations.

"We could always try the old sledgehammer method," Walt said with a shrug. "Or maybe a hammer and chisel to pry the lid open."

"Bad idea," Ange said, shaking her head. "That could damage whatever's inside."

"Ange is right," I said. "If this guy Hastings was as smart as I think he was, I'm guessing he designed some kind of contingency for people who tried methods like that."

After an hour of trying to figure out how to get into the chest, we took a quick break and shifted our conversation to our incidents that evening.

"We ran into a beast of a woman at the Hemingway House," Ange said. "About my height, shoulders wider than an Olympic rower, short black hair, tattoos. Ringing any bells with you, Walt?"

He only had to think for about a second before replying.

"Valmira Gallani," he said. "Or, as she's more commonly known in Southeastern Europe, the Angel of Death." He paused a moment and took a sip of whiskey. "She's the daughter of Isidor Gallani, a dangerous man who ran a massive criminal underworld for over thirty years. Story goes, Val put some arsenic in his vodka one night. Less than a week after his death, she put a bullet through her older brother's head. This made her the only remaining heir to the Gallani Mafia. From what I've learned about her, she took a liking to danger and fighting from an early age. She's notorious as one of the most dangerous women in Europe."

We went quiet a moment, letting Walt's words sink in.

"She went toe to toe with Ange, and she's still breathing," I said. "So that's saying a lot."

"So let me get this straight," Jack said. "Not only did you borrow money from an Albanian mafia to get funding for a salvage project, but you borrowed from a murdering criminal's daughter who just so happens to be called the Angel of Death?"

Walt didn't answer. He didn't have to. It was clear to all of us, especially to him, that he'd messed up royally.

I changed the subject, asking for the story of how Jack had managed to get them away by drowning my innocent truck. After an animated segment of storytime, we went back to the chest, using our smartphones and Pete's computer to try and decipher it.

"We should show this to Frank," Ange said at one point.

Pete nodded. "You're right. I'll see if he's in town."

I agreed wholeheartedly. Professor Frank Murchison would be just the guy to figure it out. He worked over at the nearby Florida Keys Community College and had helped us out a few times before.

I closed my eyes, squeezed the bridge of my nose, then checked the time. To my astonishment, it was nearly midnight. We'd spent over two hours looking at the chest, reading the inscriptions, looking over the symbols, and trying to figure out how we were going to get inside it. It had been a long day, and I felt the mental and physical exhaustion begin to take hold. I was also sore and bruised from the day's encounters with our friends in the Albanian mafia.

We called it a night not long after. The streets were still packed and noisy when we drove the few blocks to the marina. Walt was staying the night at Pete's house, and we decided to crash on our boats.

We told Jack we'd meet him in the morning, then climbed aboard the Baia as he made his way down the dock to the *Calypso*. We'd kept a sharp eye out for bad guys but figured that they'd had enough. At least for one night.

After saying goodnight to Jack, we climbed aboard our boat and Ange headed down into the saloon while I did a quick scan of the marina. I spotted a figure walking toward me on the dock. Gus switched off the marina lights every evening at 2100, so they were indistinguishable at first. Fortunately, my eyes had adjusted to the relative darkness, and I recognized who it was long before she reached the boat.

"It's been quite the evening," Jane said as she walked within earshot. She stopped along the starboard side and put her hands on her hips. "Even for Fantasy Fest." She looked out over the water and cleared her throat. "I've got a handful of dead guys over in Papa's backyard and two vehicles in the ocean off Fort Zach Pier. You got anything you wanna tell me, Logan?"

I told her everything that had happened, starting with when we were attacked at the lighthouse. Jane and I didn't beat around the bush with each other, and there was no sense lying to her. She'd just figure it all out anyway.

"Jeez, Logan," she said, shaking her head. "You know, believe it or not, Key West has a government organization whose purpose is to keep the peace."

"When people try to kill me, Jane, my first instinct isn't to call 9-1-1. I don't sit tight and wait for help. Just not the way I am. I defend myself, and I defend those I care about. I use whatever means necessary. You know all this well enough, Jane. This isn't the first time I've been caught up in trouble around here."

"Got that damn right," she said. She paused a moment, then added, "You guys alright?"

I nodded. "What have you found on the guys we took down?"

"We haven't been able to identify them yet. But it's only a matter of time. It's clear that none of them were here legally."

"What makes you think that?"

"No passports or IDs of any kind."

"I recommend calling the ATCs over at the Key West and Miami airports. Those guys must have arrived recently. You might be able to figure out what plane they were on."

"Who are they, Logan?"

I took in a deep breath and let it out.

"All I know is that they're Albanian mafia," I said. "And that they're led by a woman named Valmira Gallani."

"How do you know all this? What's going on?"

"It's a long story. They're after an old friend of Pete's, and they want a rare artifact that we're looking for."

She crossed her arms, looking out over the water.

185

"My job is to keep the people here safe, Logan. Can we expect any more confrontations with these guys?"

"Most likely," I said. "But we're the ones they're after. And we can handle them. That is, if we haven't scared them off already."

She shrugged.

"Just trying to do my job. If you get any tips or feel the need to maybe ask for some help sometime, the arm of the law is here to do what it does best."

"Thanks, Jane," I said.

She paused, clenched her jaw, then turned around and disappeared down the dock. I headed down into the main cabin. Ange had already passed out, and I lay down beside her. Staring up through the hatch, I thought about the words engraved in the side of the chest, and about this Valmira Gallani. Soon my eyelids grew heavy, and I dozed off to the gentle rocking of the boat.

TWENTY-THREE

The next morning, after calling ahead to make sure
that Frank was there, we drove over to the Florida
Keys Community College located on the northern end
of Stock Island. Ever since I'd first stepped foot on
the campus a year earlier, I'd decided that if I'd ever
gone to college, it would have been there. The white-
washed buildings and freshly manicured lawns are
located right on the water. It has an Olympic-sized
pool, an impressive curriculum of dive programs, and
a private beachfront for dropping beneath the waves
for training just beyond the front door of the
classrooms.

Frank Murchison was about as fitting for a
community college professor as Stephen Hawking
would be. Having taught for over twenty years at
Harvard, he'd traded in the freezing white winters in
Cambridge for the temperate white beaches of the

Keys. "Traded deep pockets for sandy pockets," as my good friend and the former sheriff of Key West, Charles Wilkes, used to say.

I'd first met Frank back in February, just after he'd finished up a lecture at Tennessee Williams Theatre. I'd been drawn to his passion, energy, and the smooth, articulate way in which he spoke. He was also one of the smartest guys I'd ever met. He'd been a great friend and asset during our various searches and endeavors throughout the Keys.

Frank could be found at Pete's at least once a week when he was in town, though he was often off on various expeditions around the world. Fortunately, we'd caught him while he was home. There wouldn't be a man in the Keys better suited for figuring out how to get into the chest than him.

Despite Walt's protestations that he was fine, Pete had driven the stubborn treasure hunter over to the Lower Keys Medical Center to get his forearm taken care of. The hospital was right across the street from the college, so we'd told Pete we'd meet him there.

His red '69 Camaro with black racing stripes was idling in the visitor lot when we arrived. Jack pulled his blue Wrangler into the space beside it, then we hopped out and greeted them.

"Looks like you got a new accessory, man," Jack said, motioning toward the dark blue cast around his left forearm.

Walt laughed. "Yeah, I've got your driving to thank for it."

"It's a good thing we went in," Pete said. "Doc Patel said it was one of the most impressive wrist fractures he'd ever seen. You guys should have seen the X-ray."

Moving through the parking lot, we headed up onto one of the sidewalks leading toward the back of the campus. Frank's office wasn't in the same building as the other faculty offices. Instead, it was on the second floor of the Diving and Underwater Technology Building. He told us not to bother with knocking since he'd be working on a project when we got there, so we opened the door and shuffled inside.

His office was big, probably close to a thousand square feet. It consisted of two adjoining rooms filled with shelves of texts, tables with artifacts from around the world, and various archeological equipment. It was like Indiana Jones's and Dirk Pitt's offices combined.

Just as the door shut behind us, he called us from the adjoining room.

"Come on in," he said in his smooth English accent, not even bothering to see who it was. "You guys make yourselves comfortable. I'll be right out."

Curious what had garnered his attention, I stepped through the propped open door. He was sitting on a roller stool, hunched over a fish tank and looking through a magnifying lens at a corroded artifact that was bubbling and slowly ridding itself of its black crust. He had alligator clips connecting the object, as well as a piece of steel that was also in the murky water, to a power source.

Frank was in his mid-fifties, with thinning dark hair and sun-tanned skin. He had a long, lean frame and wore a pair of brown slacks and a gray button-up shirt with rolled-up sleeves. He was also wearing a pair of black rubber gloves as well as an apron.

"Electrolysis," I said, nodding my head toward his work.

It was the same technique I'd used while

salvaging the remnants of the *Valiant* wreck in Florida Bay. It's simple and regarded as one of the best ways to clean metal that has been lost to the seas for years.

"Just cleaning a pistol a student of mine found while we were in Palau," he said. "It was found near a sunken Japanese Zero. You recognize what kind it is, Logan?"

I stepped closer and leaned in. It was still covered in grime, but that didn't matter. The design was distinct.

"It's a Nambu," I said.

The Nambu was the most popular sidearm used by the Japanese Army during World War II, similar to a German Luger in both appearance and function.

"I'd recommend adding some lime juice," Walt said, looking over my shoulder. "It helps yield better results."

Frank paused a moment and looked Walt up and down.

"You know, you look very familiar."

"Walt Grissom," he said, stepping toward the professor and extending a hand. "I used to motor around these islands with a rusty metal detector back in the seventies."

Frank smiled.

"Your reputation precedes you. I've heard that you found more than just old bottle caps with that rusted metal detector."

"I've had my share of luck, that's for sure."

Frank narrowed his gaze and looked over toward the blind-covered window, looking deep in thought.

"Mark Twain," he finally said. "Yeah, I believe it was good old Sam Clemens himself that said, 'The harder I work, the luckier I get.'"

Walt smiled and nodded.

Frank looked over at the rest of our group. Ange, Jack, and Pete were in the main room of his office. They were walking along the edges, looking at his many photographs and relics from around the world.

"I see you brought the whole gang today," he said. He removed the gloves and apron and rolled back from the fish tank. "Well, I need to let this settle. What can I do for you?"

Walt and I exchanged glances. I turned back to Frank and was about to reply when he beat me to it.

"Well, I recognize that look, Logan," he said. "And that means I'm officially intrigued." His eyes rested on Ange, who'd stepped into the doorway. "Does this have anything to do with the box your beautiful wife is holding?"

We followed Frank into the main section of his office and sat around a small table. Ange set the box on the table, opened the flaps, and slowly lifted out the chest. Frank's reaction was just as I'd hoped. His eyes grew wide at first, then narrowed with intense intrigue.

Ange set it in front of him, and he inspected it with the precision of a surgeon just before making the first cut.

"Where did you get this?" he asked, never letting his eyes drift from their careful scanning of every inch.

"It was buried at the downtown lighthouse site," I said.

"That chest belonged to Alfred Hastings," Pete said. The mention of the name got Frank's full attention. "We believe it could be linked to his hiding of the Florentine Diamond."

"Do you know the story?" Ange said.

He paused a moment, then nodded.

"Not very well. I just know that this Hastings character supposedly came into possession of the rare stone, hid it, then created a scavenger hunt of sorts that led to its whereabouts." His lips contorted into a smile. "I was told, however, that it was only a legend. Pure fiction and nothing more."

"We were too," Pete said. "Until Walt helped us find the compass."

Walt removed the golden compass from his pocket and handed it over to Frank.

"Extraordinary," he said. "These words here— they seem to be some kind of riddle." He paused a moment and looked up. "It led you to this chest, I assume?"

The five of us looked at each other and smiled. Frank was as sharp as they come. We'd sure come to the right guy.

"Right," I said.

He set the compass on the table and turned his attention back to the chest. Rising to his feet, he stepped over to his desk and grabbed a magnifying glass from the top drawer. He leaned in close, examining the edges of the chest even closer.

"There are words here," he said. We let him continue without saying anything. We wanted him to come to his own conclusions without regard to our own. "French here. Italian. German. And this last one's Devanagari script." He'd rotated the chest in a full 360, then paused a moment and stroked his chin. "Very interesting. And these dials here at the centers. Looks like they're supposed to be lined up with the appropriate symbols." He counted the symbols around each dial, then added, "Four dials. Twelve positions on each one." He grabbed a calculator and punched in a few numbers. "That means there are over twenty thousand possible combinations. It would take a week to go through them all."

"That is, if we can't figure out what the words mean," Pete said.

He nodded, examined the chest again, then looked off into space. After a few seconds, he smiled.

"It's a timeline," he whispered in a tone that was just barely loud enough for us to hear.

"A timeline?" Pete said.

Frank nodded. I could see that his mind was hard at work. The silence in the room seemed to drag on forever, the suspense growing with every passing second.

"In order to understand this chest," he said finally, "we need to understand the history of the diamond." He grinned and shook his head. "This guy Hastings was smart, that much is clear."

"What do you mean, we need to understand the history of the diamond?" Ange said.

Frank cleared his throat.

"Each of these languages corresponds to a point in the diamond's history," he said. "Beginning with Devanagari, the written script for Hindi which is the official language of India. My knowledge of the Florentine Diamond is minimal. But I do know that it is believed to have been originally found in India. You see, India was the source of almost all diamonds of the ancient world. In fact, until the 1700s, the only diamond mines in the world were located in India."

Without a word, he stepped off into one of the adjoining rooms and came back moments later carrying a stack of old textbooks. Setting them on the table, he also grabbed his laptop and brought up an online search engine.

"From there," he continued, "I believe the diamond fell into the hands of Charles the Bold, the Duke of Burgundy. He liked to wear his most precious jewels into battle. And during the battle of"—he paused a moment, grabbed his laptop, and performed a quick search, reading and nodding—"the Battle of Nancy in 1477, he was struck down by the Swiss, and the diamond was lost on the battlefield."

He continued reading, then performed a few more quick searches.

"From there, the diamond's history is unknown until the early 1600s, when the Medici family came into possession of it."

"Italian," Ange said.

"Right," Frank replied, spinning the chest around to reveal the side with the Italian text. "And the famous family of Florence owned the diamond until their line came to an end in 1743. At which time it fell into the hands of the Grand Duke of Tuscany, Francis I."

"Wait a second," Ange said. "Wasn't his wife Maria Theresa?"

Frank smiled. "You certainly know your European history. That's correct." He grabbed one of the textbooks, leafed through to a page, then set it open on the table in front of us. There was a picture of a woman at the top of the page. She had a pale face, rosy red cheeks, and wore an elegant dress along with an impressive tiara.

"This is Maria Theresa," Frank said. "A woman who held many titles, including that of Holy Roman Empress. She was also the mother of Marie Antoinette."

"And what did she do with the diamond?" Walt asked.

"The diamond was put on display in Hofburg Palace, in Vienna. And from there the trail runs cold. Some believe that the diamond was smuggled to Switzerland at the onset of World War I and then sold. Some believe it was sold before that and taken to South America. Others claim that it was cut down and sold off in secret." He took in a deep breath and let it out. "But it's all speculation. No one knows for sure. All we know is that the largest yellow diamond ever discovered disappeared in the early 1900s and that it hasn't been seen since."

Frank leaned back into his chair and smiled. The man had such a passion and enthusiasm for history that it was always an experience to watch him in action.

"So how does the history tie in?" I said. "How can we use the words and the symbols to open the chest?"

Frank nodded and spun the chest around so that the Hindi side was facing him.

"Well, let's start with the beginning," he said. "My Hindi is far from perfect, but I can verify with a translating program just to be sure." He examined the text carefully with the magnifying glass and read the words aloud. "From mud and water. Blood, sweat, and tears. The grand nativity of the stone."

We fell silent for a moment, thinking over the words.

"So, what does that all mean?" Pete said.

Frank read it a few more times, then wrote it down on a notepad. I leaned in close and looked over the side of the chest. Above the text was the dial along with twelve distinct symbols. I recognized a few of them, including a trident, a six-pointed star, and even a swastika.

195

"They're Hindu symbols," Frank said. "They each represent something different. For example, the swastika. Now generally regarded as evil, the symbol wasn't created by Hitler and the Nazi party. No, the symbol dates back thousands of years. To the Hindus, it represents happiness and good fortune."

"More than a little ironic," Jack said.

Frank nodded and continued, going over each of the symbols. When he got to one that looked like a flower, he paused.

"Wait," he said. "That's it! The lotus flower." He grabbed his laptop, punched a few keys, then smiled. "The lotus flower emerges from a dirty flower, blossoming pure and unblemished. It represents strength, purity, and resurrection."

"The nativity," Ange said.

That caused something to click in my mind.

"The birth," I said. Turning to Frank, I added, "You said the diamond originated in India."

"And going from a dirty flower to a pure, unblemished flower sounds an awful lot like how a diamond is formed from coal," Frank said with a smile. "I think we have the first key to this fascinating lock."

He grabbed the dial, spun it slowly until the arrow pointed at the image of the lotus flower.

"Only three more to go," Jack said with a smile.

Frank spun the chest, revealing the French side. Ange had already been able to translate it the previous day, so she said the words aloud, then wrote them down on the notepad.

"I couldn't talk. I couldn't walk. Life had only just begun."

Frank examined the symbols around the dial.

"We thought they looked like family crests," I

said.

Frank nodded.

"That's exactly what they are," he said. "Coats of arms. Trademarks of the medieval rich and powerful."

"What do you make of the riddle?" Walt said.

Frank paused a moment, then said, "Well, since it was Charles the Bold who had the diamond at this time, we can infer that Hastings was referring to him. Sounds like it's talking about his first few years of life."

We fell silent as we looked over the family crests. Frank went to work, searching to find matching crests online.

"So, this guy was born into royalty or something?" Walt said.

"One of the richest families in the world at the time," Frank answered, not looking up from the computer.

"So, I'm guessing a kid like that would've had a title at birth, right?" Walt continued.

"Undoubtedly."

"Before he could walk," Walt said slowly. "Before he could talk."

We all stopped and turned our gazes to him. It's like when you're looking for something, and someone tells you where it is. It makes you wonder how you'd manage to miss it all along.

"You're a genius," Frank said. He read a few lines on the screen and added, "Charles the Bold was born the Count of Charolais."

I patted Walt on the back.

"And which one of these crests belonged to the count?" Ange said.

Frank searched for a few seconds, then turned

back to the chest.

"This one."

He pointed to the image of a shield with an angry looking tiger on it. It had big sharp claws, and its head was turned back with its mouth opened. It looked like it was trying to bite its tail.

Frank let Walt do the honors, and he grabbed the dial and turned it to point at the crest.

"Two down," I said. "And I think we owe you a few beers for that one."

"A few?" Pete said, giving his old friend a hug. "You can have a whole keg. We'll just keep that from your doctor."

We turned our attention to the third riddle. It proved more difficult than the first two. Even with our combined efforts, it took us nearly three hours to decipher. Frank had to get a sub to fill in for his afternoon class, and we had a few pizzas delivered from Roostica to fuel us.

Frank was beyond impressed by the genius design of the chest. At one point I asked why he thought that Hastings had hidden the diamond and created the scavenger hunt to find it.

"This was a last hurrah from an incredibly intelligent and driven individual," he said after giving the question some thought.

The fourth side completely stumped us all, so Frank called a friend of his from the University of Hamburg in Germany to help us with the final part to the elaborate lock. With three of the sides already solved, it would have been easy to just check each of the twelve remaining positions until we got the correct one. But Frank, being the romantic that he was, wanted to figure out the clues thoroughly.

"It would be a dishonor to Hastings if we don't

see this through to completion," he said.

He also brought up that there could be some mechanism that prevented random guessing anyway. We consented, seeing his point and knowing that it would have taken us weeks to solve it all without him.

It was 1330 by the time he solved it, turned the dial into place, and we heard the welcome sound that signaled that our efforts had been worth it and that we'd managed to figure out the clues—a soft, nearly unnoticeable click.

Frank looked up at us and grinned.

The top of the chest was suddenly loose. Whatever secret it held was now ours for the taking.

I set aside the remaining crust of my fourth slice of pepperoni, wiped my chin, and hunched in close. The five others were huddled right beside me. We felt like we were Aladdin in the Cave of Wonders, reaching in for the genie's magic lamp.

We agreed that Walt should do the honors. My heart raced as he placed his hands softly on the lid and lifted the chest open.

From my angle, it looked like the chest was empty. I couldn't see anything inside it. But after a short pause and examination, Walt reached inside and pulled out a small rolled-up parchment.

No diamond yet.

"Look at that," Frank said, pointing toward an intricate mechanism built into the lid.

There was a narrow glass vial with a clear liquid inside it.

"It's a good thing you guys didn't try and break into this thing," Frank continued. "I'd be willing to bet that's acidic and would have ruined whatever's on that parchment."

Walt untied a string that held the small rolled-up paper in place. Opening it carefully, he flattened it on the tabletop, allowing us to see what it said. To our surprise, there were no words. Just rows of numbers and dashes. Not even a title or explanation of any kind.

"Another clue," Pete said.

Frank rubbed his tired eyes and added, "Yes. And a very confusing one at that."

TWENTY-FOUR

Valmira Gallani sat on a cushioned chair in her private jet and watched through one of the windows as a team of inspectors spoke to the captain. She smiled and sipped a glass of raki, a popular Albanian alcoholic drink, while watching the interaction. She felt anything but nervous.

Before her father had passed away, he'd taught her everything he knew when it came to running a successful crime operation. That included how to evade customs agents and local police.

Maybe he taught me a little too much, she thought, her lips contorting into a wry smile. *Winners strike first, Father. Winners are never content with second place. Winners in this business leave their morals at the door.*

A vial of arsenic and a few .45-caliber bullets had ensured that she was the winner. And as far as her morals, if she'd ever had any, they'd not only been left at the door, they'd been locked outside for longer than she could remember.

She glanced to her left at the four men seated across from her. They'd arrived in the States just half an hour earlier. Some of the best killers in her organization, Val had called for them right after shit had hit the fan the previous evening.

Just as she finished off her drink, her phone vibrated to life on the small table beside her. She grabbed it, glanced down at the screen, and read a few lines of text. She laughed and set the phone back down.

I've got you now, old man.

The men outside finished their chat. The customs agents walked off satisfied, and the captain entered the cabin.

"Ma'am," he said, "will we be leaving now?"

Val paused a moment. At first, the captain had thought that maybe his boss hadn't heard him. She seemed preoccupied with something else. He was about to ask her again when she finally replied.

"Yes," she said, "we will be leaving now."

The captain nodded. He turned and strode toward the cockpit.

"But not for home," she said, causing him to freeze in his tracks.

The four men seated across from Val raised their eyebrows and cocked their heads. The captain turned around, waiting for a moment before saying, "Where, then, ma'am?"

"Memphis International Airport," she said, reading the words off the screen in front of her. "Tennessee."

Just under two hours later, the jet's tires touched

down onto a wet tarmac nine hundred miles northwest of where they'd taken off. The sixty-degree weather was a welcome relief and was more like what she was accustomed to that time of year in her homeland.

She stepped out to the hangar and slid into a rental car. Two of her men climbed inside, and they drove to an affluent subdivision on the east side of town. It was just after three o'clock on a typical Sunday afternoon. A middle-aged woman was walking her shih tzu while chatting on the phone. A group of kids rode by on their bicycles. A UPS truck was parked a few houses down, the driver stepping out to deliver a package.

They pulled up to the curb in front of an opulent Southern-style house situated on a well-landscaped property. Judging from the home and the neighborhood, it was easy to see that the owners were well off.

Val spent a few moments scanning over the house. There appeared to be a garage around the left side, so she couldn't tell for sure if anyone was home. It looked like there were lights on, but it was hard to tell in the early-afternoon light.

"Pull into the driveway," she ordered the driver.

He didn't hesitate. Putting the car in drive, he pulled them slowly into the driveway and stopped in front of an elegant black gate.

The moment the wheels stopped turning, Val reached for the handle.

"Now are you finally going to tell us what we're doing here?" one of Val's men said. "I thought we were going to take down that old man and get the diamond."

Val tilted her head slowly, stared daggers at him.

"You question my leadership one more time, and

it will be the last thing you do." She eyed him for a few seconds to make sure that he got the message, then pushed open the door. "And leverage. We're here for leverage."

Val walked along the red brick walkway that wrapped around to the front of the house. All of the plants and hedges were trimmed neatly. There was a wreath with flowers hanging from the large front door.

She stood still for a few seconds, then reached forward and pressed the doorbell. The two guys stood at her flanks a half step behind her.

A muffled welcoming jingle rang out inside the house. A dog barked. A kid called out something. And a man walked into view.

After a quick glance through one of the small side windows, he opened the door slowly. He was tall and had neatly trimmed dark hair. He wore brown shorts, boat shoes, and a button-down shirt with the sleeves rolled up.

"Can I help you?" he asked through the partly open door.

He looked suspicious, but not enough to be worried. People going door to door in their well-to-do neighborhood weren't entirely out of the ordinary. Though it was usually a parent with kids trying to sell overpriced sugary treats.

"Yes," Val said, answering honestly and trying to sound nonthreatening. She recognized his face from the photographs her investigator had sent over. Peter Adams had no idea how bad his day was about to get. "We know your father. Walt."

Peter let out a long sigh.

"He isn't my father," he said. "Why are you here? Is he dead?"

"Not yet."

He shook his head in confusion.

"What does that mean?"

Val was getting sick of the small talk. She glanced back over her shoulder and spotted a neighbor across the street.

A close-knit community like this, everyone's up in everyone else's business.

"It means that he's in trouble and we think that you can help," she said. "May we come in?"

There was a slight pause before he answered. It was so short that it was almost unnoticeable, but it was there. Maybe a voice inside his head told him it was a bad idea. Maybe a deep, primal part of him knew that something was wrong.

But when the moment passed, he opened the door the rest of the way.

"He's always in trouble," Peter replied. "I'll do what I can. Can't make any promises, though. What are you guys, detectives or something?"

The three of them entered. One of Val's men shut the door behind them. The moment that they were hidden from view within the house, Val slammed her right fist into Peter's face. His nose crunched, and he groaned as his head snapped backward.

Before he knew what had happened or could make an attempt at retaliating, Val was on top of him. She slammed him to the floor, pounding him two more times before ordering the two guys to go after the rest of the family.

They didn't need an order. The two men were already halfway across the entryway, heading straight for the kitchen. Peter wailed and grunted. Blood dripped down his face, soaking the collar of his shirt and dripping onto the clean white carpet.

Holding him down, Val grabbed a small syringe and stabbed the needle into the middle of his right thigh. Peter struggled for a few seconds before his body went limp. Tilting his head up, he watched helplessly as his wife and two infant children were dragged into view. Their terrified faces were the last things he saw before he drifted into unconsciousness.

The three experienced criminals quickly knocked out the woman and the two kids as well. The two thugs duct-taped all of their captives' mouths, then zip-tied their ankles and wrists while Val opened the gate and drove the rental van around back.

Less than ten minutes after arriving at the house, they had the family loaded up and were back on the main road.

"Back to the airport," Val said.

That old-timer has really pissed me off now, she thought. *Too bad he has no idea that he's barely managed to scratch the surface of my ruthless potential.*

TWENTY-FIVE

I filled a mug with coffee for what felt like the twentieth time since arriving at Frank's office five hours earlier. We'd sat huddled around the mysterious parchment for half an hour, trying to figure out what the random assortment of numbers could mean.

I reached across the table, opened a pizza box, and pulled out yet another slice. Nearly all the excitement from figuring out how to open the chest was gone. It had been replaced by the disappointing possibility that Hastings had simply scribbled a bunch of gibberish on an old piece of paper.

Or maybe the man's just messing with us from the grave.

During a momentary break in the conversation, Jack coughed, appearing to choke on his drink. He made a few abnormal noises, then cleared his throat. His eyes were wide, and he looked like he had something important to say but couldn't get it out.

"You doing alright over there?" Frank asked.

We were all looking at him, making sure that he wasn't really choking.

"Wrong pipe," he said, waving a hand. He rose to his feet, stepped around the small table, and looked closely at the flattened parchment. "But I know what this is." He laughed and added, "Holy crap, I know what this is!"

We all looked at him like he was crazy. Probably because he was acting like a crazy person.

"It's an Ottendorf cipher," he declared.

I smiled, taken aback by his words. It wasn't that I knew what the hell an Ottendorf cipher was. I didn't. I was just amazed that Jack knew such a big word.

"It's been a long day," Pete said with a laugh. "Maybe we should pick this up again in the morning."

Jack punched our friend in the shoulder.

"I'm serious, man," he said.

He was laughing as well, but it was clear that he believed what he was saying.

The only one not reacting was Frank. He was sitting quietly, staring intently at the parchment.

"He's right," Frank finally said. He looked up and locked eyes with Jack. "I can't believe I didn't realize it myself." He rose to his feet, shook Jack's hand enthusiastically, then plopped back down into his chair and sighed. Shaking his head, he added, "Not that I'm complaining, and please don't take this the wrong way. But how would that possibly be common knowledge for a guy who spends most of his time diving and fishing to his heart's content?"

Jack laughed.

"It's okay, Professor," he said in a happy tone.

"You can say it. I'm a beach bum, through and through. Proud of it. And I'll grant you that one. It sure isn't common knowledge for a conch like me."

He raised his eyebrows, and we all remained silent, waiting for him to continue and wondering what in the hell they were talking about.

"You remember a few months ago when I invited you guys to the movies?" he said. If we had any expectations when it came to his explanation, he'd officially gone off that radar. "Well, I went to see *National Treasure*." He paused a moment, then grinned. "I'm not exactly the biggest Nic Cage fan, but that movie was pure entertainment."

"And this has something to do with an Ottendorf cipher?" Frank said.

"Yeah. If any of you saw it, you'd know it's about a treasure hunt with clues. Kind of like what we're doing now. Anyway, the main character, this guy named Gates, stole the Declaration of Independence and on the back of it were codes that looked just like this."

He held up the old parchment.

"Can someone please tell me what this Ottendorf thing is already?" Walt said emphatically. "I'm about to have an aneurysm over here."

Frank raised a hand.

"It's simple, really," he said. "Each of these numbers… actually, Jack, would you care to do the honors?"

Jack smiled.

"Alright, so basically these numbers correlate to words in a document of some kind," he said, leaning over and pointing to the parchment. "The first number refers to the page. The second refers to the line on the page. The third refers to the letter on that line." He looked up and shrugged. "It's actually pretty simple."

I smiled and patted my friend on the back.

I guess I need to watch more movies. Hard for me to justify a significant amount of screen time when I live in paradise, however.

After each of us expressed our gratitude to Jack for his integral realization, Ange said what all of us were thinking.

"So, what document is it referring to?"

Walt was the one who perked up this time. Grabbing the parchment, he examined the lower corners.

"These numbers are out of place," he said. "They don't go with the others above. And there are twelve of them."

"Coordinates," I said with a smile.

Before another word could be said, Frank slid over his laptop and punched in the sequence of numbers. My mind ran over possible locations. I just hoped that it was someplace nearby. From what I'd learned about Hastings over the past few days, he'd traveled extensively in his life. The last thing we needed was to have to travel to some remote region in Africa or South America to find the next clue. But glancing at the coordinates, I knew that we were looking at somewhere in the Caribbean.

"Andros Island," Frank said. "Looks like it's near Spaniard Creek."

Andros Island is in the Bahamas. Though it's technically an archipelago, or a group of many islands, it's commonly referred to as just Andros and is known as the largest of all the Bahamian islands. Though I'd only ever been there once and many years earlier, I remembered it being beautiful and knew that it was a top dive destination in the Caribbean.

Frank zoomed in on the map, then paused a moment.

"What is it?" I said, curious by his intrigued expression.

"Have a look for yourselves," he said, turning the screen around.

We all leaned in close and stared at the point on the map. It looked like it was in the middle of nowhere and was directly over a near-perfect circle of water and a tiny sandy beach.

"A blue hole," Jack said.

He grabbed the mouse and zoomed out.

"It's right on the edge of Blue Holes National Park," Walt added.

Jack shook his head. "This guy is just full of surprises."

Blue holes are geological phenomena that are formed when a sinkhole or cave fills with water and becomes a vertical aqueous void in the landscape. Some descend for less than a hundred feet, but many go on and on, seemingly forever.

I'd dived one before, off the coast of Belize. The Great Blue Hole, arguably the most famous of its kind in the world, is over four hundred feet deep. It made for an incredible dive, and the round dark blue speck is an amazing sight from the air as well.

"It's about two hundred and fifty miles from here to Andros Town as the gull flies," Pete said. "And that's just south of Spaniard. It's closer to three hundred miles if you go by boat since you'll have to motor around the northern tip."

Frank brought up a distance tracker on the GPS. It verified that the distance between Key West and Andros Town was precisely what Pete had said.

"It's almost scary how much you know about the

Caribbean, man," Jack said. "I mean, I know a lot, but if you were any more conch, you'd have a hard outer shell instead of skin."

Pete went on to inform us that there are over fifty documented blue holes in that region, and many of them are relatively untouched. Based on the satellite imagery we looked over of our destination, there didn't appear to be any structures or roads nearby.

"The tricky part will be depth," Pete continued. "These holes could be a hundred feet deep or five hundred. With an off-the-beaten-path one like this, there's no way of knowing until you get there."

I thought it over for a quick moment. My underwater drone had a three-hundred-foot tether, and I felt comfortable diving even deeper than that if necessary for a short duration.

"Ange and I will take the Cessna," I said. "We'll make it faster with just the two of us. Should be just under two hours of flight time." I glanced at Ange, who nodded, verifying that my quick math was correct. "If we get in the air within the next half hour, we can be at the hole before sundown. Maybe even make it back in time for a late dinner."

It took a little bit of convincing to get the others on board with the plan. They wanted to come, of course. But I was confident that it would be quicker just the two of us. Plus I was looking forward to the idea of spending some time just the two of us. I liked the group, don't get me wrong. But we'd spent every moment together the past few days, and a quick getaway sounded nice.

"What about the Albanians?" Walt said. "We managed to rid ourselves of some of them, but Val got away. She doesn't take kindly to failure. In fact, it only pisses her off more. She'll be back. She'll be back with more people. Just a matter of time."

"I seriously doubt she'll manage to follow us to the Bahamas," I said. "But if she does, we'll be ready for her." I paused a moment and added, "As far as you three, I'd recommend sticking close together. We can call in Jane and have her send a few guys to hang out nearby just in case. Plus I was thinking of calling in Scott, seeing if he can spare a few days."

"Scott?" Walt said, raising his eyebrows.

"An old friend and a hell of a warrior." I glanced at my dive watch, then motioned to Ange. "Time to go." I rose to my feet and addressed the others. "You guys be careful."

They each nodded, except for Jack. He was sullen and hunched over.

"You two better not find this diamond without us," he said, shaking his head. Then he smiled and added, "Because I'll be forced to kick your ass if you do, Logan."

I laughed and shook my head.

"Not to worry, bro," I said. "Remember, on his deathbed, Hastings said that the diamond was hidden somewhere in the Keys. This is just another clue."

TWENTY-SIX

I ran into Jane on the way out the front door. I told her what was going on and that I'd appreciate her helping to keep an eye on Jack, Pete, and Walt. It wasn't that I doubted their abilities to defend themselves, but I knew that having uniformed officers nearby would most likely dissuade criminals from taking action.

She'd also informed me that my truck had been raised from the water and was sitting in a salvage yard across town. As I'd expected, the truck was a total loss and would most certainly cost more to repair than to replace. Though Jack had been apologetic about his car chase escape tactics, he'd also pointed out that I was in need of an upgrade anyway.

I thanked her for taking care of it but didn't have time to worry about it then. Ange and I would need to get in the air soon if we were going to reach the hole before sundown.

After a quick stop at the Conch Harbor Marina to pick up a few bags of dive gear, the underwater drone, and an inflatable raft, Jack dropped us off at Tarpon Cove Marina. Ange had kept her Cessna there since she'd first moved in with me in the Keys.

Once loaded up, we did the preflight checks, and she called the ATCs. She gave them our flight plan and they gave us instructions for the flight. After giving us our unique transponder code to be used during the flight, they gave us the all clear.

Atticus got comfortable in the backseat. He'd flown a few times before and knew the drill. We'd decided to take him, knowing that we'd be glad to have him around when trekking into the middle of nowhere on Andros.

There was a little chop in the cove, but nothing Ange couldn't handle. She started up the 230-hp engine and had us up in the air within minutes.

She turned us around onto a easterly course, then brought us steadily up to a cruising altitude of a thousand feet. We were flying at 105 knots with an eight-knot crosswind. With the sun at our backs and just a few sporadic patches of clouds, the view was beautiful.

Using my satellite phone, I punched in a quick number, then inserted the headset so that I could hear over the roar of the engine and passing wind. Sometimes people exaggerate other people's abilities, as well as their own. But calling Scott Cooper a hell of a warrior was actually an understatement.

He'd been my division officer back when I'd first shown up to my SEAL team nearly fifteen years ago. Our friendship grew over time, and we'd gone on a handful of vacations and other adventures over the years. Smart, athletic, and presentable, he was the kind of guy that can do anything. Currently serving as a senator representing the state of Florida, he often took "vacations" down to the islands to get away from the political grind.

I told him what was going on and asked if he could offer some help. Given his government position and ties to Naval Special Forces, he had an impressive network of influential and helpful people.

"I'll get Wilson on this," he said, referring to the CIA deputy director. "See what he can do. Also, I think I'm overdue for a little fun in the sun."

I laughed. Like myself, Scott had a unique idea of what he considered fun. We were both men of action, plain and simple. Though he often claimed that the bug had worn off a little when he'd hit his forties, I wasn't convinced. Men like us don't change. We may age and get different careers, but our core selves remain what we are and always will be.

"One more thing," I said. "We need a customs agent to meet us at Fresh Creek in Andros Town. We tried calling the airport there but haven't gotten anything."

"Don't worry about it, brother. I'll take care of it."

He told me he'd be down in the Keys as soon as he could. I thanked him, and then we ended the call.

After relaying the gist of the conversation to Ange, I gazed out the passenger-side window at the dark blue ocean below. Just ahead of us, I spotted a giant stretch of turquoise with a handful of small dark specks intermixed. It was Cay Sal Bank.

I'd traveled there back in March. Kyle Quinn, a man who'd been one of my best friends before being accused of treason while serving in the Navy, had returned from the dead one evening. In order to attempt to prove his innocence, we'd traveled to the dangerous and remote group of islands and run into trouble when a Russian assassin had tried to blow us and my boat to pieces. Somehow we'd managed to come out on top, and the last time I'd heard from Kyle, he was happily living with his wife and daughter in Costa Rica.

"Alone at last," Ange said.

I glanced back and saw that Atticus was passed out on the backseat with his head under a blanket.

Ange leaned over, tilted her head, and batted her eyebrows at me. She was giving me her cute sexy look, and it was driving me all kinds of wild. It had been a busy last couple of days and we hadn't had much of a chance to spend time just the two of us. I was happy to see that she was as eager as I was to make up for the lost time.

She leaned over and kissed me slowly and passionately. Her hands traveled down my shirt, then unclasped my belt.

"Autopilot's on," she said seductively. "Care to join the mile high club?"

I smiled. The two of us had already met the requirements for that club a few times before. But I wasn't stupid enough to bring it up and possibly dampen the excitement of the moment.

"I'd love to."

TWENTY-SEVEN

By the time we finished, our bodies were covered in sweat, and the cockpit windows had a thin layer of condensation. Putting our clothes back on, we directed our gaze forward and could just make out Andros in the distance.

Ange shifted our course and called into local ATCs. Scott had messaged me back and told me to meet the agent at the Andros Escape Hotel. He said that the guy would meet us on the dock to do a quick inspection, and I thanked him for his help.

Before landing, I was able to spend a few minutes searching for information about the Bahamian paradise I'd visited years earlier. The islands that make up Andros are mostly remote, especially when compared to the rest of the Caribbean. The total population is only about seven thousand people, and most of the settlements are along the eastern coast.

To put Andros into perspective, its islands have a population density of roughly three and a half people per square mile. That's about half that of Wyoming, a state that's only second least dense after Alaska.

We flew over the massive cluster of land separated by intricate, weaving waterways. Ange brought us down over the eastern coastline and did a flyover to look for a good splashdown site. We would need a vehicle to reach the blue hole and figured Andros Town would be our best bet, though the place looked more like a tiny settlement than a town.

The largest group of buildings were to the south of Fresh Creek. Based on the maps I was looking over, it appeared to be the Atlantic Undersea Test and Evaluation Center, or AUTEC for short. The military installation has a wide deepwater channel that extends out into a region of dark blue ocean known as the TOTO. TOTO stands for the Tongue of the Ocean, a twenty-mile wide, hundred-and-fifty-mile-long trench. For most of its length, it drops nearly straight down from less than a hundred feet deep to well over six thousand. The unique geological formation is similar in size to the Grand Canyon but completely underwater.

Ange brought us down just north of the military installation, at the mouth of Fresh Creek. The water landing was much easier than in the Keys given that there were far fewer boats out on the water.

Most of the small handful of docks were private, but we spotted a small promenade in front of a hotel and dive shop that looked promising.

"Looks like the only hotel around, so I'm guessing that's it," Ange said.

As Ange brought us slowly to the dock, I

positioned two white fenders, then leapt onto the wood planks and tied us off. Sure enough, an agent met us at the plane and performed a routine inspection before giving us authorization.

"Thanks for coming to us," I said. "We tried the airport, but—"

"Nuh a problem," he said in a Bahamian accent. "Nuh much plane traffic here di past few days. Plus mi just dung di street. Gi mi regard to mista Cooper."

I smiled, told him I would, then he walked off. It always seemed like my old friend had a contact everywhere.

After a quick look around, I spotted a young woman hanging a few dripping wetsuits behind a counter. It looked about as close to an office as anything nearby.

Since the drone and dive gear were heavy, we left them in the cockpit until we could secure a ride. After locking up, we walked side by side down the dock. Atticus was excited as always and sniffing everything in sight.

It was 1700, so we still had a few more hours of sunlight left. But we'd brought our dive flashlights just in case the trip took longer than expected.

The small promenade had a dive boat tied off that shared the same name as the hotel in front of us. Andros Escape, the words on a softly flapping flag said. It was small, maybe a couple dozen rooms, and had a little restaurant with scattered people sitting in chairs and at the bar. The place had a great view of the creek and the ocean beyond.

"Nice plane," a woman's voice called out as we walked from the dock onto the promenade.

I realized that it was the same young woman I'd noticed from the dock. She was still behind the counter and was up on her tippy toes, leaning over to get a view of the Cessna.

"You both pilots?" she asked.

"Technically," I said. "But she's much better than I am."

Ange and I walked around the counter and got a good look at her for the first time. I pegged her at just over five feet with dark hair and a tan complexion that was lighter than that of the dark-skinned locals we could see.

"You guys need a slip?"

"Just for the day," Ange said. "We probably won't even stay the night."

"Careful," she replied. "That's what I said. Been here for two months now."

"You're American?" I asked, judging by her accent.

She nodded.

"Born in the Philippines and moved to the States when I was little." She motioned toward our plane and added, "It's twenty dollars for the day. But I can put it toward some food or drinks if you want. The jackfruit mango smoothies here are the bomb."

"We'll have two, please," Ange said excitedly.

She called to one of the workers, relaying our order.

After checking out every sniff-worthy thing on the dock, Atticus trotted over and headed right behind the counter to greet the woman. She lit up as she petted him. I heard the distinct patter of little paws, then spotted a small French bulldog as it ran happily into view from behind a row of avocado trees.

The two dogs smelled each other for a few seconds, then started to play.

"Aw, a Frenchie!" Ange exclaimed.

The woman picked up the little dog and handed her to Ange. She was still a puppy and had a blue brindle coat with white patches on her belly and sparkling blue eyes. Without question, she was the cutest dog I'd ever seen.

"What brings you two to Andros? It's not exactly common for people to visit just for an evening."

We told her that we were explorers of sorts and that we were looking to dive a remote blue hole. I brought up the GPS and showed her our desired destination.

"Oh, that's Hastings' Hole," she said.

The mention of the name caught both Ange's and my attention quick.

"Hastings?" Ange said.

"Some American who used to have a house near there, or so I've heard. Apparently, he used to work up and down the islands here, doing various engineering projects. Then his wife drowned, and he left. Never came back. Kind of sad, really. Anyway, I've only been to the hole once. Middle of nowhere and it's a difficult hike." She paused a moment, looking us over. "You both seem like good people, so I'll give you a tip. Just before the end of the nearest dirt road, you'll see a turnoff, a gate, and a bunch of signs. Danger, no trespassing and all that. Don't let them scare you. There's an old guy that lives up there. He's a recluse and can't stand people. But he's harmless, and that road's way faster than the normal footpath. I also haven't seen his fishing boat in a few days, so you should be in the clear."

"Isn't this place located within the national park?" Ange said.

"Yeah, but good luck telling him that. His family's lived there for generations."

222

"And if we run into this guy?" I said.

She smiled and waved a hand.

"You shouldn't, but if you do just tell him I sent you. I spotted him solo diving last month over at the edge of the TOTO. He got caught in a fishing net, and he'd still be down there if it weren't for my shears. He owes me." She paused a moment, then added, "You two got a ride?"

We told her that we didn't, and she recommended a rental place right down the street.

"Gonna be rough terrain," she said. "I recommend one of their little off roadies."

In just a few minutes, Atticus and the woman's Frenchie had become good friends and were sad that they couldn't run around more. The woman handed us our smoothies, and I gave her a hundred-dollar bill. I asked if she could use the extra to prepare us a to-go dinner for when we got back.

"No problem," she said. "I'll make sure they leave some aside."

"Thank you, Miss…?"

"Jenny," she said. "I'll see you later this evening. And be careful. Being such a remote destination has its disadvantages. Criminals tend to like remote just as much as adventurous tourists."

Following her directions, we walked down to the rental place and picked out a red four-wheel-drive two-seater UTV. After driving back to the dock and transferring our gear from the Cessna into the storage space in the back of the UTV, we headed out of town.

"Hastings' Hole," Ange said. "Sounds like we've sure found the right place."

We took the Queen's Highway north for seven miles, then turned onto a dirt road. The small off-road vehicle was a blast to drive, and I pushed it up over forty miles per hour for most of the trip. The wind whipped past us as we took in the scenery and enjoyed the seclusion. Tall ironwood and mahogany trees littered the landscape on both sides, providing a canopy for the lush vegetation below.

I felt like a kid again, racing a go-cart or riding a bike down a steep hill. My face clearly showed my excitement, which caused Ange to smile and giggle as she kept her arms wrapped around Atticus.

"My husband's twelve years old," she said with a grin.

"Don't pretend like you don't want a turn."

Following the GPS, we turned west onto an even smaller dirt road and eventually came to the turnoff Jenny had told us about.

I brought the vehicle to a stop right in front of the gate. The young woman hadn't been kidding about the signs. There were eight of them in all, ranging from Keep Out to Beware of Rabid Attack Dog.

"No Trespassing," I said, reading one of the signs. "Violators will be shot. Survivors will be shot again."

I laughed and shook my head.

"Nothing like a little good old island hospitality," Ange said.

I patted my holstered Sig.

"At least we're ready in case his bite is as bad as his bark."

Following Jenny's advice, I drove us slowly between the edge of the gate and the trunk of a palm tree. Neither of us were about to turn down an easier route to the hole. And we were both armed, of course, just in case there was any truth to the signs.

After a quarter mile, the road turned into little more than a barely noticeable footpath. Zigging and zagging around sharp corners, we soon reached the end of the line at a thick patch of bushes and a giant tamarind tree.

"Alright," Ange said, looking at the GPS in her hands. "The hole's just through there. Looks like just a few hundred yards."

We grabbed all the gear and slogged through the thick foliage. As usual, Atticus took off ahead of us to check the way. There's something comforting about having a dog with you when you walk through a dense jungle. I imagine it goes back to our hunter-gatherer ancestors. The four-legged mammals have far superior senses of smell and hearing, and they can move much quicker through just about any terrain. There's a reason they're called man's best friend.

After ten minutes of navigating the difficult terrain, we caught our first glimpse of blue in a clearing up ahead. Moments later, the beautiful sight came into view as we stepped to the edge of a twenty-foot cliff.

We gazed upon a nearly perfect circle of crystal-clear freshwater gathered in a carved-out hole in the limestone. It was small, I estimated just a few hundred feet across. One of the edges was shallow, but most of the hole was dark blue.

We made our way to the western shore and set our gear onto a small beach. Using a manual portable pump, we inflated the raft, then loaded everything inside and paddled for the center of the lake.

The place was incredibly quiet and serene. The only sounds beyond our paddles dipping into the water were the slight breeze through nearby palm fronds and the songs of a few Bahama mockingbirds.

Blue holes are popular among freedivers, and they're common locations for holding their competitions. Clear, calm, and devoid of obstructions, the natural anomalies provide the perfect setting for testing your limits with a single breath-hold. But Hastings was isolated and too difficult to access for most people. Out of the way, we had the place entirely to ourselves.

"I think we're gonna have to come back here sometime," Ange said. "This island's a true paradise on earth."

It didn't take us long to reach the coordinates. Looking around, I saw that we were smack-dab in the middle.

"I know he had a house here at one point in his life. But how in the hell did a man in his eighties travel all the way here back in the early 1900s?" Ange asked, completely puzzled.

It was a good question. All I could think about were Frank's words back in Key West. "This was a last hurrah from an incredibly intelligent and driven individual," he'd said.

There was no current, of course, so all we had to combat to stay in place was the breeze, which I estimated wasn't even five knots. Reaching into my waterproof backpack, I grabbed my depth finder and powered it on.

"Two hundred and forty feet," I said, reading the depth from the screen once it appeared.

Handing Ange the paddles, I grabbed the black hard case, opened it up, and pulled out my top-of-the-line underwater drone. It was white, about the size of a briefcase, and had up, down, forward, and reverse thrusters. It also had two built-in cameras, LED lights, and a three-hundred-foot tether.

After hooking it up to a tablet and running a few quick diagnostics, I dropped it into the water. We both gazed at the screen as I quickly descended into the dark depths of the hole. There's something exciting about exploring the unknown. So far off the beaten path, it was unlikely that anyone had ever seen what we were about to see.

"Dive technology was nearly nonexistent back in Hastings's time," Ange said. "So whatever we're about to find, he must have simply chucked over the side."

It reminded me of diving the blue hole in Belize. Sheer underwater cliffs on either side. A magical drop into the abyss.

Soon, we spotted something below by the glow of the two front lights. The rugged, sediment-covered bottom came into view. After a few passes, we spotted a shape that caught our eye. It was flat and had right angles, something that's rarely seen in nature. Moving the drone in closer, I used the bottom thrusters to try and clear away the light coat of sediment.

As the cloud settled, we both smiled as we saw what looked like a stone tablet come into focus. It looked to be about three feet tall by two feet wide and three inches thick. Looking closer, we spotted a rusted chain attached to what was probably the top of it.

"He must have had a buoy or something to mark its location," I said, pointing at the chain. "Probably intended the finder to use the chain to pull it up. Like you said, diving technology was nearly nonexistent compared to today."

"And no one passing by would think anything of a random buoy in the middle of the lake?"

I shrugged.

"He probably made it so that the buoy floated

just beneath the surface. That way it would only be visible to those who came close, which, in a remote place like this, I imagine would likely never happen unless someone had these coordinates."

We used the thrusters to clear the tablet one more time. Clearly, it was the next clue to finding the diamond. The only problem was that it was completely blank.

Again, I wondered if maybe Hastings was just playing a big joke. Then Ange knocked some sense into me.

"It's upside down," she said, shaking her head. "Must have flipped over when he eased it to the bottom."

Before the words had left her mouth, I was already sliding off my tee shirt and grabbing my scuba gear from the bag. The water looked great, and I was sweating under the late-afternoon tropical sun.

"Probably won't be able to bring it up," I said as I dipped my 3mm wetsuit into the water, then slid it on over my swim trunks. "I'll take the underwater camera, and you can record with the drone as well once I flip this thing over."

Ange strapped a trimix tank to the back of my BCD. Jack used his own special mixture of oxygen, helium, and nitrogen for deep dives, allowing him to dive deeper and safer than most operations in the Keys, though he only allowed it for advanced divers with at least a few hundred dives under their belts.

Once I had all my gear on, I sat down on the starboard pontoon.

"Should be about twenty minutes," I said. "Keep a sharp eye out," I added, scanning the shoreline surrounding us.

I petted Atticus, who'd been sitting quietly and

watching everything intently since we'd shoved off from the beach. He had a stick in his mouth that he'd found on the shore, but he let it drop while I petted him.

"I'll toss it a few times when I come back, boy," I said.

"Be careful," Ange said, kissing me on the lips before sliding my mask up over my face.

I grinned, gave the OK sign, then flipped backward. I hit the water with a soft splash. The water felt good, and I bobbed on the surface for just long enough to let Ange know that I was all good before venting my BCD.

The water on the surface was over seventy degrees. But as I descended into the dark blue void, I soon passed through the thermocline, a thin layer where the water temperature drops dramatically. Within seconds, it felt like, the water around me plummeted down to fifty degrees. It was the reason why I'd decided to wear the wetsuit. Without it, the cold of the deeper water would cause me to shiver within minutes.

I kept my high-powered dive flashlight aimed ahead while my eyes scanned eagerly between my dive computer and the water below me. It felt like drifting through infinite space, or a dream where you're falling into an endless pit. The visibility was about as good as it gets, over a hundred and fifty feet. It wasn't long before the dark bottom appeared, vague and blurry at first, then clearer the deeper I got.

I kept close to the tether, using it as a guide all the way to the ROV, which was still situated right beside the tablet. When I reached the bottom, I vented the remaining air out of my BCD. This allowed me to plant my feet firmly on the lake floor. I clipped my dive light onto my shoulder, keeping the beam of light pointed in front of me.

Bending down, I wrapped my fingers under the tablet and lifted. It was heavy, much heavier than I'd expected. Using my legs, I managed to lift it up and set it on my knee before pushing it over the rest of the way.

A cloud of sediment whooshed up into the water as it fell. I waited for it to clear, then grabbed my light and moved in for a closer look. My lips formed an uncontrollable smile behind my regulator.

The backside of the tablet was covered in lines of text. Three distinct paragraphs, each with five lines. At the top of the stone was a name: Gladys Hastings, along with birth and death years. I shook my head as I gazed upon it. I remembered what Jenny had said about Hastings's wife dying while they were on Andros. This was her memorial.

I collected myself, wiped away the settled dirt, and snapped about a dozen pictures with my waterproof camera. Other than the name, years, and rows of text, there was also a symbol etched into the bottom. It was the same familiar symbol that was on the compass as well as the chest—the symbol representing the irregular double-rose-cut Florentine Diamond.

I glanced over at the ROV, which was floating right beside me, its lights aiming at the tablet to help me get better shots. I gave a thumbs-up, knowing that Ange was watching, then motioned my thumb up and down, indicating that I was going to begin my ascent.

I sent a few quick hisses of air into my BCD, then took one more look at the tablet before pushing off the bottom and finning for the surface. I ascended at a controlled rate, breathing steadily in and out with each kick.

Rising out of the dark abyss and into the light above, I switched off my flashlight. I leveled off at fifteen feet to perform my safety stop. The ROV passed me, and I watched as it broke the surface and Ange lifted it out of the water. My dive computer kept track of the time for me, and once it beeped, I finned for the surface.

I broke out of the water, handed Ange the camera, then removed my fins and swung up into the small inflatable. Eagerly, I unstrapped and slid out of all my gear. Atticus wagged his tail and licked every inch of my face. As I set my BCD aside, he grabbed his stick and dropped it in front of me.

I laughed and grabbed hold of it.

"It's freshwater, boy," I said. "You're gonna have to swim harder."

His tongue sticking out, he glanced back and forth between me and the water.

"Alright," I said, tossing it just fifty feet or so from the raft to see how he'd do.

He jumped over without hesitating and splashed into the lake. It took him a few seconds to get used to the less dense water, but he quickly got the hang of it and reached the stick without a problem.

"Any activity up here?" I asked while wiping the water from my brow and scanning the shoreline.

The sun was setting below the trees, shooting rays of light through the fronds and glowing the sky.

Ange shook her head. She held the camera in her hands and was clicking through the images.

"It's a memorial to his wife," she said. "She died years earlier, so that means he probably dropped this tablet years before finding the diamond."

I nodded, grabbed the tablet, and quickly brought

up the picture of the rolled-up parchment we'd found in the chest. Ange read the words from the tablet aloud first. They were emotional. Powerful. A testament to the love and passion shared by the two of them.

A tear streaked down Ange's cheek, and I wiped it away. I was struggling to keep composed as well. From the words, it was clear that this was a man who'd been broken by the loss of his wife. A man who'd found it difficult to find the strength to keep on living.

After reading it, we made quick work of the cipher. The numbers corresponded to a paragraph, a line, and then a letter. After a few minutes, it was solved.

"F-T-J-E-F-F," Ange said, reading the letters aloud. "M-U-D-D."

We thought for a moment, then Ange smiled.

"Fort Jefferson," she said.

I nodded and smiled back, my heart racing from the excitement of the moment. Fort Jefferson was located in Dry Tortugas National Park, just seventy miles from Key West.

I kept Atticus busy, tossing the stick farther and farther each time until he finally shook the water off his coat and plopped down in the raft for a rest.

"MUDD?" I said, confused by the rest of the letters.

The word, and it's relation to Fort Jefferson, sounded vaguely familiar, but I couldn't place it.

"Must be short for something, given the spelling," Ange said. She grabbed her smartphone and woke up the screen. "No signal."

Her eyes gravitated back toward the shore. She slid her phone into her pocket and set the camera aside.

"Looks like it's time to head back," I said, grabbing the paddles. "I had a few bars back at Andros Town, so we can search when we're there."

She nodded, and I started rowing us back to the beach, the four letters dancing around in my head.

TWENTY-EIGHT

Walt stepped out to get some fresh air. He headed down to the end of the dock and looked out over the calm, dark water. He was excited and anxious to figure out the next clue. The Florentine Diamond was close, he could feel it. One last treasure, one last payout, and then he'd put an end to his wild and unpredictable career.

He hoped he could settle down and dig in his roots as Pete had recommended. Hoped that he could quell the burning passion within him that always strove for just one more search. He also hoped that he could rid himself from the mobsters who were hell-bent on making him pay.

Maybe the fight last night scared them off, he thought. *Maybe they've lost all taste for this fight and have written it off.*

He knew that it wasn't like them to relent and

wave the white flag. But he also knew that their death toll was stacking up. At some point, you cut your losses and move on. At least, that would be the logical thing to do.

He grabbed a flask from his pocket, unscrewed the cap, and took a few swigs. After wiping his lips, he looked out over the water and felt better. For the first time in a long time, he could see a light at the end of the tunnel. It was dim and shrouded by potential impediments, but it was still there.

He downed another sip, then took in a deep breath of fresh air and turned around. After just two steps back down the dock, his phone vibrated to life in his pocket. Unlike Jack, he'd left it on the boat the previous day, so it hadn't been claimed by the sea.

He reached into his pocket, pulled it out, and looked at the front screen. It wasn't one of his contacts, but it was a number that he knew well. Too well.

With each vibration, he debated whether or not he should answer. He decided that whatever she had to say, he didn't want to hear it.

No good can come of talking to her, he thought.

After what felt like an eternity, the vibrating stopped. He let out a long sigh, then nearly smiled.

Good riddance.

He was about to drop the phone back into his front pocket when it shook to life once more. This time it was a message. It was from the same number, and he didn't need to flip open the phone to read it. The words were displayed on the small front screen.

"Peter Adams," was all it said.

Nothing else needed to be said. The first and last name was all it took to cause Walt's heart to go from a resting pulse to throbbing like mad in an instant.

How did she find him? How did she figure out he even existed?

With a handful of uncomfortable questions spinning around in his mind, he quickly flipped open the phone and called the number. Two rings. Three. Four. He gritted his teeth, knowing that Val would be enjoying every second of the cruel waiting game she was playing.

Finally, she answered.

"I thought that might get your attention, old man," Val said slowly.

"Where is he?" Walt said frantically.

"He's right here," she replied, her tone ice cold.

There was a short pause.

"Walt, what the hell is this shit?" An angry male voice came over the line. "What the hell did you do? How dare you—"

The voice turned muffled, and Val's returned to cut him off.

"That's enough, Peter," she said.

"What have you done to him?" The words rushed frantically out of Walt's mouth.

"Relax. All we did was rough him up a little. He's fine for now. They're all fine." She paused a moment, letting Walt come to the painful realization on his own. "That's right. We didn't just take your son. We took his pretty wife and their two little brats."

"I swear," Walt said, anger boiling over inside him, "if you hurt any of them, I'll—"

"Shut the fuck up," she cut him off in a loud, stern voice. "I'm doing the talking here, understand? I'm in charge, and you'll do as I say or I'll cut each of them apart, piece by bloody piece."

Walt nearly fell over. His eyes welled up with

236

tears. He felt helpless. Utterly and completely helpless.

"Alright," he said, clearing his throat and gripping the phone tighter and tighter. "You can have the diamond. I'll make sure of it. Just don't hurt them. Please don't hurt them."

Val paused again. More than anything else in the world, she liked this. Manipulating people, watching them squirm as she broke them down. It was a sadistic form of pleasure for her, one she'd enjoyed for as long as she could remember.

"That's not enough, old man," she finally replied. "If you want to save them, I'm going to need more than just the diamond."

Walt couldn't bring himself to ask the rest of her demands. He already knew what they'd be. If he was going to save his son, his daughter-in-law, and his grandchildren, he'd need to sacrifice others.

"Your friends," Val continued, her tone filling with more anger every second. "The assholes who killed so many of my men. In order for your family to live, they will need to die."

Walt fell silent. His hand was shaking. His breathing erratic. He'd stood face-to-face with danger many times throughout his life. Not once had he ever allowed it to get the best of him. He had no problem gambling his life on a roll of the dice now and then. But the mention of his son, his son's wife, and his two grandchildren struck a nerve he didn't know he had. They were in severe danger, and he couldn't stand it. He needed to do whatever he could to save them.

"I'm not a patient woman," Val said menacingly. "If you don't make up your mind soon, I might have to—"

"Alright," Walt said, summoning the strength to speak through the swarm of powerful emotions.

"Alright, what?"

"I'll... I'll make sure you get the diamond. And..."

"And your friends die," she said, finishing his sentence.

"Yes."

"Good boy," she said. "Now, what can you tell me?"

"I don't know much for now," Walt said. "They went to the Bahamas to find the next clue."

She fell silent for a moment.

"The second you learn where the diamond is, you call us," she said sternly. "You call us and tell us your plans to retrieve it, or else they die."

The line went dead.

Walt was squeezing his phone so hard he was nearly breaking it. He stared at the screen, in disbelief at what had just happened. His knees wobbled, and he nearly toppled over. He pressed a hand to his chest, felt like he was dangerously close to having a heart attack.

Keep it together, he told himself. He took in a few deep breaths. *You have to keep it together, or they're dead.*

Just as he turned around, he saw Jack fast-walking toward him on the dock.

"They figured it out, man," Jack said once he was within earshot. "And you're not gonna believe it. The diamond's practically been right under our noses the entire time." He froze when he got close to Walt and took a good look at him by the dim marina lighting. "Hey, man, are you okay?" he said, stepping over and placing a hand on Walt's shoulder. "You don't look

238

so good."

Walt waved him off, trying to collect himself.

"I'm fine," he said. "Where's the diamond?"

Jack paused a moment, not even close to being convinced.

"He said it's at—"

"Come on, you two," Pete said from down the dock. He was walking toward them excitedly. "Hurry up, let's get a move on. I wanna meet them when they land."

Jack shrugged. "I'll just let them tell you. Sounds like we're in for a nice payday here soon. The children's shelter will be set till the end of the century."

Walt followed them toward the shore, a few steps behind them. While they were eager and excited, he was lost in a whirlwind of emotions. But by the time he reached Jack's Wrangler in the parking lot, he'd pulled himself together. He had no choice but to comply with Val's demands. He had no choice but to lead Pete and his newfound island friends into a trap.

TWENTY-NINE

"Dr. Samuel Mudd," Ange said, staring down at her phone as I motored us along the Queen's Highway less than a mile outside of Andros Town. "Holy crap, this is it, Logan," she added enthusiastically while continuing to read. "This Dr. Mudd helped John Wilkes Booth after he assassinated Lincoln. After Booth shot the president, he jumped down onto the stage and broke his leg. This Mudd guy helped him and was later arrested for conspiracy."

That's right, I thought, shaking my head. I've never actually been inside Fort Jefferson, but I must've read or heard something about it's connection to this Mudd guy. It rang a bell deep inside my mind, but I hadn't been able to grasp it fully.

I listened intently as I brought us back into town, heading toward the dock to drop off our stuff before returning the rental.

"This has something to do with Fort Jefferson?" I said.

She nodded.

"Mudd was convicted and sentenced to life in prison. His sentence was carried out at the fort."

"Incredible," I said, shaking my head. "So, I'm willing to bet that if we search this guy's prison cell, we'll find our next clue."

Ange nodded, then smiled.

"Or the diamond."

It was well after 2200 when Ange splashed us down back at the Tarpon Cove Marina. Filled with excitement and fueled by a delicious to-go meal of pigeon peas and rice from back at Andros Town, we'd been wide awake the whole trip back. Only Atticus managed to doze off on the backseat, and he'd only awoken when we descended toward Key West.

Scott had messaged me again, letting me know that Wilson said not to worry about US customs on the way back into the States. A quick call to ATCs and that was all it took. They gave us the all clear to land back where we'd taken off earlier that day. Sometimes, it sure was nice having friends in high places.

Ange brought us up alongside her usual spot on the dock. I jumped out and tied us off, then we unloaded the gear.

"Welcome back," Pete said enthusiastically.

He strode down the dock alongside Jack with Walt right on their heels. Atticus ran over and greeted them as they walked up and helped us with the gear.

"So, how was the Bahamas?" Jack said.

"Beautiful," Ange replied. "And you should see Hastings Hole. It's stunning and remote. We had the

241

place to ourselves."

"Hastings Hole?" he said, raising an eyebrow.

"He lived there for a time apparently," I said. "You guys run into any trouble here?"

"Nothing, bro," Jack said. "There's been a squad car parked over at the marina this whole time just in case. But I think they might've run off."

I wasn't so sure. Based on our interaction, this Val Gallani woman didn't seem like the type to back down. But it had been over twenty-four hours since we'd seen them. There was no way of knowing for sure if they hightailed it out of here or were just waiting for the right moment to strike.

"I sure hope so," Walt said. "I've had those people on my ass long enough. I'm sick and tired of them."

"We can't rule out the possibility that they're still here," I said. "If anything, we have to be overprepared and ready for the worst."

We grabbed all of the gear, locked the Cessna, then loaded everything into Jack's Wrangler. He drove us over to the marina, and we carried everything to the Baia and gathered in the saloon.

We uploaded the images of the tablet onto my laptop, then showed them to the others while a pot of coffee brewed.

"It's a gravestone," Pete said, examining the images closely.

Ange nodded, and the three of them kept looking.

"What did you find from the cipher?" Walt said, glancing up at us.

I grabbed a notepad and scribbled the letters.

"F-T-J-E-F-F. M-U-D-D," Pete read out loud.

"Fort Jefferson," Walt said, only needing a few seconds to think it over.

"And M-U-D-D must be referring to Dr. Mudd," Pete added.

Walt and Jack both nodded at the mention of the doctor. Ange and I glanced at each other and smiled.

"That's what we got too," I said. "Had to do a search to figure out the Mudd part."

"Man, it all ties in perfectly," Jack said, leaning back into the couch.

I shrugged.

"What do you mean?"

The three of them paused a moment, then Jack motioned for Walt to do the honors.

"While you guys were in the Bahamas, we did some more research on Hastings," Walt said. "Being an engineer by trade, Hastings had been hired to work on many local construction projects around the Keys. Sure enough, one of them was a partial renovation of Fort Jefferson in 1905. He was the lead engineer for the job."

"Now it looks like he did a little more than just renovate," Jack said. "He added a sparkling new addition to the old fort."

I grinned and nodded.

"And his sparkling addition must be hidden well," I added. "Given that it's remained untouched for so long."

If I'd learned anything about the guy from his scavenger hunt so far, we were in for a well-orchestrated surprise.

"Incredible," Pete said, looking over the pictures of the stone tablet. "All this time, the famous diamond has been right here. Hidden in the old fort." He shook his head. "Now, all we've got to do is go and find it."

Ange slid the laptop in front of her and

performed a quick search. She brought up a top-view schematic of the fort.

"Fort Jeff itself is open to the public from sunup to sundown," she said. "So if we want to guarantee some time to ourselves in there, we should get there early in the morning. Looking around without drawing too much attention could be tricky regardless of when we go, though."

I looked at the map and agreed with her.

Fort Jefferson is a hex-shaped fortress constructed of over sixteen million red bricks that form a thick wall surrounding an area of over sixteen acres. Construction began in 1846 and never technically finished. The primary purpose of the fort was to protect one of the world's busiest shipping lanes. Its guns, and especially the ships that could anchor in its deepwater harbor, made the fort a vital American strategic asset for many years.

But I remembered reading that the fort was abandoned by the Army in 1874 and subsequently used as a hospital quarantine site, a bird reserve, and eventually a national monument until President Bush made it a national park in 1992.

The fort has since become a popular tourist attraction. Its impressive design, along with the beautiful nearby beaches and its seclusion from the busier part of the Keys, draws over fifty thousand visitors every year. There's a ferry service that runs from Key West every day and private plane charters for those who prefer a quicker and pricier alternative. Dry Tortugas also offers some of the best diving and snorkeling you'll find anywhere in the world.

"Once we're inside, then what?" Jack said. "We're just supposed to search every inch of the doc's old cell or what?"

The five of us exchanged glances.

"Yeah," I said with a nod. "This is the clue, so we follow it and see where it takes us."

I stepped in the main cabin, took a quick shower, then changed into fresh clothes. Ange did the same, and when we came back out into the saloon, Jack and Pete were still going over all of our gathered information.

"Where's Walt?" I asked.

Pete nodded toward the saloon door. "Went to get some air."

A few minutes later, he returned. As he stepped below deck, he had a strange look on his face, like something was bothering him.

"You sure you're alright, man?" Jack said. "You looked like you were about to drop dead earlier and now you need air?"

Walt waved him off.

"Just caught something, but it's nothing major." He filled a glass with water and took a sip. "It would take much more than a stomachache to keep me from finishing this search."

"I've got Tylenol and Pepto Bismol in that cupboard there," I said, pointing above the sink.

He thanked me and popped a few pills.

We spent another half hour going over the plan. There wasn't much to it. We'd head over early in the morning, search the cell, and play it from there. Just before hitting the sack, I got a call from Scott. I told him all about our little side trip to the Bahamas and about Fort Jefferson. He was intrigued, and he let me know he'd be in the Keys the following morning. When I asked if he needed me to pick him up from the airport, he told me that wouldn't be necessary.

"I'm gonna put that old trawler over at

Blackbeard's into the water," he said in his articulate, confident voice. "She's long overdue. I'd like to stretch her legs."

The trawler he was referring to was a sixty-footer that had been confiscated by the government after we had taken down its Russian assassin owner. By outward appearance, the vessel looked like a rundown fishing boat that was well beyond its last legs. But beneath its decrepit exterior, the trawler had a lot of expensive surprises, especially in the engine room.

"I'll meet you guys at Tortugas at sunrise," he continued.

"You gonna be alright finding the place?" I said with a laugh. "It's been a while, Senator."

He chuckled.

"I think we're due for a little sparring match, you and me, Dodge. It's clearly been too long since I showed you who's still top dog."

"Just making sure," I said in a friendly tone.

We hung up, and when I headed back down into the saloon, everyone was getting ready to call it a night. Pete and Walt decided to stay in the guest cabins on Jack's Sea Ray. I didn't blame them. The Baia's built more for speed than anything else, and though it's comfortable on the inside, there's not a lot of space compared to the *Calypso*.

"Zero four thirty," I said to them as they stepped down onto the dock.

"That diamond's ours, bro," Jack said, petting Atticus, then waving as he strode down the dock alongside the others.

THIRTY

My alarm woke me up at 0400. After switching it off, I rolled out of bed, cleared my mind, then rose and got ready. Ange got up a few minutes later and headed for the galley. We ate a quick breakfast, and each downed a mug of coffee.

I met Jack, Pete, and Walt topside, and they helped me secure my small white Zodiac inflatable dinghy to the Baia's swim platform. After a quick check of the weather and the tides, we cast off and motored out of the marina. I'd filled up both the main and aux gas tanks the previous day, so we had more than enough fuel for the trip.

Once clear of the no-wake zone, I rocketed us up to the Baia's impressive cruising speed of forty knots. We flew into the Northwest Channel, storming into the Gulf.

It was shaping up to be a good day out on the

water, with little to no chop. The sky had only a few small patches of clouds, and there was just a six-knot breeze blowing in from the east. The waxing gibbous moon cast a sparkly glow over the dark water. Looking up, I could see the sparkling stars of the constellation Pegasus. The mythological Greek winged horse twinkled in the dark sky alongside Pisces and Aries.

Just under two hours after shoving off in Key West, we reached Dry Tortugas. I piloted us between Iowa Rock off our port side and Hospital Key off starboard, then wrapped around to the south, cruising right past the massive red brick walls of Fort Jefferson on Garden Key. The fort's size and resiliency after all these years always astounded me. It was an impressive feat of architecture and engineering, especially considering its location.

I eased back on the throttles and brought us into the same deepwater channel that's used by the *Yankee Freedom* ferry. There were two boats anchored in a small cove beside us. One looked like a thirty-four-foot Catalina sailboat, and the other was a large yacht. Both vessels were devoid of any visible activity. I kept my distance from them and idled the Baia as far north as I could get without being in the ferry's path.

Jack was already up on the bow, unclipping the safety lanyard for the anchor. Operating the windlass from the cockpit, I slowly dropped the forty-pound anchor into the water. Once clear of the deck, I reversed the throttles to set it into place on the sandy bottom, then let out another fifty feet of rode.

With the Baia anchored down, I killed the engines, then climbed up onto the bow to take a look around. It was 0630, and the first traces of the soon-to-be-rising sun were making their appearance over

Long Key and the open Atlantic beyond. The scene was calm and quiet. There was no movement aside from a guy unzipping his tent and walking to the bathroom over at the campground, a flock of early-rising frigate birds, and a handful of sandpipers rummaging about in the softly crashing waves.

I downed another mug of coffee for the road, then grabbed my waterproof backpack. Inside, I had a few essential items stowed, including my waterproof flashlight, satellite phone, and two extra loaded magazines for my Sig.

Since we all reasoned that there'd likely be a little demolition required, I grabbed my fourteen-inch, five-pound sledgehammer and stowed it securely as well. I also grabbed my crowbar, which Pete put in his longer duffel bag along with a few extra flashlights and a small collapsible shovel.

Ange had an idea to close off the cell, just to keep any wandering early riser tourists away. We grabbed a coil of nylon rope, and she created an "Area Closed" sign. I stowed both in my backpack, then zipped it up and stepped out to the main deck.

Stepping down into the engine room, I grabbed the small 4-hp Mercury outboard engine for the Zodiac, and we hoisted it up onto the deck. After tightening it down to the Zodiac's transom, we unlashed the lines and eased it into the water.

I made sure Atticus's water bowl was filled, then petted him behind the ears and said, "Alright, boy. You stay and keep an eye on the boat, alright? We'll be back before you know it."

I said it but knew it wasn't true. Stepping out of sight for more than five minutes is like a lifetime for a dog. I can drive down to the grocery store, and when I get back, Atticus will jump and lick me like he hasn't seen me in ages. He never ceases to show his affection. One of the many things I love about having a dog.

"I'll stay with him, bro," Jack said, his words catching me off guard. Before I could ask why, he added, "That dingy cell creeped me out as a kid. You know how I am with confined spaces. Besides," he added, lounging on the sunbed and taking a sip of coffee, "somebody's gotta stay and keep a lookout."

I smiled as I scanned the area around us. The scene looked about as threatening as a butterfly exhibit at the zoo, but I knew from experience just how quickly that could change and reasoned that it was probably a good idea.

"We'll take the radio," Pete said. "Channel seven. There's no phone service here."

Jack nodded, and the rest of us climbed aboard the Zodiac. I plopped down at the stern. Before starting up the outboard, I glanced over at Walt. He'd been uncharacteristically quiet all morning.

"Hey," I said, patting him on the shoulder. "You feeling any better?"

He looked over at me and nodded unconvincingly.

"A little," was all he said in reply.

"I think you're gonna feel a hell of a lot better when we find this diamond," Pete chimed in.

I started up the engine while Pete untied the line.

"You gonna be alright here all by yourself, Jack?" Ange said from beside me.

"Hey, he's got Atticus," I said with a grin.

Jack feigned a laugh.

"You guys call me if you run into trouble and need me to save you." He leaned back and propped his feet up. "But I hope you don't, 'cause I've got some boat bum relaxing to catch up on."

We cut across the channel and tied off to an empty spot on one of the handful of small docks lining the shore beside the boat pier. Climbing up onto the hardwood planks, we headed onto the white sandy beach toward a footpath that led to the fort's entrance.

We crossed a narrow wooden bridge with brick supports that traversed a sixty-foot-wide moat that surrounded the entire fort. A middle-aged woman dressed in a park ranger uniform was walking beside the entrance when we approached. She paused and looked us over.

"The park doesn't open for another—" She cut herself off when she saw Pete. "Pete Jameson?" she added with a smile. "Why I'd recognize that hook anywhere."

Pete laughed and greeted the woman. One of the many good things about Pete was that he knew just about everybody in the Keys. The woman informed us that the park didn't technically open until sunrise, but she allowed the exception.

We thanked her and headed up a nearby staircase. Mudd's old cell was located on the second level, just above the visitor center, between Bastions Charlie and Delta. Up on the second level, I looked out over the center of the fort. Most of it was just grass and trees, with a few sporadic structures around the edges.

Just down the corridor, we turned and came to the walkway leading into Mudd's old cell. Above the entrance was a wooden sign with white letters.

"Who so entereth here leaveth all hopes behind," Ange said, reading the words aloud. "Well, that's comforting."

Inside, the cell was much larger than I'd expected it to be. I estimated that it was around three hundred square feet. It had solid stone floors, faded brick walls, and a few small windows that allowed the dim dawn glow to bleed in. There was a sign and a placard that contained information about how Mudd had provided medical care during an outbreak of yellow fever in the fort.

"Looks like he redeemed himself," Ange said.

Pete nodded. "He was eventually pardoned by President Andrew Johnson."

We spent ten minutes examining every inch of the cell. We were looking for something, anything even remotely abnormal. A loose brick, an unusual feature, a strange marking. But we came up empty.

"Maybe wherever Hastings hid it has been covered up," Pete said. "There's been a handful of renovations over the years to keep this place in such great shape."

A deep uncomfortable feeling overcame me. Maybe we'd come all this way, followed all the clues and narrowly escaped deadly encounters only to come up empty-handed right at the end.

"Well, you guys are sure here early," a male voice said from behind us.

I turned and looked toward the entrance of the cell. A young guy, maybe early twenties, wearing a park ranger uniform, strolled toward us. He had short red hair and freckles, and his face was reddened from the sun. He wore glasses and had an awkward gait.

He stopped just inside and looked around.

"Ah, checking out Mudd's cell, huh? You guys have any questions about it?"

I massaged my chin and smiled as I looked over the others.

"I heard he tried to escape," I said.

He nodded.

"Yeah. A few times, actually."

"But he never got out?" Ange said.

He looked over at Ange, shooting her an awkward smile.

"Well, officially, no."

That sparked my interest.

"What about unofficially?" I said, raising my eyebrows.

He paused a moment.

"You know, I'll let you all in on a little secret," he said, stepping toward us. "This may have been Mudd's cell at first, but after an escape attempt, he was taken elsewhere."

"Elsewhere?" Pete said. "Can you show us?"

He smiled, then nodded. He led us out of the cell down to ground level and across to the other side of the fort. We headed into Bastion Alpha, the northernmost fortification. Instead of heading up, he led us into the bowels of the structure and eventually to a ground-level room that was smaller than the Baia's saloon. This cell only had one tiny window.

After a few minutes of looking it over, Pete found something. He nonchalantly showed us a faded and barely legible symbol on one of the bricks. It was the same symbol we'd seen on the compass, the chest, and the tablet in the Bahamas. The symbol representing the Florentine Diamond.

We all looked at each other and smiled.

"Did Mudd ever try and Andy Dufresne his way out of here?" Pete asked.

The young guy looked back at him, confused.

"Andy who?"

Pete smiled and waved him off.

"Did he ever try and dig his way out of here?" Ange asked, not relying on the young guy having seen one of the greatest movies ever made.

He lit up as he looked at Ange again.

"Through the rock? There's no record of that. Besides, there's a cistern under here." He tapped his dirty tennis shoes on the ground. "Even if he had managed to break through, the only thing he would've accomplished was adding a private swimming pool."

We examined the symbol again. Hastings's message was loud and clear. We needed to break through the brick and stone. But we sure as hell couldn't do it with this kid looking over our shoulder.

"Mudd was held captive in this cell for most of his time at Fort Jefferson," the young ranger continued. "He was held here until 1869, when he was pardoned."

He kept talking, but we ignored him. He'd been helpful in showing us the new cell, but it was quickly becoming apparent that he wasn't going to leave us alone anytime soon. If we were going to break through the wall, we'd have to get rid of him.

He stepped out of the small space for a few seconds, going on about something I couldn't hear and allowing us to talk without him eavesdropping.

"We're gonna need someone to distract this guy," Pete said.

Our eyes gravitated to Ange. When she saw that we were looking at her, she shrugged and stepped closer to us.

"Ange, we need you to get rid of this guy," I said.

She looked over at me and shook her head.

"What? You want me to—"

254

"Jeez, Ange I don't mean knock him out," I said with a smile. "Just sweet-talk him and walk around with him a little bit."

Nothing distracts a straight man more effectively than a beautiful woman. Pit them up against fast cars, major sporting events, boats, video games, or whatever the particular guy's thing may be. Nothing compares to the effect of a woman. And no woman compares to Ange.

"What if he's gay?" she said.

"Then we've got Logan as a backup," Pete said, patting me on the back.

She let out a big sigh.

"Fine. But you all owe me for this. Run me around the Keys all week looking for this thing and now I gotta leave right before the big ending?"

"I'll make it up to you, Ange," I said.

She winked.

"You'd better."

The kid returned just as the words left her lips. He was still talking, not having skipped a beat since we'd arrived at the cell. I had to hand it to him, he was sure passionate about history.

Ange slid off her wedding band and dropped it into the front pocket of her denim shorts. She turned around and stepped toward the young park ranger.

"Connor," she said in her sexy voice. I wondered how she knew his name, then spotted the small name tag on the left side of his shirt. "Could you be a strapping, capable young lad and show me where the little girls' room is?"

The kid lit up like a firework, and I couldn't blame him. I'd have acted the same way if a woman talked to me like that when I was his age. I grinned as he struggled to speak. This kid was straight as an arrow.

"Of course," he said, finally managing to get something out. "This way."

He turned around, and Ange placed a hand on his shoulder as they walked out of view.

"She's almost too good at that," Walt said with a chuckle.

I turned around, turning my attention back to the worn symbol in the brick. Kneeling down, I felt the dried mortar along the edges of the brick, then rapped my knuckles a few times against it with my ear close.

"You think it's hollow on the other side?" Walt asked.

"Only one way to find out," I replied.

I grabbed a coil of rope from my backpack. Moving about thirty feet in front of the cell's entrance, we secured the rope at chest height across the passageway and set up the handwritten sign that said "Area Closed." The morning ferry from Key West wouldn't arrive until around 0900, but we wanted to make sure we had the cell to ourselves for the time being.

I moved back into the cell, reached into my pack, and pulled out the sledgehammer. Stepping across to the spot where Pete had spotted the symbol, I dropped to one knee beside the brick wall.

Demolishing part of a historic site for the second time in just a few days, I thought while eyeing my desired target at the edge of the brick.

Rearing back the hammer, I swung it nice and easy, letting gravity and the five-pound head do most of the work. The flat metal face struck the dried mortar with a loud crash, causing broken pieces to fall to the floor and a small bit of dust to burst out into the air.

I continued, relentlessly beating the wall again and again. After half a minute of powerful strikes, I slammed the head into the brick, and it broke free. Instead of falling toward me, it fell back and tumbled into a dark space.

I looked up at Pete and Walt and smiled. Grabbing my flashlight, I switched it on and peered into the opening. I gazed upon a short, narrow crawl space.

Turning back to face the others, I said, "I think we may have just found the way."

THIRTY-ONE

After five more minutes of hacking away at the old wall, we'd smashed a space big enough for us to crawl inside. Broken pieces of bricks and crumbled mortar rested in a pile beside us. We'd pulled most of it out, allowing us to move inside without having to crawl over the jagged obstacles.

I took one more look around, listening intently for any sign of someone else. When confident that the coast was clear, I shined my flashlight ahead of me and looked back at Pete and Walt.

"You sure you wanna go first, kid?" Walt said.

I smiled. "Fortune favors the bold."

I was also the youngest of the group and in significantly better shape than the others. It made more sense for me to go first and make sure it was safe. Selfishly, I also enjoy being the first to lay eyes on something that has been lost for years.

Keeping the light shining in front of me, I crawled into the space. Up ahead, it looked like the tunnel ended abruptly. But as I moved closer, I realized that it cut hard to the left and the floor dropped down.

Shining the light around the corner to make sure it was safe, I slid over the edge, landing on my feet. The tunnel was taller in there, but still not tall enough for me to stand up straight, so I kept my knees bent.

I took a few steps down the corridor, then reached a large stone cube at the end. Aside from the random block, there was nothing else. In all directions, the tiny space was completely empty.

"What is it, Logan?" Pete said.

I shrugged.

"I don't know. The tunnel just ends here."

"Wait a second," Walt said, sliding beside us and dropping down to examine the stone. "The symbol."

He aimed his flashlight and pointed at the side of the stone. There, carved into its flat face, was the same symbol Hastings had put on every other clue and the same one that had led us down into there.

Examining the stone more thoroughly, we saw that there were grooves dug into its sides. I slid my fingers around the back where the stone made contact with the wall. Instead of resting flat against it, the stone appeared to jut into the wall.

"There's a space behind the stone," I said, putting the two clues together. Turning to look at the others, I added, "We need to slide it back."

Fortunately, it appeared to be some kind of artificial rock. I estimated it to be about five hundred pounds, versus the thousands it would have weighed if it were real stone.

The three of us squeezed into the narrow space,

and each grabbed along the indent. On the count of three, we pulled with all our strength and just managed to budge the stone. After a few strong heaves, the stone slid toward us again. Just as it inched out of place, the sound of flowing water filled the narrow space.

We froze and listened as the water trickled out and quickly rose up over our feet. Shining the flashlight, we saw that it was pouring out from beyond the stone at a steady rate.

"I think it's safe to say we found the cistern," Pete said. He tasted some of the water, then immediately spat it out. "It's salty. There must be a crack someplace letting seawater in."

Within seconds, the water reached our knees. Shining through the opening, I saw that the flow was slowing and that there was a foot of headway for us to crawl inside and still be able to breathe. Crouching down, I shined the light as far as I could down the opening. It was hard to tell, but it looked like it opened up to a larger space beyond.

"Come on," I said, grabbing hold of the stone once more. "We need to keep pulling it back."

My muscles ached, and we grunted with each pull as we slid the stone farther back. Soon we'd slid it back far enough for us to crawl through. We paused and caught our breath.

"How in the hell did Hastings keep this passageway a secret?" Walt asked, shaking his head.

I didn't know. It was incredible, to say the least, and it was still unclear whether Hastings had built it or had discovered it and kept it hidden after hiding the diamond. Either way, moving forward was our only way to the diamond. And we'd come too far to hesitate now.

I crouched down and raised my flashlight. Sloshing through the water, I reached a small chamber on the other side and nearly tumbled over a sharp corner. Shining the beam of light, I saw that the water was deep. There was only about a foot of empty space between the water's surface and the ceiling.

Slowly, I slid over the edge and splashed into the water. It was about five feet deep, reaching up to my shoulders. I scanned my light around the water-filled chamber as Pete poked his head through behind me.

"This guy sure had a flair for the unique and dramatic," Pete said with a grin.

I smiled back and nodded. From the wild scavenger hunt he'd sent us on so far, I hadn't expected anything less.

He shuffled out of the crawl space and splashed into the water beside me. Walt followed right behind him, and the three of us searched the chamber, shining our lights into every corner.

The space for us to breathe was getting smaller and smaller with every passing minute.

"The tide's coming in," Pete said. "It'll be high just before noon, and it's about a two-foot tidal range right now."

I glanced at my watch and saw that it was just after 0700.

"This whole thing's gonna fill up," I said, looking around.

Pete nodded, and we continued our search of the chamber with increased motivation. If we couldn't find the diamond before the chamber filled up, the rangers would figure out what we were up to, and our window of opportunity would close.

As I moved across the narrow space, my right foot caught on something, and I nearly tripped. After

261

stabilizing myself, I turned back and shined my light through the water. It only took a few seconds of searching to realize that I'd brushed up against a brick that was raised slightly above the rest. Glancing side to side, I saw that the brick was located right in the middle of the floor.

I smiled as my mind raced back to when we'd first been learning about Hastings and the diamond. The whole search began at his deathbed, when he had spoken to his niece. I thought mainly about what Walt had said were the last words to come out of his mouth.

"Of all the secrets in my life," I said, recounting Hastings, "I hid the greatest at the bottom and in the center."

I took in a breath, dropped down into the water, and grabbed the brick. Biting down and aiming the flashlight with my mouth, I squeezed tight with both hands and tried to pull it free. Though it was sticking up a few inches, it was secured in place, and I couldn't budge it an inch.

I surfaced, unzipped my bag, and pulled out my sledgehammer.

"What'd you find?" Pete asked.

I smiled, shrugged, then took a breath and dropped back down. Three strong strikes were all it took to loosen the brick. Letting go of the sledgehammer, I reached down and grabbed the brick a second time. Gripping as hard as I could, I shimmied it back and forth, then lifted it free.

Setting the brick aside, I reached into the small revealed space and grabbed a tin box. I straightened my legs, broke free of the water, and took in a few breaths. I wiped the saltwater from my eyes and held the box out in front of me.

I could see only the dim glow of their faces, but I knew that they were both smiling just as big as I was.

"You're the one who believed in this more than anyone," I said, looking at Walt. Holding out the box, I added, "You should do the honors."

He hesitated a moment, then Pete nudged him.

"Go on, old friend," Pete said. "Logan's right. After all the years I made fun of you for believing in this legend, you deserve this and many more moments of glory."

Again Walt hesitated. He seemed conflicted for a few seconds, then nodded and finally grabbed the tin box.

Maybe he's in shock. Maybe he can't believe what's happening.

I had a hard time believing it myself.

Pete and I shined our flashlights toward the box as Walt grabbed the lid and pried it open. He reached inside and pulled out a small leather pouch. Just as he emptied its contents into the palm of his hand, his eyes lit up, and he gasped. I waded through the warm water, peeking around for a look inside.

Walt wrapped his right hand into a fist around the contents. Holding up and rotating his hand around, he opened his fingers, revealing a massive yellow diamond.

I smiled triumphantly and laughed as I patted the two of them on the back. Pete was lost in the tremendous heat of the powerful moment as well. He cheered and laughed more heartily than I'd ever heard him before.

Walt stood stunned, staring at the rare twinkling gem.

I thought about the past couple of days, the work we'd done and the knowledge we'd gained in order to reach this point. Starting out in Snake Creek, sifting through acres of seafloor in order to find the lost compass. Then using the jackhammer to dig up the old chest and fighting off the ruthless Albanian mafia bad guys. Flying to the Bahamas and diving two hundred and forty feet down to photograph the memorial to Hastings's wife. And finally, breaking into a secret passageway hidden within one of America's oldest and impressive forts.

I smiled as I grabbed and examined the stone by the glow of my flashlight.

"The Florentine Diamond," I said, in awe that I was holding one of the rarest diamonds in the world.

It was heavy, much heavier than I'd expected. And its sparkle was almost too intense to look at, even when reflecting nothing but the flashlight.

"Lost no more," Pete said, his smile bigger than any smile I'd ever seen before.

Walt looked over his shoulder toward the crawl space entrance into the chamber.

Before I could ask what was wrong, he said, "We should get moving. The water's rising and somebody might figure out what we're up to."

He was right, though it was hard for me to take my eyes off the diamond. I wasn't normally a sucker for fine jewels. I'm more of a simple man. I like my guns, boats, and good food. But the incredible stone had me mesmerized. It was perfectly shaped on all sides, its double-rose cut flawless.

I handed the diamond to Walt, and he put it back into the pouch, closed it inside the box, then slid the box into his pocket. He took the lead on the way back, with Pete in the middle and myself in the rear. I took one more look around the chamber, then pulled myself up out of the water and into the small crawl space.

As I sloshed back through the water, keeping my head craned up in order to breath, I thought I heard footsteps coming from far ahead. The steps sounded too far away to be Walt, so I called out, making sure that he was alright. I got no reply from Walt. Not even an acknowledgment that I'd said anything.

"Walt, can you hear us?" Pete called out.

I watched as Pete rose to his feet, then climbed over the stone block ahead of me. I heard the shuffling of feet, the splashing of water, and a few loud grunts.

Something's very wrong.

It was like a switch went off in my mind. In an instant, I went from ecstatic and feeling like I was in a dream to focused. I reached for my Sig, held it out in front of me with my right hand while I pointed my flashlight forward with my left. It was challenging to move forward in that position, so I lowered the flashlight as I crawled and called out.

"Pete!" I yelled. "Are you alright?"

My heart was pounding, my vision narrowed.

What the hell happened? And why in the hell aren't either of them replying?

"Logan!" Pete yelled back, struggling to get the words out.

I could still hear shuffling and the loud sloshing of water.

"Shut up," I finally heard a voice say sternly in the darkness.

It was Walt.

My heart sank. I rose up from the other side of the stone block and shined my flashlight forward. Walt was standing behind Pete, his left arm wrapped around Pete's neck. His right hand gripped Pete's

265

Taurus .44 Magnum, and he had the barrel aimed straight at me.

THIRTY-TWO

"Walt?" I said as our eyes locked. "What the hell are you doing?"

I felt a powerful rage storming deep inside me. Walt was taking the diamond for himself. After everything we'd done for him, he was betraying us right at the end.

How in the hell can he do this? How in the hell did we allow him to do this?

Pete was gasping for air, his eyes big and bulging. He was angry and had a hard time believing what was happening.

I was surprised by Walt's expression, however. He didn't look angry at us but instead conflicted. Like he was doing something that he didn't want to do, but had to.

"Drop the gun, Logan," Walt said. I swallowed hard but kept my Sig raised, the barrel staring him

267

down. "Drop it now! I'll shoot."

I controlled my breathing, trying to slow myself down so I could make the best move.

"What is this, Walt?" Pete exclaimed, struggling for every word. "We've been friends all our lives and now this?"

I watched Walt carefully, seeing the conflict within him. He was struggling to justify his actions. I could see it all over his face and in the way his gun hand shook.

"What's the game plan here, Walt?" I said. "You shoot us and take the diamond? We're already willing to split it and give you half. That not enough for you?"

He opened his mouth, then shut it. He looked like he was going crazy, and I wondered if maybe he was. He opened his mouth again, but just as he started to speak, a voice overtook his.

A woman's voice.

"For him, maybe," the voice called from the darkness behind Walt and Pete. "But it's not enough for me."

I directed my gaze up in an instant as footsteps echoed from just down the corridor. I didn't need to see her face to realize who it was. Her powerful Albanian accent was unmistakable. The big woman with short black hair who'd fought Ange back at the Hemingway House stepped into the beam of my flashlight.

Valmira Gallani, I thought, remembering the name Walt had said a few days ago.

She was the leader of their mafia. A woman who'd murdered her father and brother in order to get in control. She'd engaged in a fight with Ange and was still standing, which meant she was both brutal and tough as nails.

Val held a black Beretta in her right hand, and the two guys with her each held stockless AK-47s. They all switched on high-powered flashlights that illuminated the space, forcing me to cover my eyes it was so bright.

"You're the old-timer with the hook for a hand," Val said, glaring at Pete. "So that means you must be the mercenary. Dodge, is it? Yes. You're the asshole who killed a handful of my men." I gave a nod of my head and a short, sarcastic bow. She smirked, looked over at Walt, then added, "Looks like you've picked the wrong friends. Now, drop the fucking gun before we blow your ass to pieces!"

How can I drop it? It's the only card we have, the only bargaining chip.

I couldn't take all four of them out before they shot me, which meant that Pete and I were both goners if I couldn't think of something quick.

"I'm going to count to three," Val said, growing irritated. "One… two… th—"

"Alright," I said, having no other choice. "But let him go first," I added, motioning toward Pete.

Val looked calmly back and forth between her two men, then stared daggers at me.

"You've got some stones," she said with a sly smile. "I'll give you that." A moment later, she shrugged and added, "Let him go, old man."

Walt slid his broken left arm from around Pete's neck with a wince and pushed him toward me. He nearly fell in the darkness and turned around right beside me.

I kept my eyes locked on Val. She clenched her jaw and motioned toward my Sig. Still facing four loaded guns, I had no choice but to let it go. The grip slipped from my hands and tumbled to the floor at my feet.

"Grab it, Walt," Val ordered.

He did so, snatching it as best he could with his left hand, his mobility limited by the cast, and ruling out the possibility that I could make a desperate attempt to grab it.

"I'm sorry," Walt said, choking up. "I'm so sorry. I… I had no choice. They have my son. They have my daughter-in-law. And they have my two grandchildren."

My heart sank, and I let out a breath. It explained everything. How he'd backstabbed us, how he'd looked conflicted the entire time. It also explained why he hadn't been acting like himself since the previous evening.

I could understand why he'd done it, but he had to have been out of his mind if he thought for a second that he'd be getting out of this alive. I knew Val's type. She was evil and heartless. I was confident that the moment she got what she wanted, she'd kill Walt's son in front of him and then put an end to him as well.

"The diamond, old man," Val said, holding out her left hand.

Now that Walt had my Sig, neither Pete nor I were armed, and Val's attention had shifted away from me.

Walt did as he was ordered. He reached into his pocket, pulled out the small tin box, and handed it to Val. The mafia leader smiled after opening and examining the stone, then dropped it into her own pocket.

"Wally," Pete said, shaking his head. "You could have told us. We could have—"

"You're past that now," Val snarled. "The game's over. You have lost, and I have won." She glanced at the two men squeezed beside her. "And as for your wife," she added, narrowing her gaze at me, "the one who thought she could challenge me and get away with it." She laughed. "Once you two are dead, we will find her and we will kill her as well."

I felt an uncontrollable flood of anger rush over me. I knew Ange could hold her own as well as any woman alive, but the idea of these thugs taking her by surprise made my blood boil.

"Call the yacht," Val barked to the guy on her right. "Have them bring it over to this corner of the fort."

"What about the guy on the boat?" he replied.

Her lips formed an evil smile, and she eyed me. "Kill him, and the damn dog too."

I gritted my teeth upon hearing her words.

The big thug did as he was ordered, grabbing his radio and relaying the order to one of their guys outside the fort. Val eyed both Pete and me up and down. She was enjoying this, enjoying watching our anger boil over.

"You have both fucked up royally," she said. "Unfortunately for you, this isn't a mistake you will live to learn from." She relished the moment for a few impossibly long seconds. "Now," she added slowly, "it's time for both of you to die."

She raised her weapon. This was it. If we were going to have any hope of getting out of this, we'd have to act now.

As fast as I could, I bent my knees, twisted my body around in a blur of rapid motion, and tackled Pete. We flew over the large stone and splashed into the water just as bullets exploded out from their barrels like thunder, shaking the small corridor to life.

Just as we hit the water, I kept my arms wrapped around Pete and forced him to roll alongside me into the narrow crawl space. We splashed and flailed as we kicked and clawed our way through the water. In a haze of dark confusion, we reached the other side and fell over the edge, splashing into the deeper water of the inner chamber.

I planted my feet on the bottom and broke free, gasping for air. My heart was hammering violently, my adrenaline full throttle. I splashed alongside Pete as we moved out of sight of the crawl space. The incessant barrage of gunfire finally ceased, and we heard muffled yelling from the other side.

"Holy shit," I said, breathing heavily. "Pete, are you alright?"

I was about to ask how in the hell we'd manage to make it without getting shot, then I saw the look on Pete's face through the light bleeding down the crawl space. He was wincing and had his hand pressed to the upper part of his right leg.

Examining closer, I saw blood spilling out like dark food coloring into the clear water. As I tore one of my shirtsleeves to create a makeshift tourniquet, I heard a low, grinding rumble coming from the opening. A moment later, the sliding stopped, and the muffled voices went silent. In a second the chamber was plunged into utter and complete darkness. They'd put the stone back in place. Pete was shot, and we were both stuck. And the water was rising higher by the second.

THIRTY-THREE

Jack lounged on the Baia's sunbed, wearing nothing but a pair of boardshorts and dark sunglasses. In his right hand, he held a chilled strawberry daiquiri. His propped-up feet swayed to the rhythm of Eric Clapton singing "Forever Man" through the topside speakers. A gust of fresh ocean breeze danced through his curly blond hair, and he let out a smile, relishing the temperate southern Florida morning.

He glanced over the port bow and watched as the sun peeked over the horizon, sending brilliant streaks of light across the sky. He loved lounging out on the water. He liked to keep his music down low so he could listen to the calming lapping of the ocean against the hull, the distant small waves against the shore, and the sounds of passing gulls. He was a conch alright. Tropical sky, salt, sand, and sun flowed through his veins.

He took another sip of his frozen concoction and glanced over at Atticus, who was relaxing on the shaded deck beside him. In half an hour, if the others weren't back yet, he'd take a dip and toss the energetic Lab's tennis ball for a few rounds.

Glancing over at the massive hex-shaped nineteenth-century fort, he thought about what the others were up to. He hoped that this was the last leg of the search. That they'd show up any second and hand him the diamond they'd been looking for all this time. He'd already had to reschedule a few charters, and he was looking forward to getting back to "work."

The song ended, and just as Jack took another sip, Atticus stirred suddenly. He quickly lifted his head, his ears perking up as he glanced toward the bow.

"What is it, boy?" Jack said, watching the Lab intently.

Just as the words left his lips, Atticus jumped to his feet and vaulted up onto the sunbed beside him for a better look. Jack set his drink aside, turned around, and rose up onto his knees to see what all of the fuss was about.

Probably a dolphin or something, Jack thought.

Whatever had piqued his interest, it couldn't be the others. He was looking southeast, away from the fort and toward the entrance into the deepwater channel.

Shielding the left side of his face from the rising sun, Jack focused his gaze on the anchored yacht. There was a lot of activity on board, and to get a better look, Jack slid off the sunbed and snatched the binos from the cockpit dashboard. Peering through the lenses, he watched as the yacht's captain brought up the anchor while a group of guys lowered an RHIB into the water. The RHIB, or rigid-hull inflatable boat, looked roughly twenty feet long and had two large outboards clamped onto its stern.

Atticus barked as the guys piled into the small boat and started up its engines. Focusing closer, he could see that they were all carrying guns. Jack's heart raced as the boat accelerated straight toward him.

He lowered the binos and quickly ran through his options. There weren't many. The guys were clearly part of the Albanian mafia they'd run into before. And they were clearly motoring over with the intent to start a fight.

He glanced up at the approaching boat again. They were only about a football field away from him, and closing in fast.

With no time to bring up and secure the anchor, Jack snatched his dive knife from the dinette and climbed up onto the bow. Kneeling down, he manually disengaged the windlass, allowing the remaining chain to fall rapidly into the water below. Once the chain rode was gone and the rope rode appeared, he re-engaged the windlass, then slashed the taut line with his knife. In an instant, the rode snapped and splashed into the water.

With smooth agility, Jack flew back down into the cockpit and exchanged his knife for his compact Desert Eagle. Holding the handgun with his left hand, he moved into the cockpit and quickly started up the Baia's engines.

"Atticus—down, boy!" he said, and the jumpy pooch dropped down to the deck beside him.

Jack watched as the boat quickly approached. He saw three guys aboard, and two of them were armed.

As they motored closer, he could see them pointing toward him and yelling out words he couldn't understand.

He kept low, trying to remain out of sight as the boat slowed and eased toward the Baia. Sensing that it was now or never, he gunned the throttles and roared the big engines to life. The propellers surged, accelerating the boat rapidly and causing the bow to rise up out of the water.

He could see the looks of surprise on the guys' faces and hear their yells even over the loud engines as he flew right past them. Jack brought the sleek speed machine up on plane, then rocketed up to fifty knots. Looking back over his shoulder, he watched as the RHIB accelerated into a wide sweeping turn.

Wanting to try and outrun them until he thought of a better plan, he wrapped around the shallow reefs surrounding Garden Key and the fort. Turning onto a northeasterly course, he looked back and saw that his pursuers were gaining on him.

More power than I assumed, he thought. *Way more power!*

Flying right past shallow reefs off the starboard side, he thought back to a similar predicament he and Logan had been in a year and a half earlier. While being chased by the notorious Mexican drug cartel, Black Venom, Logan had used their knowledge of the area to their advantage.

I'm not gonna outgun them, he thought, glancing at the Desert Eagle snug on the dash in front of him. *But maybe I can out pilot them.*

Still gunning the engines full throttle, he skirted around Hospital Key and headed back toward the fort. As the RHIB passed by, the bad guys aboard fired off their automatic weapons.

Jack dropped to the deck as the repetitive explosions echoed across the water. Bullets slammed into the hull and shattered holes in the windscreen just inches above his head.

As his pursuers were forced to turn around, Jack rose and focused his gaze on his destination less than half a mile ahead of him. Slowing just enough to let the RHIB fly into the Baia's wake, he gunned the throttles again, roaring toward a large patch of shallow water.

Iowa Rock sat mere inches below the surface off the northern shore of Bush Key. It formed a few whitecaps, but not enough to draw suspicion. Staying over fifty knots, and with the RHIB right behind him, Jack navigated into a narrow channel that only locals knew about.

Bullets rattled the air again, and he dropped down moments before cutting a hard right, the engine groaning as the Baia's hull tore through the water less than ten feet from the dangerous shallows.

Come on, baby, come on!

He completed the turn with a gasp and turned around just in time to see his pursuers play right into his hands. Trying to cut the distance between them, they took the inside on the turn, the fiberglass hull of the RHIB slamming into the massive jagged rock with a loud crash. The sudden impact smashed the hull to pieces and flipped the small vessel. It spun violently over the rock and water, sending metal, fiberglass, and bad guys flying. The accident had occurred so suddenly that they hadn't had time to scream.

Jack watched the seconds of chaos unfold. When the sprays of broken boat and water settled, there was nothing left but spread-out wreckage all over the shallows. As would be expected, none of the three guys were moving.

Jack eased back on the throttles, turning around and idling the Baia. He let out a triumphant yell and pumped his chest with his fist. Atticus jumped up and down, then sprang up to the sunbed for a better view. Jack smiled and grabbed his Desert Eagle before taking a survey of the water surrounding them.

"Not a single shot fired, boy," he said proudly, patting Atticus on the head. "Wait till I tell Logan about this."

He paused a moment, then lit up and moved for the radio.

Logan, he thought. *If those assholes came after me, what kind of trouble are they in?*

He had to warn them. Had to do everything he could to help his friends.

Grabbing the radio, he tried to call them but got no answer. Three more times he tried, and each time he came up empty.

Am I too late? Are they already...

"Get down, Atty," he said, grabbing the helm and throttles once more. "We gotta get to the fort."

He pushed the throttles forward. Instead of the healthy roaring engines and adrenaline-inducing acceleration, the engines moaned and sputtered. They sounded terrible, and if the Baia had accelerated, he hadn't noticed.

He stepped aft, grabbed hold of a flush lift ring in the deck, and pulled up the engine hatch. A plume of thick black smoke engulfed him, and he had to turn away to protect his lungs. The bad guys on the RHIB might have failed, but they'd managed to put the Baia out of commission with their rounds.

After waiting a few seconds to let the bulk of the

smoke clouds disperse in the ocean breeze, he peered down into the engine room and saw that the damage was beyond repair.

Great, he thought. *Absolutely fantastic.*

He glanced over the bow at Fort Jefferson and the white, sandy northern tip of Garden Key. He was about a mile off. A swim he could make in less than twenty minutes if he needed to. But that would mean abandoning the Baia, and Atticus if he didn't take him along.

He quickly thought over the situation. Stepping over and grabbing the radio, he was about to make another attempt at contacting the others when he heard an engine in the distance. It was coming from behind him, to the east, and he gripped his Desert Eagle before turning to take a look.

Let me guess, more bad guys coming to ruin my day out on the water?

He turned, prepared to raise his weapon and take aim in a heartbeat. But as he looked over the stern, he kept his pistol at his side and smiled. A boat he'd recognize from miles away was thundering straight toward him.

By outward appearance, the vessel looked like an ordinary fishing trawler. Sixty feet long, the decrepit-looking old boat was in serious need of a paint job. It had rust all over and broken-looking topside equipment. But Jack knew from personal experience that it was a lot more than met the eye. Beneath its grimy façade were large, powerful engines and top-of-the-line technology.

As it motored up alongside the Baia, Jack could see Scott Cooper at the helm. When it came to an idle, the six-foot-tall, athletic Florida politician and former Navy SEAL commander stepped out. He was wearing cargo shorts, a black tee shirt, and sunglasses.

Seeing the wreckage and no doubt hearing the explosion, Scott's face was all business.

"Where are the others?" he said, his voice low and powerful.

After a quick catch-up on what was going on, Jack and Atticus came aboard the trawler and Scott thundered them toward Fort Jefferson.

THIRTY-FOUR

Angelina walked with her hands on her hips alongside the young, energetic park ranger. She looked incredible, her tank top and denim shorts doing justice to her toned, tanned frame. Her looks, combined with her interest, were driving the young guy mad and causing him to get sweaty and talk really fast.

"So that's basically how and why the fort was approved by the government," he said, finishing a few deep breaths worth of history. He pointed at the large brick walls surrounding them and added, "Then construction began, bringing on a whole new set of—"

"It looks like that lady over there's calling you," Ange interrupted, motioning toward a middle-aged woman dressed in a park ranger uniform standing in front of a small group of people over by the entrance.

The woman was waving toward them and calling Connor's name.

He looked over at the group, then back at Ange.

"Oh, no, she's fine," he assured her. "That's just the sunrise tour. I usually do it, but it's about time she learned to do that by herself. Have you seen the hotshot furnace?"

Ange grinned and let out a soft sigh. The plan of distracting the curious kid had worked well. Too well. She'd hoped to lead him away from Mudd's secret cell, then head back to join in on the party. But glancing at her watch, she saw that it had already been twenty minutes since she'd left them.

Probably missed my chance.

She shrugged and smiled when she thought about how she'd have Logan make it up to her.

The young ranger led her over to the hotshot furnace and enthusiastically explained how it worked and what it was used for.

"The fire was built down at the bottom," he explained, motioning toward the bottom of the rectangular brick structure. "Then cannonballs were loaded in through this opening and eventually rolled down to this position here at the other end due to gravity." He walked to the other side, then paused a moment, clearing his throat. "By the time they came out this end here, they were cherry-red hot. These superheated balls of iron were then fired by the cannons and were more effective against the wooden warships of the time."

Ange nodded and gave a childlike smile. Despite wanting desperately to be somewhere else, she'd never heard of the hotshot furnaces and found them fascinating.

As the ranger led Ange to the next stop on his

little private tour, Ange froze suddenly as she heard the loud growling of distant boat engines. Turning around, she realized that the sounds were coming from the channel where they'd anchored the Baia. They were far off, but it sounded like the Baia's engines, and like they were being gunned full throttle.

What reason could Jack have to haul ass out of here? Unless…

No, she needed to see for herself what was happening before drawing any conclusions. She took two strides toward the other side of the fort while the young ranger spoke behind her.

"Hey, what the heck?" he said. "You can't have guns in here."

Ange froze in her tracks. She spun around suddenly and gasped as she laid eyes on Val, Walt, and two other mafia members. They were just outside the entryway into Mudd's cell, heading for the nearest stairs.

Before Ange could do or say anything, Connor yelled out, "Hey, you! You guys—"

Hearing the young guy call out, Val's head snapped to look straight at them. In the blink of an eye, Ange grabbed Connor and jerked both their bodies behind the hotshot furnace. Just as they vanished from Val's line of sight, a barrage of gunfire echoed across the air. Bullets struck the edge of the brick, sending shards and dust into the air.

Ange expected the young kid to be scared out of his mind from all the action and noise. But when the shooting stopped, and Ange looked him over, he just looked pissed off.

"Stay here, ma'am," he said, shaking his way out of Ange's grasp. "I'll take care of this."

"You're a brave kid." Ange peeked around the

corner as Val and the others moved toward the other side of the fort and ran up the stairs to the top level. "But I think you've played one too many video games. This is way over your head."

"No, I need to stop them—"

Ange snatched him again, placing him in a quick chokehold, then twisted his right arm back.

"Make one move toward those bastards, and I'll break your arm," Ange said, pulling his arm dangerously far back into a position it wasn't intended. He winced, and Ange added, "What are you going to do, huh?" Ange grabbed her Glock 26 with her free hand and held it so the young guy could see it. "Now, head over to the visitor center and get help. Call the police. Call the Coast Guard. Hell, call anyone and everyone and get them here now!"

The young man froze for a moment, then nodded. Ange loosened her grip, helped him to his feet. He turned around and sprinted for a cluster of trees in the center of the fort for cover. Once he reached them, he veered left, heading toward the visitor center. The small group of people and the other ranger had vanished, running away after hearing the gunfire.

Ange gripped her Glock with both hands and peered around the corner. Scanning the area around them, she saw no sign of Logan or Pete. Val's head popped into view, followed by the others as they reached the top level. Ange raised her Glock and fired off a quick succession of rounds that caused them to hit the deck and disappear from her view.

Seizing the minuscule window of opportunity, Ange took off. She darted from the back of the furnace to the base of Bastion Alpha, reaching the lower staircase in seconds. Without a moment's pause, she flew up to the second level.

When she reached the staircase to the top level, she slowed and held her Glock out in front of her. She controlled her breathing and listened intently as she took the stairs two at a time.

She swiftly reached the top and, before stepping out the entryway, glanced through a thin partition and saw the two big thugs heading around the corner to cut her off. Taking aim quickly, she fired off two rounds straight into the first guy's chest. Blood splattered out, and he whipped sideways, crashing to the floor.

Seeing his buddy go down, the second guy dropped to the side and fired a rapid series of automatic bullets in Ange's general direction. She was forced to take cover as a few of the rounds ricocheted through the partition and slammed into the brick wall behind her.

Moving in a low crouch while hugging the wall, she paused at the edge and waited for the second thug to make his move. It didn't take long. The first thing she saw was the barrel of his AK-47 as the big guy swung it around. Ange grabbed the middle of it with her left hand and forced it up. The thug held the trigger, spraying bullets into the ceiling while Ange fired a 9mm round into his leading foot.

He yelled out in pain from the blow and lurched forward. Ange used his momentum to her advantage, sliding into his path and throwing him over her body. He hit the hard ground with a loud thump and dropped his weapon.

In quick retaliation, he slammed his fist across Ange's face. She managed to go with it, but it still hurt like hell and caused her lip to bleed.

Pissed off beyond belief, Ange grabbed him from behind, put him in a chokehold with his arm back, and pressed her Glock into his temple.

"On your feet!" she said forcefully.

He did as he was told, wincing in pain and keeping all his weight on his good foot.

"Now walk."

He staggered around the corner with Ange holding him from behind, keeping her weapon jammed in place. She spotted Val and Walt standing over at the far corner of the bastion. Walt was wrapping a rope around a narrow section of what looked like a type of battlement and tightening it in place. The other end disappeared over the wall toward the ocean. Ange couldn't see what the other end was tied to, but she imagined it led down to their yacht.

They're making their grand escape attempt.

Val stood beside Walt, facing Ange and her human shield. Her eyes were shooting daggers, her jaw was clenched, and she had her Beretta .45 raised.

Ange forced the injured, bleeding thug to move until they were within fifty feet of Val and Walt. The old man raised Pete's Taurus .44 Magnum as well and said something to Val that Ange couldn't hear. He looked spooked and anxious to get out of there.

Damn well should feel that way, Ange thought as she faced them, aching for them to make a move.

"You really are a pesky little vermin, aren't you?" Val said. "I figured you would have gotten the message when we fought a few days ago."

"Clearly not," Ange replied, tightening her grip on the bleeding thug in her grasp. "I guess you're just not as tough as you thought." Val was about to spit out a rebuttal when Ange beat her to it. "Where are they?"

Her eyes slid back and forth between Val and Walt. She'd take an answer from either one of them.

"Your husband isn't here to save you this time," she said. "In fact, he won't be saving anyone ever again. I hope you said your goodbyes."

Ange's eyes narrowed to slits. Her pulse quickened.

"What the hell did you do?"

"Not just me," she replied coldly, patting Walt on the back. "Walt here led you all right into our hands. He's been playing you all this time. He deserves a lot of the credit."

Ange locked her eyes on Walt. He was angry, but more than that, he just looked worried.

"So, you're a traitor, huh?" she yelled. "You sold out your only friends for what? A damn rock?" She shook her head. "Some hero you are—"

"Enough chitchat," Val snapped. "Drop your fucking gun, or I'll blow your brains out just like I did your pathetic husband."

Ange's anger was rapidly delving into new territory. She could feel it overflowing inside her with every word out of Val's mouth.

Is she lying just to get me to react? Whether she is or not, it's working.

After a few stretched-out seconds of tense silence, bullets echoed from far across the water. Beyond her enemies, Ange could see two blurry boats far in the distance. One was the Baia, and the other clearly wasn't the good guys.

"They have my son!" Walt shouted, catching all of them off guard.

"Shut up, old man!" Val barked. "Or I'll feed them to the sharks."

He bowed his head slightly, staring down at their feet. Slowly, he lifted up his head and looked right at Ange.

"Help them," he said, tears welling up in his eyes.

Val looked like she was about to tear him a new one. But before she acted against him, a loud crashing sound thundered across the air. Val glanced over her shoulder momentarily and watched as the small boat her men were piloting blew to pieces in the shallows a mile away.

With Val distracted, Walt suddenly sprang into action, no longer able to justify what he was doing. He swung his body to aim the Taurus at Val, but the experienced mafia leader saw what was happening and punched the weapon from his hands at the last second. Ange knew that it was now or never. Her trigger finger was just starting to flex with the barrel aimed at Val when the big thug in her arms yelled and slammed his shoulder into her chest. She lurched forward and loosened her grip enough for him to knock her Glock out of her hands.

Val's weapon fired into the air as Walt engaged the menacing mafia leader. Ange blocked a blow from the bleeding thug in front of her, then put him out of commission with a blinding roundhouse kick that snapped his neck and caused his body to collapse.

With the thug dead, Ange directed her gaze back to the others. Val was on top of Walt. Blood flowed from his chest. He gasped for whatever breath he could get and tried to force Val away.

Val looked over at Ange, a sick smile forming on her face before she raised her blood-soaked Albanian jambiya dagger and stabbed its razor-sharp tip through Walt's heart. It was over quickly. His head lowered and he breathed his last before going limp in the grass.

Ange rose to her feet. Val wiped the blood from

her blade on Walt's shirt, then did the same. They were only twenty feet from each other. The nearest handguns were too far to go for, but that didn't matter. Staring each other down, the two experienced fighters knew how it had to end.

"Let's dance," Val said.

Ange stepped toward her and raised her fists.

"Last dance of your life, bitch."

Ange didn't hesitate, didn't wait for her opponent to make the first move. She strode quickly toward Val and engaged her with a rapid barrage of punches and kicks. Val was fast and strong, with the skilled technique of a master martial artist. She managed to block or redirect all of Ange's blows and strike back with a few of her own.

Sliding quickly to the side and catching her opponent off guard, Ange landed a punch to Val's gut. But the big, hard woman was seemingly unaffected. Ange felt as though she'd hit a concrete wall and not a body.

Angered, Val sprang toward Ange in a powerful flying kick. Just before her leading heel crashed into Ange, she stepped to the side, grabbed Val by her tactical pants, and slammed her back against the corner of a short brick wall.

Val grunted and retaliated by landing two quick blows, one to the shoulder and the other to the side of the face. Ange felt dazed as Val continued a relentless combo that ended with a kick to the chest that sent Ange flying backward.

Ange managed to keep herself from falling over, regaining her balance just in time to react to Val grabbing her bloody knife and flinging it through the air. Ange hit the ground and could hear the blade as it spun through the air, dangerously close to her head. It rattled against a brick wall behind her, and Ange jumped to her feet.

Val let out a loud, barbaric yell, then took off toward Ange, barreling straight for her like an angry linebacker heading for the quarterback on third down. Instead of facing the furious, sprinting woman head-on, Ange turned and took off away from her. After a few quick strides, Ange lunged high into the air, planted her right foot onto the brick wall, then launched herself back toward Val. Before Val could react, Ange slammed a hard right square into her face, causing the big woman's body to whip backward and nearly knocking her unconscious.

Val grabbed hold of Ange's tank top as she fell, ripping it halfway up the seam and pulling Ange on top of her. The two women rolled as they struggled to subdue the other while throwing occasional elbows.

They quickly reached the edge of the wall, and Ange's head dangled over the brick, hovering dangerously over the shallow moat thirty feet below. From that angle, Ange could see in her blurry peripherals where the rope led. Sure enough, it was attached to the yacht they'd seen anchored earlier that morning. It was a hundred yards off, idling close to the shallows along the outer wall.

In a quick, desperate attempt to swing the fight, Ange managed to force the strong woman into a kimura hold. Without hesitating, she pulled back forcefully and snapped Val's elbow.

Val screamed and cursed. Ange didn't let up. She dug her feet into Val's chest and kicked, sending her flying and crashing into the grass. Sore and bleeding, Ange rose to her feet. She locked eyes with Val as the woman winced and struggled to recover.

The injured mafia leader staggered to her feet,

glanced to her right, and smiled.

"You lose," she said as she patted the diamond in her pocket.

Lunging to her right, she snatched a large carabiner from her belt loop and secured it around the rope that led down to their yacht.

Ange took off, moving with everything she had as Val ran and jumped over the side. Ange wasn't about to let her enemy get away that easily. She followed right behind the mafia leader, diving through the air and wrapping her arms around her lower body. Somehow, Val managed to hold them both up, and they zipped down the line, quickly picking up speed.

As the wind flew past them, Ange held on tight and reached for her dive knife that was sheathed at the back of her belt. Pulling the blade free, she stabbed it as hard as she could into Val's chest.

Val yelled out again, this time even louder as blood flowed out.

Glancing toward the stern of the yacht that they'd reach in seconds, Ange spotted two thugs standing and aiming their weapons toward her. She had no choice but to drop. Taking in a deep breath, she let go and splashed into the water fifty feet behind the yacht. Kicking and pulling with everything she had, she reached the shallow bottom and swam ferociously in the opposite direction of the boat as bullets torpedoed through the water all around her.

Summoning all her strength and ignoring the pain from the fight, she held her breath and kicked as hard and as long as she could. When she finally surfaced, she took in a few much-needed deep breaths and turned to look toward the yacht. To her surprise, it was motoring full throttle away from her, heading west.

To her amazement, she heard a second boat and looked off to her right toward the sound. Relief came over her face as she saw a familiar trawler approach with Jack standing on its bow. She swam toward it, reaching the swim platform right at the edge of the shallows surrounding the fort.

"Holy shit, Ange," Jack said while offering her his right hand. "Are you alright?"

He pulled her up. She was breathing heavily, her cheek was bleeding, and her shirt was ripped. She looked like a UFC fighter who'd just gone the full five rounds.

"Better than Valmira," she said.

"Where's Logan?" Scott asked, stepping out from the pilothouse.

Ange gasped.

"He's not with you?"

She turned back and gazed toward Bastion Alpha, focusing on the single tiny window of Mudd's cell. All she could think about was her husband, and all that she could cling to was a hope that he was still alive.

THIRTY-FIVE

I secured the torn piece of fabric around Pete's upper leg, slowing the bleeding as best I could. The makeshift tourniquet was far from ideal, and he'd need medical care soon if he was going to pull through. But Pete's being shot wasn't our only big problem.

We were trapped inside the chamber with no light source, and the water was steadily rising. There was just under a foot of clearance, and it wouldn't be long before the incoming tide filled the space entirely. We needed to do something, and we needed to do it fast if we were going to have any hope of getting out of here.

Pete was grunting and yelling out curses at our situation. It was clear that the gunshot wasn't what was bothering him the most.

"We trusted him," he said. "He was my best

friend for years. I—"

"Pete, there will be a time to dwell on what happened," I said, holding tight to one of his shoulders. "But it sure as hell isn't right now." He slowed his breathing as I examined my work to try and slow the blood loss from his leg. "You've lost a significant amount of blood, but it looks as though your femoral artery wasn't struck."

Pete pulled my hands off him.

"I'll be fine, boyo. Just a scratch. You and I have bigger fish to fry."

I stepped away from him and looked around. It was pitch black. Not even a tiny trickle of light bled in from anywhere. We were stuck in total darkness with water rising around us. The situation was about as bleak as it could get. But my father had always taught me that no situation is hopeless until you believe it is. Even as a kid, I'd known what he meant. No matter how bad things get, no matter how high the odds are stacked against you, nothing's over until you keel over and let the fates have their way with you. As long as you have air in your lungs, the fight isn't over.

"Strap up your boots, tighten your fists, and rise," he used to tell me. "Far better to go down swinging."

As I moved across the chamber, trying to come up with any possible course of action, my foot came into contact with something on the bottom. It was the brick. The same loose brick that I'd stumbled upon earlier.

I froze midway through another step.

Did anyone grab the sledgehammer? 'Cause I didn't.

I took a breath, splashed into the water, and reached around the floor of the chamber. After a few seconds, I felt the handle of the heavy tool and rose back up with it firmly in my hands. I moved back to the entrance of the chamber and told Pete what I was going to do. Before taking a breath and dropping down, Pete grabbed me by the shoulder.

He could have reminded me that the stone easily weighed over four hundred pounds and that I was out of my mind for thinking I could move it on my own. But he didn't.

"Godspeed, Logan," was all he said.

I took a breath, dropped down, and swam into the crawl space. After a few strong kicks, I reached the large flat side of the big stone. I moved into position and reared back the sledgehammer.

Here goes nothing.

Gripping the wooden handle tight, I swung as hard as I could, slamming the heavy face into the stone. I winced at the moment of contact. The vibration was painful. It sent a shock wave through my hands and all the way up my arms. Worse, the massive stone hadn't budged at all.

I slammed it two more times, each just as painful as the first. The task appeared utterly futile, but I pushed back the little voice that told me that all I would accomplish was an impressive cluster of blisters. I had no choice. Either I found a way to move the stone, or we'd both die right there.

I used the few inches of overhead space to take a few breaths. Feeling an overwhelming surge of resolve, I gripped the handle harder, reared it back farther, and swung it with everything I had. Then I did it again, and again, and again. I beat the stone with reckless abandon. I felt like a lumberjack in the nail-biting final event of a logging show.

After what felt like an eternity, the stone budged

slightly from the force of a blow. It was minuscule, nearly imperceptible, but it had happened. It wasn't much, but in a dark room, even the smallest light can make an astounding difference.

I kept at it, beating relentlessly over and over. The minuscule budge soon grew into an inch. Then two inches.

"How's it going in there?" Pete yelled while I paused a moment to catch my breath.

"We're not out of this fight yet," I replied. "How's the leg?"

"Hurts, but probably not as bad as your hands do."

He was right. My hands were raw, blistered, and bleeding. But whatever pain I felt, I channeled it toward the task at hand. I wasn't about to die there. No, I was going to see Ange again. I was going to see many more sunrises and sunsets.

I pushed through, continuing my incessant barrage on the stone block. With every strike, the block slid farther, and my resolve grew stronger. My muscles screamed, and my lungs burned, but I kept at it, ignoring my body and pushing through.

Soon, the block slid back far enough for us to squeeze through. I dropped the sledgehammer and nearly passed out from exhaustion. After calming myself and catching my breath, I laughed out of sheer joy as I gazed through the darkness at the faint glow of light beyond.

Turning around, I sloshed back into the chamber.

"We've overstayed our welcome," I said.

He didn't reply.

I moved toward where he'd been and grabbed his body.

"Pete!" I said, shaking him.

He mumbled a few incoherent words back to me.

"Dammit, hang in there, Pete. We're about to get out of this."

He was fading from consciousness. It was still pitch black in the chamber, but I didn't need to see anything to know that he'd lost a lot of blood. Too much blood.

I grabbed him and, with every ounce of strength that I had left, dragged him into the crawl space. He came to a little as water splashed onto his face. He was in pain and delirious but somehow was able to make it through and climb out over the small opening I'd muscled for us.

Free from our flooded tomb, we made it over the stone, and I carried most of his weight as we trudged back up toward the cell. I was nearing the end of my rope as I crawled and pulled Pete through the final portions of the passageway.

With a final surge of strength, we reached the small cell, and I pulled Pete out alongside me. Catching my breath, I looked around the empty cell, having a hard time believing what had just happened.

After a few much-needed deep breaths, I grabbed hold of Pete again.

"Come on, Pete," I said. "We need to get you to help."

Just as I tried to lift him, I heard footsteps coming from around the corner. Instinctively, I reached for my waistband, but of course, my Sig was gone. I reached behind me, pulled out my dive knife, and prepared for the worst. I was in no position to put up a fight, but that wouldn't stop me from trying.

With my hands bleeding, my muscles throbbing, and an arm around Pete to help hold him up, I raised my blade.

"Logan!" a beautifully familiar voice said as Ange appeared into the light of the entryway.

I gasped, smiled, and dropped my dive knife. She sprang over and wrapped her arms around us, keeping us both on our feet. I'd never been so happy to see anyone in my entire life.

"Are you okay?" she said, squeezing me tight and looking me over from head to toe. "Val said… I thought you might be…"

She was breathing like she'd just won a 5K. Her eyes stopped when they reached my mutilated hands.

"I'm fine," I assured her, looking deep into her eyes. "But Pete needs help. What happened to you?"

She was soaked from head to toe. Her cheek was bleeding, and her tank top was ripped and dirty. Somehow she still managed to look amazing.

"Val," she said.

"Where is she?" I asked, narrowing my gaze.

"She's running," Scott said as he stepped toward us.

"But she's badly injured," Ange added.

"And she's lost a bunch of her goons," Jack chimed in.

I felt a wave of relief upon seeing that Jack and Scott were both unscathed as well. They both ran over and took hold of Pete. We carried him down to the ground level and across the fort to the visitor center. The rangers and a few tourists had locked themselves inside, and Ange managed to get the young guy from before to open the door and let us inside.

"We need a medivac right away," Ange said sternly.

The young ranger nodded, grabbed the phone, and called it in. They'd already notified the Coast Guard as well as the Key West Police Department about an incident at the fort after hearing the gunshots.

The other ranger grabbed a first aid kit from behind the counter, and we went to work, cleaning Pete's wound and stopping the bleeding. He was far gone from his usual self. The substantial blood loss had made him delirious, and he had a hard time saying much of anything, let alone a coherent sentence.

"I think he'll be alright," Jack said after we moved Pete onto the grass under a gumbo-limbo tree.

I nodded. He was in rough shape, but he was also one of the toughest guys I knew. I glanced up at Scott and extended my right hand.

"Looks like you showed up at the perfect time," I said. "Thanks for coming."

"Of course, brother," he replied, shaking my hand, then patting me on the back.

"You said Val's running?" I asked.

"On their yacht," Ange replied. "Heading southwest out of here, full throttle."

"And she's injured?"

"To put it mildly," Ange replied. "I fractured her elbow and buried my knife in her chest."

I smiled. Just when I thought Ange couldn't get any more badass, she went toe to toe with the spawn of Satan and taught her a painful lesson.

"Walt's dead," Ange said. "He had a change of heart and tried to kill Val when I confronted her. And she has the diamond. Though I don't think she'll be breathing long enough to sell it."

The mention of Walt's name brought on a surge of anger, though I was glad to hear he'd come to his senses, even though it was short-lived. Then I thought about the encounter down in the bowels of the fort.

How Walt had mentioned that Val had taken his family. My eyes narrowed, and I let out a breath.

"We need to go after them," I declared. My eyes drifted back and forth between Ange and Scott. "Walt's son, his son's wife, and his two young grandkids are on that yacht."

"Shit, he did mention his family," Ange said. "How do you know they're on the yacht?"

"I just know," I said. "Val needed leverage. And now with Walt gone, she has no reason to keep them alive." I looked over toward the docks. "With the Baia, we can track them down, save the family, and bring the rest of these assholes to justice."

I glanced over at Jack, who had a slight lump in his throat.

"I'll stay with Pete, bro," he said. "And the Baia's currently dead in the water."

I didn't have the time or the energy to ask what had happened or to even care about my boat. I couldn't get Walt's innocent family out of my mind.

"I've got the Darkwater trawler," Scott said.

I smiled and nodded. "Let's move."

THIRTY-SIX

I stood up on the bow of the trawler, wind pelting against my body as I caught a glimpse of our quarry through a pair of binoculars. I could see the sleek white-hulled yacht and its long wake spread out ahead of us. They were less than a mile away, and getting closer with every passing second. Scott was gunning the trawler's two 800-hp Mercruiser engines, and the big boat was flying through the water at just over forty knots.

We were twenty miles from Dry Tortugas, heading due southeast. Based on the yacht's course, they were either wrapping around the western coast of Cuba, or they were heading for the Yucatan. My money was on the latter. Either way, it didn't matter. They weren't going to reach their destination.

"What's the plan here, Logan?" Scott asked as I stepped into the pilothouse.

Normally, I'd just motor up alongside them and let them have it. A hailstorm of bullets to take down everyone on deck and force them to give up. Rambo style. But it wasn't as simple as that. They had hostages aboard, and we couldn't just go in there firing at will. We had to be careful and precise if we were going to take them down and save the family.

"Bring us in close," I said. "We'll keep a sharp eye out for tangos. Once the deck's clear, we'll board the yacht."

"How many do they have left?" Scott asked.

Ange and I looked at each other, then just shrugged.

We didn't know how many men they had left, but we did know that they'd suffered many casualties over the past few days.

With Scott staying at the helm, Ange and I moved back out onto the bow and kept our eyes glued to the approaching yacht. We had our pistols at the ready and were prepared to use them at a moment's notice.

As Scott brought us right up to the yacht, we kept our eyes peeled for any sign of movement. The windows were tinted, making it impossible to see inside. But every exposed portion of the deck, as well as the yacht's open flybridge, was devoid of bad guys.

I instructed Scott to pull right alongside the starboard side and match her speed. Then Ange and I climbed up on top of the trawler's pilothouse. I scanned the yacht one more time, then got a quick running start and launched myself over the edge. I just cleared the railing and landed as smoothly as I could onto the deck of the yacht's open flybridge.

After a quick look around with my Sig aimed

chest height, I gave Ange a thumbs-up, and she vaulted over as well. She timed the rising and falling of the boats better than I had and cleared the gap easily.

I stepped into the flybridge cockpit, disengaged the autopilot, then idled the throttles and shut off the engines. The large yacht slowed to a stop while Ange and I kept our weapons raised toward the stairs. We thought for sure that turning everything off would cause someone to stir, but it didn't.

Covering each other, we moved down to the main deck. Scott idled the trawler, threw over the fenders, and we tied a line to keep the two boats together. Gripping his Glock 19, Scott jumped over and nodded toward the sliding glass door.

With Scott to my left and Ange to my right, I moved in, feeling like I was a member of the A-team and we'd just assembled the squad. There weren't two people alive who I'd rather have watching my back than them.

To our surprise, the sliding glass door was unlocked. After shoving it open, we quickly searched the saloon. The entire pristine, luxurious interior was as quiet and empty as a tomb.

"Where the hell are they?" Scott said after we'd searched every inch of the main level.

As if to answer his question, we heard a sudden high-pitched cry. It came from below deck and was quickly silenced. I motioned toward the narrow staircase, then headed straight for it.

I made quick work of the stairs, keeping my eyes peeled for bad guys or booby traps. Scott and Ange were right on my heels when I reached the bottom step.

Suddenly, a shotgun blast splintered one of the

cabin doors to pieces and blew a massive hole in the wall right beside me. As the thug cocked the weapon for another shot, Scott jumped into the cabin, snatched the shotgun barrel, then grabbed our attacker by his hair and slammed his face into a mirror.

He gave the guy a chance to surrender, but the thug only used the time to try and stab Scott with a hidden blade. Scott knocked it away, slapped him across the face with his pistol, then sent two quick shots through his chest. The thug shook and grunted as he fell back and collapsed onto the deck.

Just as the guy fell, a door slammed open behind me and a second thug grabbed me from behind. He jerked me back into the head and wrapped an arm around my neck. I sent a 9mm round into his leg, then bent my knees and threw him over me. Ange dropped down and knocked him out with a powerful side kick.

The three of us turned our gazes down the passageway in an instant as we heard the whining sounds again. They were coming from the main cabin. Its door was shut, and we approached it slowly with our weapons raised.

After a quick nod to Scott and Ange, I reared back and kicked the door open. It broke free of its hinges and rattled to the deck at the foot of a queen-sized bed. The room was packed. There were five people in all. A man, woman, and a young boy were sitting against the headboard, tied up and gagged. Their eyes were big, teary, and filled with fear.

On the other side of the bed, Val leaned against a cupboard with a young girl held in front of her. The mafia leader was clearly in bad shape. She had blood-drenched clothes and had trouble staying on her feet. Her breathing was erratic, but her face displayed the rage-filled resolution of a murdering psychopath.

My eyes locked on the Beretta she had pressed against the scared little girl's head. I had my Sig raised when I entered, and its sights were zeroed in on Val. I didn't have a good shot. The evil woman was doing her best to keep the terrified child right in front of her.

I'd been trained in hostage situations many times before. I knew the best course of action to take. I just needed the right moment.

A brief life-or-death moment passed. Then Val opened her mouth.

"Drop the gun and—"

Her struggled words were interrupted by the sound of my Sig's firing pin striking the primer. A round exploded out of the barrel, flying just inches beside the young girl's head, and striking through Val's right eye. Blood and bone splattered out the back of her skull as the loud boom rattled the small space. Her body went limp in an instant, and she collapsed to the deck, bringing the young girl down with her.

I stormed into the room with Ange and Scott right on my heels. We made quick work of the ropes and gags, and the young family embraced each other in a chorus of cries and sobs. Ange watched them while Scott and I checked over the rest of the boat, making sure that there weren't any more stray thugs or rigged explosives of some kind.

When we returned to the main cabin, Ange helped calm the young family.

"Thank you," the man said with tears in his eyes.

It was one of the most sincere thanks I'd ever received, and we told them that we were happy to have played our part.

"You're not the police," he said.

305

"No, we're not," Ange replied. "But we are the good guys."

Ange escorted them up into the saloon. I stepped around the bed with Scott right behind me. Glancing down to look at Val's bloody lifeless body, I spotted something on the deck against the side of the bed frame. I knelt down, grabbed the small tin box, and smiled.

THIRTY-SEVEN

The days following the events on and around Fort Jefferson were a blur. Scott called in a few of his high-level contacts, including CIA Deputy Director Wilson, the Secretary of Homeland Security, and a few of the local Coast Guard and Navy commanders. The yacht was seized by the Guard, and the mafia bodies were transported back to Albania for official identification. Having Scott in our corner made the whole process much less painful than it would have been otherwise.

We brought Peter and his family to Key West and took care of them as best we could. After being cleared by the hospital, they spent a night at the Sheraton before catching a flight back to Memphis.

Using the trawler to tow the damaged Baia, we brought it to Blackbeard's Boatyard in Marathon for repairs. Our first stop once back was to head over to the Lower Key Medical Center to check up on Pete. He'd been airlifted there from Fort Jefferson during our pursuit of Val and her remaining criminal posse.

Pete had received an impressive blood transfusion and a surgery to remove the bullet fragments and to repair the internal damage. Thankfully, the doctors assured us that he should be just fine after a few weeks of rest and rehabilitation.

While visiting him in his hospital bed, I looked around to make sure no one outside our group was looking, then handed him the diamond. While he examined it, we told him all about what had happened.

He nodded, then motioned toward my bandaged hands and asked how they were.

"Raw and hurt like hell," I said. "But nothing that won't heal."

Pete handed me back the diamond and shook his head.

"Still can't believe you moved that stone all by yourself," he said. "That was some next-level cowboying up. Even for you."

"Fortunately somebody left the sledgehammer," I said.

"Forgot it, more like. Never thought my aging and negligent brain would save our skins."

I glanced over at Ange. "I gotta say, though, if anyone was John Wayne this time it was you, babe." I glanced over at Pete and added, "She's the one who took down Val. I just put the final nail in her coffin."

After a few more minutes of talking and joking around, Pete asked how exactly we planned to sell the diamond. I'd given it a little bit of thought on the boat ride over and thought I knew the perfect buyer.

"I have this wealthy collector friend," I said. "His

family stumbled upon some oil in Saudi Arabia. Haven't spoken to him yet, but I think this might be right up his alley."

Pete smiled.

Arian Nazari was a billionaire oil tycoon who'd helped us during our fight with Black Venom over the Aztec treasure. He also had one of the most impressive private collections of rare jewelry and artifacts in the world. I managed to get ahold of the smooth-talking, respectful Arabian the following day. As I'd hoped, he agreed to have a few of his guys check out the diamond, and the purchase was made just a few days later.

It was a lot of money, and the first thing we did was send half to Walt's son. A deal was a deal. As the treasure hunter had predicted, the diamond had been worth twenty million dollars, and his share would set up his son for life if he was smart with it. A stipulation was put that a percentage of the money be placed into a college fund for his grandchildren. We made sure that his son knew that it was all thanks to Walt and that he'd loved them more than they would ever know.

I decided to take just enough from the sale to fix up the Baia and buy a truck to replace the one Jack had drowned.

I spent a few days poring over online ads, then Ange and I drove Jack's Wrangler up to Homestead to test-drive a few trucks. After giving several other manufacturers a chance, I ended up choosing another Tacoma. It was a couple of years newer than the one I'd lost, but aside from that, it was nearly identical. Black four-door 4x4 with a six-foot bed.

Ange tried to get me to buy a new one, but I've never been able to justify buying new. I had my dad and his savvy financial wisdom to thank for that. Besides, I'd be too concerned with scratching a new truck and getting it all dirty. I like a truck with some miles under its belt before I buy it. A proven truck.

Some of the money was also used to create an impressive exhibit at Salty Pete's dedicated to Walt Grissom and his salvaging adventures. It included artifacts from many of his trips around the Keys, the rest of the Caribbean, and around the world. It also included information about Hastings and his incredible scavenger hunt.

Anonymous donations were also made to both the Key West Lighthouse as well as Fort Jefferson to pay for the damages we'd caused.

After giving Ange, Pete, Jack, and Frank small portions of the money as well, the rest was donated to the children's shelter on Tavernier. Needless to say, the shelter wouldn't be closing its doors anytime soon. In fact, the anonymous endowment was enough for them not only to stay open for years but to expand to other much-needed services and add another location.

A few weeks after ridding our island paradise of the unwelcomed mobsters, things started to get back to normal. Pete recovered enough to get back to his usual restaurant-owning duties. Jack was busy running charters. And Ange and I were swinging comfortably back into our normal lifestyle. Spearfishing, island hopping, and working out were the typical orders of the day.

In mid-November, Scott managed to get away again, this time for a proper tropical sun, sand, and sea vacation. Frank was also in town and managed to get away for a day out on the water. To Jack's surprise, we invited Lauren Sweetin, making it a full group. Ange and I both thought she and Jack would be a good fit, and I encouraged my beach bum friend to ask her to dinner sometime in the near future.

We took the *Calypso* out to one of our secret lobster honey holes in the morning. After bagging our limits, we motored over to Joe's Tug for some afternoon scuba diving. The seventy-five-foot tug rests in sixty-five feet of water and is always a great dive with near-perfect visibility year-round.

"It's a shame we had to sell it," Pete said as we cooked up some lunch after the second dive. "That sure was a pretty rock."

I looked around at my wife, my good friends, and the tropical paradise surrounding us.

"There are much more important things in life than diamonds," I said, smiling and feeling a little sentimental.

"Yeah, like twenty million big ones," Jack said, raising his beer.

The group laughed. It was especially funny since Jack was about as money-driven as a sea snail.

"I was thinking more along the lines of good friends," I said. I took a sip, cleared my throat, and added, "When I moved back here last year, I didn't know what to expect. You've all welcomed us into your island family, and there's nowhere I'd rather be."

There was a short pause of smiles and nods and drink raises. Then Jack spoke.

"Easy on the sap, bro," he said. "You're gonna stick to the deck."

I grinned. Glancing at Ange, we gave each other a quick nod, then grabbed our blond-haired beach bum friend and threw him into the water.

After a long day out on the ocean, we sat up on

the bow to watch the sunset. I had Ange in my arms as we stared in awe of the beautiful display of vibrant, streaking colors.

"There's nowhere else I'd rather be," I said again, this time whispering it into her ear.

THE END

Logan Dodge Adventures

Gold in the Keys
(Florida Keys Adventure Series Book 1)

Hunted in the Keys
(Florida Keys Adventure Series Book 2)

Revenge in the Keys
(Florida Keys Adventure Series Book 3)

Betrayed in the Keys
(Florida Keys Adventure Series Book 4)

Redemption in the Keys
(Florida Keys Adventure Series Book 5)

Corruption in the Keys
(Florida Keys Adventure Series Book 6)

Predator in the Keys
(Florida Keys Adventure Series Book 7)

Legend in the Keys
(Florida Keys Adventure Series Book 8)

Join the Adventure!
You can sign up for my newsletter to receive updates
on upcoming books at my website:

matthewrief.com

About the Author

Matthew has a deep-rooted love for adventure and the ocean. He loves traveling, diving, rock climbing and writing adventure novels. Though he grew up in the Pacific Northwest, he currently lives in Virginia Beach with his wife, Jenny.

Made in the USA
Columbia, SC
21 August 2022

65789805R00188